Devon watched F... ...his mother.

Here was a man who wo... ...a commitment or a duty. A good son, a tolerant brother and a caring uncle. What would he be like, she wondered, as a husband? Or a father? Would he look at his wife the way Theo had yesterday at Maura? With adoration? That question instantly begged another—would she herself ever be on the receiving end of such feeling?

"Devon?"

She blinked, realizing at once that the man in her head was standing in front of her, a light smile on his face. She flushed, as if he'd had access to her thoughts.

"I asked if you could be ready to leave in, say, ten minutes."

She nodded.

"Great. I'm just going to send off a couple of emails. Do you want help going upstairs?" He held out his hand.

Dear Reader,

Welcome to Maple Glen, Vermont, a village alongside the Appalachian Trail nestled between the Green Mountains and the Taconic.

Rescuing people is Finn McAllister's full-time job, as a firefighter and a volunteer trail keeper, but it's also his passion. So when he finds Devon Fairchild, frightened and injured on a section of the trail, Finn's instinct, after assessing her injuries, is to continue watching over her.

When he discovers that the mystery woman has a deep, possibly dark, secret, Finn is more determined than ever to protect and guard her. But the woman who's won his heart doesn't want rescuing. Ultimately, it takes the whole community to help Finn show Devon the way to a different future and, most of all, to a love she can trust.

Rescued at Christmas is the second book in my new series, Home to Maple Glen, but you don't need to start with the first book, *A Small Town Fourth of July*, to discover the joys of life in the Glen. You can begin right here...

Enjoy!

Janice Carter

RESCUED AT CHRISTMAS

JANICE CARTER

Harlequin

HEARTWARMING

Harlequin®
HEARTWARMING™

Recycling programs for this product may not exist in your area.

ISBN-13: 978-1-335-05132-5

Rescued at Christmas

Copyright © 2024 by Janice Hess

For questions and comments about the quality of this book, please contact us at CustomerService@Harlequin.com.

TM and ® are trademarks of Harlequin Enterprises ULC.

Harlequin Enterprises ULC
22 Adelaide St. West, 41st Floor
Toronto, Ontario M5H 4E3, Canada
www.Harlequin.com

Printed in Lithuania

MIX
Paper | Supporting responsible forestry
FSC® C021394

Janice Carter has been writing Harlequin romances for a long time, through raising a family, teaching and on into retirement. This is her eighteenth romance and she has plans for many more—along with plenty of personal family time, too.

Books by Janice Carter

Harlequin Heartwarming

For Love of a Dog
Her Kind of Hero
His Saving Grace
The Christmas Promise
The Officer's Dilemma

Home to Maple Glen

A Small Town Fourth of July

Visit the Author Profile page
at Harlequin.com for more titles.

For Scott Carter—retired firefighter,
rescue-protocols fact-checker and
my awesome brother—with so much love!

CHAPTER ONE

"WE HAVE A saying here in Maple Glen," warned the owner of the Shady Nook Bed and Breakfast, "'sunny at daybreak and raining by noon.' Or in this case, *snowing* by noon. My opinion? Wait till tomorrow."

Devon Fairchild peered out the picture window of the small dining room. It was sunny, and despite the pillowy white clouds on the horizon, there was plenty of blue sky. She'd put off this day long enough and had traveled many miles to fulfill the promise she'd made in a highly emotional state four months ago. She turned from the window to look at Bernie Watson, standing with hands on hips in the kitchen doorway, his brow furrowed beneath a thatch of gray hair.

She could see that he was concerned, but he didn't really know her. She'd only checked in yesterday afternoon, and his weather advice probably stemmed from an overabundance of caution. He'd noted her Chicago address and drawn a conclusion. *City slicker* and *greenhorn* were probably the first two words that popped into his head when she told him her plan at dinner last night. Still, he'd sat down with her when she'd finished her meal and sketched a rough map, showing her how to get to the path leading from Maple Glen to link up with the Long Trail arm of the Appalachian Trail.

"I'll be fine, Mr. Watson… Bernie. Trust me. I'm not inexperienced." Devon hoped her ears weren't bright pink at the slightly misleading implication of those last two words. "Not inexperienced" didn't equal "experienced." She sat on one of the chairs to lace up her hiking boots, feeling his eyes on her the whole time.

"Do you have crampons for those?"

"I'm not going up the mountain," she told him for the umpteenth time since last night. "Just to the conservation area and along the valley to the base."

"Best avoid the ice beds, then."

Devon kept her head down, hiding an eye roll. Bernie Watson, a man she'd known for less than twenty-four hours, was channeling some mythical parent. She'd fought too long—since she was a teen—to manage her own life as much as possible. The last thing she needed was a surrogate parent.

"I will." She reached for the daypack on the floor, zipped up her down vest, then pulled her Gore-Tex parka over her fleece-lined water-resistant pants and cast a big smile at the large gray-haired man. "I'm hoping to be back for a hearty lunch. What's on the menu today?"

"French onion soup with my sourdough bread."

"Sounds amazing. I may be late, so please save me some." Slinging her pack over one shoulder, Devon headed out of the dining area toward the front door. She heard Bernie shuffling behind her and wondered what further advice would sound before she left. It came as she placed her hand on the doorknob.

"Cell phone coverage is sketchy, especially in the valley."

"Thanks. I'll keep that in mind." Closing the door behind her, Devon felt a rush of both relief and trepidation.

The early morning sun reflected off yesterday's snowfall, shooting out prisms of color, and Devon blinked against the brightness, reaching into her coat pocket for her sunglasses. Bernie's warning about more snow seemed far-fetched right now, but Devon decided her mission today should be accomplished as quickly as possible. She stood for a moment, peering up and down the main drag of the village, thinking how unearthly quiet the place was on a Wednesday morning two weeks before Christmas.

Her research had informed her that Maple Glen predated its closest neighbor, the town of Wallingford, about ten miles north. After picking up her rental car at the airport in Rutland yesterday, she'd made a brief stop at a tourist information kiosk for maps and pamphlets. Not that she planned to stay in the area any longer than necessary, but her natural curiosity about places and things often guided her rare impulses. It was her first time being in Vermont that she could actually remember, so best to take in the local scenery while she was here. Besides, none of this was for her. Holding steadfast to that fact was the best way to endure whatever challenges arose in the next twenty-four hours.

Adjusting the weight of her daypack on her shoulders, Devon turned away from the small intersection that was the heart of Maple Glen and headed for the large tract of forest in the near distance. It was cold enough for her expelled breath to puff tendrils of vapor ahead of her, but the crisp air felt good. Winters in Chicago were seldom pretty or refreshing, and as she walked, the unspoken mantra that had been spooling in her head since she'd made her decision urged her on: *You can do this*.

The scattering of houses she passed were a range of white and pastel frame buildings—mainly Colonial and Federal with more contemporary houses—similar to the architecture she'd seen in nearby Wallingford. There was a bakery beyond the Shady Nook with a tiny post office attached to it, and the aromas wafting out were

tempting, but Devon had opted for the full breakfast at the B and B in case her hike took longer
than expected. She'd easily managed five-mile
walks in the past, but not in the winter and not
alone. Plus, Dan had always been her cheerleader,
egging her on whenever she wanted to quit. *You
can do this*, he'd urge. And she could. By the time
she was a teenager, Dan's coaching had instilled
her with enough self-confidence to assert her independence and step out from her brother's nurturing shadow.

There were few street signs in the village. She'd
noted yesterday that the B and B was situated on
Church Street, the main drag, and sure enough,
there was the church straight ahead. Its white
framed structure was topped by a modest steeple
and sat imposingly on the crest of a small hill with
a pretty house next to it. The reverend's, Devon
assumed. The village seemed to be awakening
now, as a car and a pickup rolled down the street
heading for the exit to Route 7, which Devon had
taken out of Wallingford yesterday. She imagined
many of the residents commuted to that larger
community and even beyond, to Rutland in the
north or Bennington to the south. There'd been
a few farms along Route 7, and on the cutoff to
Maple Glen, some dairy farms with cows wandering intrepidly through snow-covered pastures,
but she'd also spotted fields of dried cornstalks
from last autumn. Just before she reached the

village, she noticed a horse farm—at least she thought the four-legged creatures standing in a far-off paddock were horses, though their shapes were stockier.

A footbridge spanning a shallow creek marked the end of Church Street, yards away from the woodland ahead. This was the end of the village and the start of the access that linked eventually to the Long Trail, as Bernie had mentioned. On the opposite side of the road, Devon saw a large two-story framed house with a wraparound veranda, a white picket fence and a couple of outbuildings. *The quintessential chocolate-box country home*, she thought. The creek curved around the property, separating it from the woods it bordered, and she crossed the road for a better look at the place.

An old wooden sign, its faded lettering reading The Manor, had been hammered onto the gate post next to a typical rural mail stanchion. The name on the mailbox was clearly defined—McAllister. Perhaps one of Maple Glen's original homesteaders, Devon figured, since the house looked old. She was about to turn away to cross the footbridge into the woods when she spotted a small figure in the large bay window. A child waving to her. Devon smiled, taking this as a good omen for her mission today. She waved back and, straightening her backpack once more, stepped onto the bridge and left the village behind.

The path was immediately obvious, and a mere

six feet or so in, Devon came upon a tree with a laminated sign reading Off Trail to the Long Trail and the blue painted slash mark, or "blaze" as Bernie called it, that would lead the way to the main trail, marked by white blazes. Once she met up with that main trail, the White Rocks National Recreation Area was an approximate seven miles away. The path was covered with the heavy wet snowfall from last night, but some patches were already melting beneath the sun's rays. By the time she returned along this same route, hopefully in a couple of hours or so, Devon figured those patches would have frozen over. She'd have to be careful. But the goal today was to keep her promise to Dan.

Ten minutes into the walk, the path angled uphill and the composting leaves on its surface gave way to sedimentary rock, slabs and pieces of all sizes and shapes. Devon realized that longtime caretakers of the trail had fashioned as accessible a path as possible, and she felt some of her apprehension fade. Her boots didn't have cleats or crampons, but she figured she'd be okay as long as she watched her footing. She could easily have driven to the recreation area, where there was a large parking lot and a well-marked route for less committed hikers, but she knew Dan would have expected—no, *wanted*—her to walk the whole way, and so far, it was a beautiful day for a hike.

The forest was quiet at first, except for the

crunch of snow beneath her boots and the rhyth-
mic exhalations of her breath, but soon Devon
could hear birdsong and the rustling of small
mammals somewhere in the trees flanking the
trail. She'd brought bear spray just in case but
knew there was little chance of encountering one.
They're hibernating right now, she reminded herself, but still she was startled by a flutter of movement somewhere in the dense vegetation. About
an hour after she'd entered the woods, she reached
the fork where the off trail joined up with the
main Appalachian/Long Trail and spied the first
white blaze. Some thoughtful person had long ago
posted a wooden sign pointing the way to White
Rocks Mountain and Devon felt herself relax.

"You can do this," she quietly muttered.

There was a reason why Dan had chosen the
section of the trail beyond the conservation area
to mark the twenty-fifth anniversary of their new
start in life. *It's symbolic*, he'd said in the low,
raspy voice of his last days. *The place where we
left behind our childhood, our original names and
our family. In a sense, it's where we were reborn.
We were never the same after.*

Devon also knew she'd never be the same after
fulfilling her promise.

No doubt about it, Maple Glen was a winter
fairyland today, Finn McAllister thought as he
peered out the front bay window of his childhood

home. As magical as the scene might be for his seven-year-old niece, Kaya, who'd been entranced by it at breakfast, the sight of new heavy snow draping tree branches and electricity wires meant only one thing for Finn—a potentially busy day. He hoped any hikers would sensibly stay indoors, but if there was one thing he'd learned during his four years on the volunteer search-and-rescue team operating out of Wallingford, many would not. Some foolhardy souls might even view last night's snowfall as an extra challenge for hiking to the section of the White Rocks National Recreation Area closest to the Glen. But Finn knew all too well how visibility on the trail could quickly shift or how fresh snow hid treacherous obstacles.

Checking the time, he realized the school bus would be arriving any minute. He moved away from the living room window to the bottom of the staircase. "Kaya! Time to go. Are you ready?"

His mother heard him from the kitchen, where she was clearing breakfast dishes, and came to the open doorway off the hall. "Are you going to drive her?"

"Huh? Mom, we only have to walk a few yards."

"Sure, but you know Kaya."

Kaya and her mother, Finn's younger sister, had only been living with them six months, but that was definitely long enough to know his niece. Those few yards to the bus stop took a lot longer to walk than usual with the easily distracted seven-year-old. Still, Finn balked. Kaya needed to learn to focus and this was a learning opportunity for her.

Seconds later, Kaya practically tumbled down the stairs, followed by her mother, Roxanne, and they dashed for the mudroom at the back of the house. Finn mentally counted as the snowsuit donning commenced. He marveled at his sister's patience, always smiling at Kaya's nonstop chatter or her sudden interest in a scrap of paper in her snowsuit pocket or a small toy that had been dropped and forgotten days ago. The daily routine was a whirlwind of talk and movement, one that left Finn exhausted even as a mere bystander.

By the time he got to fifteen, they were scurrying back along the hall to where he waited at the front door. "I can drive her," Roxanne said.

Finn shook his head, determined not to give in. "I'll walk with her. Mom wants some bread from the bakery anyway." He noticed his sister bite down on her lip and regretted his tone. She'd been through enough in the past several months and didn't need a brother to hand down parenting advice. Or any kind of advice, for that matter. Biting his own lip when it came to speaking up had been his ongoing challenge since they'd moved in, and although he knew this bad habit was improving, there were still moments when he reverted to that know-it-all older brother from their youth. When Roxanne yielded, he felt even worse.

"Okay, I'll help Mom clean up," she mumbled and headed for the kitchen.

Finn noticed Kaya's glance from him to her mother. Could a child pick up this vibe? he wondered. Probably, he thought, feeling even guiltier. Surely, Kaya, too, had been through enough since her parents split up six months ago. He stifled a sigh. Maybe a freshly baked cookie from the bakery would make up for his churlishness this morning.

"Okay, shrimp?" he quipped, reaching for his down jacket draped on the stair newel post. When she grinned and stuck her tongue out at him, Finn knew he'd been forgiven.

They paused briefly on the veranda while Kaya pulled her mittens on. Finn realized he should have cleared last night's snowfall, but his mother's waffles—a special treat for Kaya that morning—had been too tempting. The shovel was right there, propped next to the door, but he knew they couldn't spare the time. The bus taking Maple Glen's elementary school kids to Wallingford would only wait an extra five minutes.

"Let's do this," he announced in the "go get 'em" voice he assumed for his team of volunteers.

Kaya gave him a thumbs-up and descended the steps to the sidewalk leading to the gate and Church Street. Finn smiled at her waddle, the padding from her snowsuit adding extra surface area to her skinny frame. Fortunately, the snowfall was only a few inches deep, but one glance at the eastern sky told Finn more would be coming, and soon. He didn't notice the footprints until they were at the gate.

"Hmm," he muttered, staring down at the single set of prints leading from across the road to their gate and then toward the footbridge. Not a good sign, he thought. At this time of year, hikers typically entered the trail from the entrance closest to Wallingford. Even in spring and fall, tourists rarely stumbled on the Glen's access to an off trail leading to White Rocks Mountain. Few guidebooks bothered listing the small village, focusing on the more accessible and convenient Wallingford, though Finn knew some trekking and hiking websites mentioned the route from Maple Glen.

Kaya must have noticed his attention to the footprints. "It was a lady," she said.

He looked up, frowning.

"I saw a lady go into the woods when we were about to have breakfast."

"Was she a hiker?"

"She had a backpack and was in a snowsuit, too. But not like mine," Kaya quickly added.

Great, Finn thought. Only a newbie to the trail would head out today, given the ominous sky and the forecast. His next shift at the Wallingford Fire

Department wasn't until Saturday, and he planned to do some training with a couple of new volunteers for the area's search-and-rescue team. In fact, one of them—young Scott Watson, Bernie's nephew—was scheduled to hike out with Finn after lunch. Well, whoever the hiker was, he wished her luck.

By the time they reached the village's main intersection, the bus was already loaded. Kaya ran ahead, her backpack swaying against her frame. As she mounted the bus steps, she turned to wave goodbye. Finn had hoped to buy that cookie for her as a school snack, but a welcome-home treat at the end of the day would be just as good. The bus door closed and the driver made a U-turn to head for Wallingford, where the only elementary school in the area was located. The high school serving the small local communities was even farther away, not that Roxanne and Kaya would still be living in Maple Glen by that time. At least Finn hoped not, for their sakes. He watched the bus until it turned onto the side road to Route 7, and the realization of how much his life had changed—not only in the past six months but the last four years—struck him again.

When he'd moved back home to help his mother, who'd been recently diagnosed with macular degeneration, cope with his father's move to a care facility in Rutland, Finn had expected to sort things out and return to Burlington shortly to resume his job as a captain in one of the city's fire stations. That was before he knew the gravity of his mother's vision problems or the hopelessness of his father's dementia. Around the same time, he also resigned himself to the collapse of his marriage, though its demise had been long coming. He'd simply been ignoring the warning signs. *That was then and this is now*, he told himself, sighing.

He pushed open the bakery door and was immediately assailed by a burst of steam and mouthwatering fragrance. The owner and chief baker, Sue Giordano, called out from the rear of the store where all the goodness happened. "Right with you!"

Finn browsed the stainless steel racks displaying trays of everything from muffins to bagels. There were no fancy French pastries—"Too finicky," Sue said—but Finn guessed the residents of Maple Glen were plenty satisfied with the daily offerings.

"Hey, Finn, how're things?" Sue asked, drying her hands on a tea towel as she came out of the kitchen.

They'd been schoolmates, and Sue was one of the few who never left, staying behind to take over her parents' bakery when they passed. Her husband, Tony, ran the post office next door, and the two had married a couple of years after Tony had been transferred to the Glen from Postal Services in Bennington.

"Great," Finn replied. "And you?"

She shrugged. "Can't complain. Getting ready for the holiday season."

Christmas. Finn's stomach lurched a bit at the reminder that the biggest holiday of the year was a mere two weeks away. It would be Kaya's first Christmas without both parents. Another major adjustment for her and for Roxanne as well. For all of them, really.

"What'll it be, then?"

"A loaf of multigrain, sliced, and if you happen to have a cookie? Something special for Kaya."

"Sure." She ran the bread through the slicing machine and inserted it in a plastic freezer bag. "I just made a batch of gingerbread men, perfecting my recipe before the Christmas rush. One of those do?"

"Excellent."

The store's doorbell tinkled, and a couple Finn didn't recognize entered, exclaiming loudly over the enticing aromas. Sue came back from the kitchen with a wrapped cookie and, handing it to Finn, winked as the couple checked out the baked goods. At least the Glen still attracted a few tourists in the dead of winter, if only to the bakery. *Tourists who were savvy enough not to go traipsing into the woods on their own.* As he left, Finn realized he could have asked Sue about the woman, but she was busy now with her new customers.

When he got home, he noticed Roxanne's car was gone. She had a part-time job at the library in Rutland three days a week, which Finn and his mother, Marion, considered a blessing. When Kaya and Roxanne moved back home last summer, Roxanne hadn't resembled the chatty, extroverted sister Finn had grown up with. Finn and Marion had given her the space and time to heal from the breakup of her marriage, and eventually, Roxanne had become a wiser, though perhaps more cynical, version of her old self.

He dropped the bakery bag inside the front door and shoveled the sidewalk, then tackled the driveway. Roxanne could have done this, he grumbled to himself as he worked. But then, that was Roxanne, whose distracted, almost flighty nature had been a family legend since she was a kid. Around Kaya's age, Finn thought, smiling at the connection.

When he finished clearing the snow, he retreated to his bedroom and booted up his laptop. His duties as Long Trail section head and leader of the volunteer search-and-rescue unit for the county kept him busy during his off shifts from the fire department in Wallingford. Initially, he found juggling both a challenge, but after four years, he'd managed to perfect a routine that accommodated the needs of his regular work—firefighting—

and trail volunteering. Besides, the two occupations overlapped. His recent promotion to captain meant more administrative work, and his volunteering called for the same kind of organizational and search-and-rescue skills he'd acquired through firefighting. When his mother called him down for lunch, he noticed that the impending snow had arrived.

The knock at the front door just as they were finishing lunch announced Scott's arrival.

"Wasn't sure if you were gonna cancel," the younger man said, stamping his snowy boots on the mat inside the front door.

Finn smiled at the idea. "This is the perfect weather condition, Scott, for a practice run. Or walk, I guess I should say." Finn had set out his hiking clothes before lunch and was putting them on when his mother appeared behind him and Scott.

"Do you two men need any food for your session today?"

"We're good, Mom," Finn answered. Then, glancing at Scott, he added, "Unless…"

"I'm good," Scott said. "Oh, by the way, Uncle Bernie asked me to pass on a message."

Finn looked up from lacing his boots. "Yeah?"

"He asked if we could look out for one of his guests. A woman left for the trail early this morning and was supposed to be back for lunch. She was headed for the conservation area. He thinks it's not a problem, but just in case…"

The woman Kaya had seen. Finn was about to reply when Scott went on to say, "She's from Chicago, so…you know…"

Yep, Finn mused. *What I thought. A city slicker.*

By the time Finn had hoisted his working backpack with its kit of safety and rescue equipment onto his shoulders and adjusted Scott's smaller one for him, snow was pelting down from the gun-metal sky. They marched down the sidewalk, which was filling up again with snow, and crossed the footbridge. The woman's boot prints were long gone, and Finn remembered for the first time since spotting them that she hadn't been wearing crampons. Another rookie mistake.

Scott had been training with Finn long enough to know not to chatter as they walked. Talking was a distraction, which meant you weren't paying attention. As lovely as a walk in the woods could be at any time of the year, Finn knew all too well the potential dangers of a preoccupied mind. They'd been walking in silence almost an hour when they reached the fork in the path and the shift from blue blazes to white. There were more off trails ahead, also blazed with blue streaks and branching off from the main trail to White Rocks, and when they reached the next one, Finn decided to let Scott take the lead.

This second blue trail would take them lower

into the valley, away from White Rocks Mountain and toward the Ice Beds Trail. They wouldn't go that far, though, because the area was risky even in spring and summer. Only a fool would tackle it during what was now a full-out snow squall. *A fool like some woman from Chicago*, Finn thought, when a strange sound rose above the wind. He froze. Sensing he'd stopped, Scott turned around. Finn raised his finger to his lips. There it was again. A high-pitched cry. Human, Finn knew. And maybe female.

CHAPTER TWO

CHAPTER TWO

DEVON DIDN'T KNOW how long she'd been lying on the ground. She'd been careless, stopping on the path to stow her phone in her backpack. Then without hoisting the pack onto her shoulders, she'd held on to it a moment longer, taking one step forward without looking down. That had been her mistake. The cluster of composted leaves had covered a slick of ice, and her instinct to stop herself from falling had misfired badly. She'd felt the sharp pain in her ankle as she twisted it on the way down. The backpack she'd been holding flew into the brush alongside the path, the phone inside. Not that it would have been any use, as Bernie Watson had reminded her. After the first agonizing seconds, when she knew she wasn't going to carry out her mission that day, Devon tried scootching toward the pack using her arms and hands, but the pain was too intense and the effort left her exhausted. Panting, she lay back down, staring up at the gray sky. Then the first large flakes of snow began to flutter down.

Her winter clothing kept her warm for a while until her body heat began to melt the ice beneath her and the dampness seeped through her jacket and snow pants. Using her hands and arms, she managed to slide her bottom toward a tree slightly off the path and sagged against its trunk. Reclining was more comfortable than lying flat, and she closed her eyes in relief as the falling snow gradually covered her legs and shoulders. Somebody would find her, she kept telling herself. Eventually. Bernie would notice. He'd raise an alarm. She hoped. When her stomach began to growl, Devon guessed lunch—French onion soup—was probably being served. She'd asked Bernie to save her some, implying she might not be back in time. So no alarm being raised yet, she thought.

She closed her eyes, letting herself drift drowsily into the bizarre thoughts and images flitting across her mind. When she was back at the B and B, she'd have a long hot bath. She'd ask Bernie to cook her a steak with fries, the kind of meal Dan would order. Any kind of pie for dessert. Maybe Bernie would bake one especially for her. She'd eat it with ice cream. No, maybe not, she decided, shivering. A gust of wind roused her and she shook her head, forcing herself to stay awake.

When and how could she carry out her promise to Dan now? The few objects from their childhood were tucked safely in her backpack, along with a candle and matches that she'd added at the last minute, visualizing a small ceremony. A private memorial of the day twenty-five years ago when they were found in these very woods off-trail and not far from the village. The memorial had been important to her brother, but not so much to her. She'd been five years old and scarcely remembered the events leading up to their getting lost and being rescued. Her flashes of memory had faded over the years, replaced by Dan's stories, which gradually became their two-person-family folklore. The promise she'd made him as he slowly succumbed to cancer was for his sake, his peace of mind. Not hers.

If only she'd carried out his request at the actual anniversary in September. There would have been no ice or snow. Maybe bears, she thought, and her soft chuckle broke the silence of the woods. But she'd kept delaying, half thinking if she waited long enough, the promise would eventually get lost in the day-to-day business of work—she was a social worker in Chicago—and, most of all, making a life without her brother. She tried to quell the rise of anger at herself for all the misguided decisions that brought her to this moment—injured in the woods in a winter snowstorm. She swiped at the tears that welled up, her mittens leaving a wet streak across her cheek. Then she began to cry.

"Is it her, that woman? Is she alive?"

Finn ignored the pitch of anxiety in Scott's voice,

but he felt a lurch in the pit of his stomach. At first, he couldn't tell if the snow-shrouded figure leaning against a tree was human or not. The soft moan confirmed his fears but was also a good sign. She was conscious. When he crouched in front of her, brushing away the snow from her face, her eyes flicked open and her jaw moved as she tried to speak.

"We're here to help you," Finn said as he continued brushing away the snow from her head, arms and shoulders. "My name is Finn and my colleague is Scott. I don't want you to use up any more energy than necessary, so just nod or shake your head at my questions. First, are you hurt?"

A slight nod.

A quick scan of her reclining figure and the snow around it was reassuring. No sign of blood. Then his gaze reached her legs and feet, noticing the unusual position of her right ankle.

"Your ankle?"

Another nod.

"Anywhere else?"

A slow head shake.

"Are you with anyone?"

Another shake of her head.

"Okay. Scott and I have a portable stretcher with us and we're going to set it up. Then we're going to transfer you onto it and take you out." He craned round to Scott, who'd removed his pack and was delving into it for the Mylar blanket, which they quickly wrapped around her. They'd adjust it once she was on the stretcher.

She nodded and closed her eyes.

"Stay with us. It's better if you're awake." He gently pushed aside the scarf around her neck to feel for her pulse. It was faint but steady. Another good sign.

Scott was unfolding the stretcher. It was a new one Finn had purchased for the local chapter of the Green Mountain Conservancy, where he volunteered. It was super light but able to carry a full-grown man. There were lots of straps along with head and chin restraints, which he hoped wouldn't alarm her. Its narrow width made it perfect for the trails. He and Scott had already practiced assembling it, and as they worked silently and quickly, Finn kept his eyes on the woman. He saw that she was making an effort to keep her eyes open but figured once on the stretcher she'd give in to sleep. That was okay, he decided, because she'd be easier to carry if she was unaware of the inevitable low-hanging branches or steep inclines, up and down. When the stretcher was ready, they laid it on the ground parallel to the woman.

"Scott and I are going to lift you up and place you on the stretcher. We'll be as gentle as possible, but your ankle might be moved, so be prepared for that. Okay?"

A faint nod.

"The other thing is, we will be strapping you onto the stretcher. All of you, including your head and chin. Try to stay calm and don't resist. It will feel strange and maybe a bit uncomfortable. Okay?"

This time her nod was barely perceptible. Finn signaled Scott with a raised eyebrow and murmured, "On the count of three."

Scott had practiced with other volunteers lifting and placing real people on stretchers at their meetings, but he'd yet to assist someone who was injured. Finn knew the woman would be a dead weight, that the extra pain she'd feel as they lifted her and positioned her onto the stretcher would cause her to flinch or, worse, jerk away from their grasp. He hoped Scott would keep his cool, ignore whatever unexpected movements she might make and focus on staying steady himself. He was tempted to remind him but knew they'd done this exercise countless times. He had to trust that the twenty-year-old would come through.

Moving as close to her as the tree trunk permitted, Finn placed one hand under one of her shoulders and stretched across her back to the other armpit. He nodded at Scott, who stood at her feet. "Under the calves, close to the knees," Finn instructed lest Scott inadvertently try to lift her by the feet. "One, two, three," and they raised her off the ground.

Finn winced at her sudden cry as they set her

onto the stretcher and strapped her in, tucking the Mylar blanket around and beneath her so it wouldn't slip while they carried her out. When she was secure, he and Scott slung their backpacks on. Finn stooped to lift the stretcher handles at the front and saw that her eyes were already shut. It was good that she was relaxed but not so good if she was hypothermic, and he figured she was close. If they'd found her any later...

He didn't want to think about that. He turned to see that Scott was in position at the end of the stretcher. "Set your feet slightly apart to handle the weight, and on the count of three, we'll lift her up." Scott knew the training drill, but doing this with an alert and conscious volunteer was another matter.

"One, two, three." She was light, in spite of her padded winter clothing. Finn was grateful for that, because they had almost an hour's walk ahead of them. He was also grateful for his crampons, especially now that the path was covered in snow, hiding any ice. He shifted his mind away from the horrifying scenario of falling with her on the stretcher. He began to walk, glancing down at each footstep and then focusing on the path ahead. Except for their labored breathing, the woods were silent.

Every few minutes Finn looked back, checking on her. Her eyes were still closed, but he noticed that the few snowflakes landing on her face were melting from her exhaled breath. Still, he decided they should stop every twenty minutes so he could check her pulse. "Scott, when we get to the junction, we'll set her down. I want to do a quick vitals check." The wind picked up Scott's reply and carried it off, but Finn assumed he'd heard.

Reaching the fork where the off trail led toward Maple Glen, Finn gave a hand signal to stop and slowly pivoted around. He nodded at Scott, and they lowered the stretcher to the ground. Brushing aside the scatter of snow on her chin and forehead, Finn loosened the Mylar blanket tucked around her neck and felt for her pulse. Steady but still weak. He figured they were at least another twenty minutes to their destination. "Let's go all the way now," he told Scott. "She's doing okay. No change."

On the count of three again, they lifted the stretcher and pressed on. By the time they reached the slope leading down to the bridge over Otter Creek, the snow was so thick Finn could hardly see the path. This was a tricky part. The slabs of limestone rock had been entrenched years ago, when the path leading out of the village had been reconfigured. They were firmly set but covered in snow and slippery. Finn craned round to Scott. "Nice and slow. Make sure your footing is stable before taking each step."

"Got it."

He was lucky to have the young man as a trainee, Finn thought as he tentatively stepped forward. Unfortunately, after the holidays Scott would be heading back to college in Burlington but, with any luck, would resume his volunteering and possibly a paid job next summer. The kid had a good shot at one, and Finn's recommendation would help, or so he hoped. The county chapter of the conservancy was located in Rutland, and most volunteers worked in that area. Right now, Maple Glen had Finn, Shawn Harrison and now Scott to manage the off trail and the section of the Long Trail proximate to the Glen. Sometimes, Theo Danby joined in, but his position as one of only three doctors at the medical clinic in Rutland complicated any fixed schedule Finn could organize. Once the new clinic in Wallingford was completed, Theo might have more flexibility.

Finn's foot suddenly slid, but he caught the misstep before it could lead to disaster. He needed to keep his thoughts focused. When they reached the bridge, he saw that the road leading from it was thick with snow. There'd be no trip to the clinic in Rutland today and maybe not even tomorrow.

He shifted the stretcher handles as he turned around to Scott. "We'll take her to my place to wait out the storm."

He barely caught Scott's nod through the swirling snow, but relief surged through him now that they were in the Glen. They were all safe. Now his job was to ensure she had a good recovery, and where better to do that than his family home, with the help of his mother and sister?

WARMTH. DEVON REVELED in it, sinking into its soft comfort. Her mind pulled away from the dream of falling and icy cold pain followed by distant voices and then floating above the earth. When her eyes blinked open, a small face was hovering over her. Blue eyes, golden hair swept up in pigtails that framed a big smile. Was Devon still dreaming?

"She's awake!"

Devon flinched at the shout.

The face inched forward, close to her own. "They're coming. Do you want something to drink? Water or juice? Uncle Finn said you'd be thirsty."

Devon ran her tongue along her dry lips. She tried to speak, but her entire mouth was parched, as if she'd been crossing a desert instead of a snowy forest. The memories were coming back but jumbled together, like a collage. She now saw that the face belonged to a little girl, and as Devon slowly turned her head from side to side, she realized she was lying on a sofa in a room that smelled faintly of woodsmoke. A thick duvet covered her, and when she raised her head as far as she could, she saw that someone had removed her snow pants and jacket. Her right leg, inside the sweat pants she'd put on that morning, was propped up on large, firm cushions. Her foot was bare and the ankle wrapped in some kind of fabric. She tried to move it and cried out in pain.

The little girl backed away, her face alarmed. "It's okay. You're okay, but you shouldn't move."

Then before Devon could speak, the girl was gone. Devon dropped her head back onto a pillow and waited for the pain to ebb. She had no idea where she was but knew it wasn't the B and B. Someone's home, judging by the collection of family memorabilia around her—framed photographs on the side table at the end of the sofa, a sweater draped over the back of the armchair by the door and a basket of books on the floor next to it.

She closed her eyes and tried not to think about this miserable situation she'd gotten herself into. She was no health care specialist, but she knew her ankle—either fractured or sprained—wouldn't be used for walking anytime soon. Would she be able to drive, make it back to Rutland to catch her flight back to Chicago in three days' time? Show up for work in a week? How could she make good on her promise to Dan? Tears welled up, and she blinked hard to stop the flow. Crying wasn't going to answer those questions, much less solve her current problem—*Who was going to look after her?* If Dan were still alive, he'd be here in hours to whisk her away, but she was on her own. A wave of self-pity washed over her, halted only by the sound of footsteps rushing along a hallway.

She turned her head to see an impossibly tall man with broad shoulders and a worried expression followed by a gray-haired woman and the little girl. "Hello, Devon. My name is Finn McAllister, and this is my mother, Marion," he said, gesturing to the woman drawing up next to him, "and my niece, Kaya."

Devon scarcely heard the introductions, her gaze fixed on the man whose face, with its hollow unshaven cheeks, seemed familiar. He looked exhausted, and she realized at once that this must be the man who had emerged from the curtain of snow back on the trail. Her rescuer. She opened her mouth to speak, but he preempted her.

"You're okay. Sprained ankle rather than a fracture, I think, but the village doctor, Theo Danby, is on his way. The clinic where he works is in Rutland, and no one is leaving the village today or maybe even tomorrow. Fortunately, this is his day off. He's bringing some pain meds for you and a proper tension bandage, as well as a pair of crutches." Finn paused, wiping a hand across his face. "I think you should stay here until Theo's had a chance to check you over, and if he recommends that you be monitored for a day or two, it might be best if you stay with us a bit longer rather than going back to Bernie's. We can move you to a room upstairs. Is that okay with you?"

It took a few seconds for his question to register, and as much as Devon wanted to curl up somewhere quiet all by herself, the thought of enduring the pain alone in a small room wasn't appealing. She nodded.

"She can have my room!" blurted Kaya.

"I've already made up the guest room for her, Kaya, but that's a sweet gesture. When Devon is feeling better, perhaps you can visit her or fetch things for her until she can operate the crutches."

The older woman—Marion?—smiled at Kaya and then Devon. "Would you like anything to eat or drink, dear?"

"Wait till Theo comes, Mom, to find out about food. But maybe some water?" Finn's gaze shifted from Marion to Devon.

He had nice eyes, she thought. Concerned and warm. His sandy-colored hair spiked up as if he'd run his fingers through it, or else he hadn't smoothed it down after removing the hat he'd been wearing. She ran her tongue across her dry lips. "Water?" she croaked.

"I'll get it," Kaya quickly said and rushed out of the room.

It seemed as if they couldn't do enough for her, Devon thought, and felt a small rise of emotion.

"Do you want to call anyone, Devon? Or maybe we can call for you?" Finn pointed to her phone sitting on a coffee table a few feet away.

Who was there to call? Her boss in Chicago?

Her best friend, who'd be at work? She bit down on her lip, fighting tears. There was no one, really. The one person she'd always had to call on was her brother, and he was gone. "I don't have anyone I can call." The flash of sympathy in their eyes brought tears again.

"Well then," Marion announced in a steady but kind voice, "you'll just have to put up with us." She turned aside to take the glass of water that Kaya handed her and perched on the edge of the sofa, slipping her left arm beneath Devon's neck to help raise her head. Then she tilted the glass as Devon's mouth opened.

To Devon's relief, the water was room temperature, and after the first noisy slurp, she managed to drink slowly and steadily until the glass was empty. Devon sank back onto the pillow and closed her eyes until the bustle of movement in the room roused her again.

Devon watched as Finn and Kaya left the room. The heavy stomping of feet suggested someone new had arrived. The doctor, she guessed, and sure enough, Finn strode into the room followed by a slightly shorter man, whose serious expression shifted into a warm smile as he made eye contact with Devon.

"Hi, Devon. I'm Theo, as Finn probably told you. Unfortunately, because of the storm, we can't take you for an X-ray at my clinic, but I'll have a look at your ankle, and hopefully we can make you comfortable until we can organize a trip to Rutland. Okay?"

"Okay," she murmured. Her voice sounded strange to her, thin and frail. She saw him exchange a look with Finn.

"Any signs of hypothermia?"

"She was shivering and her voice was weak, but she was coherent. No shaking."

"Good." Then the doctor pulled up a chair to sit at the end of the sofa and gently began to pull away the fabric wrapped loosely around her ankle. "Ice packs?" he asked, turning to Finn.

"Yes, but we thought we'd take her up to the guest room first. It'll be quieter and more private. Did you bring the crutches?"

"They're folded up in that canvas bag in the hall. Luckily, I had a set at home."

Devon had been following the conversation, turning slightly from doctor to Finn, but she was now exhausted from the effort and closed her eyes. When her foot was unwrapped, she felt the doctor—*What is his name again?*—gently run his fingers along and around it, and she bit her lip, stifling a moan.

"I'm not feeling anything but swelling," he said, "which is a good thing, but she could have a hairline fracture, so she'll need an X-ray. Whenever we can get to Rutland," he added, sighing.

"It's lucky you were off today, though I'm not

sure of the chances of a trip to Rutland even to-morrow."

Devon groaned. A sprained ankle and a snow-storm. She had a feeling she definitely wasn't going to be flying home in three days' time. The two men were murmuring to one another—deciding what to do with her, she guessed—and then Theo said, "I'm going to give you some pain meds, but perhaps you should stay here with the McAllisters until Finn can bring you to the clinic for an X-ray. I think you ought to have someone close by to help you with your mobility and also to monitor any changes in your injury."

"Okay," she whispered. She saw him rummage in a bag at his feet, and seconds later, Finn was helping her sit up. She sagged against his arm as he slid it beneath her upper back, but the strength of his grasp didn't waver. After swallowing the pill, he gently lowered her back onto the pillow.

"Theo and I are going to set up the stretcher, and when the meds are working, we'll carry you upstairs to the guest room, and later, or maybe to-morrow, I'll get your things from Bernie's place. Is that okay?"

Devon nodded. She appreciated their constant asking if everything was okay, but deep inside, she wanted to cry, *No, nothing is okay now!* Everything was messed up and she had no one to blame but herself. A single tear rolled unexpectedly from one eye, and she felt Finn gently thumb it away. For the first time in a long time, Devon was content to let someone other than her brother help her. She let out a long, slow sigh and closed her eyes.

CHAPTER THREE

SHE WAS... Finn searched for the right word, but all he came up with was *plucky*. An old-fashioned word, one his father might have used. That thought took him instantly to the days when his father was the man Finn remembered and not the one he visited at the care home in Rutland. A surge of nostalgia flowed through Finn, but he quickly shook it off. Now wasn't the time for sentiment. After they carefully set Devon onto the bed in the guest room, Finn drew the duvet up over her, and noticed her eyes were already closing. He nodded at Theo and tilted his head toward the door.

Once they were out in the hall, Theo said, "Except for a possible sprain, which I think is a moderate one judging by how much I could move the ankle, she's okay. Heart rate is fine and no sign of hypothermia, as you'd feared."

"That's good. So what's the prognosis on recovery?"

"When the roads are clear, bring her to the clinic for an X-ray to be sure. I have a special boot, something like a walking cast, that she can use after the swelling goes down. It'll be easier than manipulating crutches, especially outside. In the meantime, pain meds when she needs them, elevate, ice. You know the drill." He frowned. "What do you know about her? Other than her name and that she's from Chicago."

"That's it. At least, that's all Bernie knew."

"It just seems odd that she's got no one to call. Most people have at least one person." He paused. "A bit sad, really, especially at this time of year."

Finn, too, had been struck by her reply—*I don't have anyone.* He'd been grateful for his mother's immediate response because anything he might have said was stuck behind the lump in his throat. He'd mulled over his atypical reaction while Theo was examining her. What happened to the neutrality of his well-established EMT training? Was he distracted by the tousled raven-black curls and those big sky-blue eyes, the only lights in her ashen face?

He took a deep breath. "Thanks for coming out in a snowstorm, Theo. I hesitated to wait till tomorrow, in case I missed something. Mom made muffins earlier. Can I offer you a couple with coffee?"

Theo shook his head. "Thanks, Finn, but a guy from Wallingford is coming to plow us out. Fortunately, the snow tires on my pickup are new and got me here okay."

"Don't be surprised if Mom hands you a packet of them on your way out. And let me know what I owe you."

"Nothing, Finn. Friends, right? Plus, you're taking Luke on a winter hike over the holidays. It all evens out one way or another."

Finn's face heated up. He'd forgotten about his impulsive offer to show Theo's thirteen-year-old son some of the Long Trail. They'd hiked last summer when Theo and Luke had come to Maple Glen to deal with Theo's inheritance of a farm. The intended two weeks had turned into a lifetime commitment when Theo fell in love with Maura Stuart, who owned the neighboring farm and donkey-riding business with her twin sister. Now they were married and expecting their first child together. Funny how life goes, Finn thought, as he watched Theo get into his winter parka and snow boots.

He handed Theo his leather doctor's bag and was about to open the door when his mother rushed along the hall from the kitchen.

"Wait a second!" She was holding a plastic container, which she handed to Theo as she drew up to them. "Muffins with our raspberries frozen from last summer."

"Aw, thanks, Marion! We will all enjoy them, especially Maura, who seems to be eating for—"

"Two?" quipped Marion, smiling. "How is she doing?"

"Good, now that the first trimester is over, along with her nausea. She'll appreciate these, believe me." He turned to Finn. "Let me know if Devon's condition changes in any way at all. You know the signs. She was lucky you were the one to find her and not some other foolhardy wannabe trail hiker."

Finn grinned. The expression echoed his own thoughts earlier in the day when he'd first spotted Devon's tracks in the snow. But it was only months ago that Theo himself had been a wannabe hiker, returning to the village years after he'd left as a teenager. Now he was a true Glen resident. He caught the glint in his mother's eye and winked. The McAllister clan had been Glen residents since its very beginning more than a century ago. Everyone was a newbie to them.

After Finn closed the door behind Theo, he said, "I'm going to do some more shoveling. Have you heard from Roxanne?"

"She's spending the night with a colleague and hopes to return in the morning, if the roads have been cleared."

"Too bad we're at the end of Route 7 and always the last section to be plowed out. A good thing Kaya's school closed at noon, otherwise a lot of kids would be sleeping in the school gym tonight."

"I remember a couple of times when you and Roxanne had to bunk with families in Wallingford when the buses couldn't get through. Kaya and I are making a hearty chicken noodle soup for Devon and for us, too. It feels like that kind of day." She reached up to pat her son's cheek. "Good work, honey. Proud of you." Then she turned and bustled back to the kitchen.

Finn felt that lump again. There had been a few misunderstandings when he'd come back home almost four years ago, but he and his mother had finally established a workable routine, one that was slightly upended six months ago when Roxanne and Kaya moved in. They'd finally managed to establish a way to coexist without treading on too many toes or dashing too many expectations.

Occasionally, though, Finn had a what-if moment. *What if his ex hadn't cheated on him? What if they were still happily married? Would they have their own family and still be living in Burlington?* As much as he loved the family he had, there were times when Finn wondered what it would be like to have one of his own.

Another long sigh. What was with him today? he wondered. All these sentimental musings. Were they due to the holiday season with its inevitable memories? Or perhaps his mood was connected to Devon's tearful face when he'd asked if he could call someone for her. *There was no one.* Which begged the question, what was a big-city woman doing hiking on an obscure section of the Long Trail, in the winter, by herself? At some point, he knew he'd get the answer. She wouldn't be leaving Maple Glen anytime soon.

Kaya helped set the table in the kitchen for supper, placing the soup spoons at interesting angles, Finn noted, and he was about to correct her when his mother, ladling soup at the stove, shook her head at him. He got her message.

"I'll check on Devon, see if she's awake and ready to eat something," he said.

Marion thought for a minute. "Are those crutches upstairs?"

"No, but I'll take them with me and unfold them for her. She may need some practice."

"And some help washing and getting ready for the night." The look he shot his mother prompted her to add, "I can manage that, and hopefully Roxanne will make it home tomorrow."

Okay, he thought, that's one problem solved. "If you get her soup into a bowl now, it'll cool off enough for her to safely eat. She may still be a bit shaky, so…"

"I'm way ahead of you. It's on that tray with a biscuit and a glass of water."

Finn looked to the counter next to her and grinned sheepishly. "I should have known." He went for the tray and tested the soup's temperature with his little finger. "It's good, so I'll take it up to her and help her with it. You and Kaya go ahead and eat."

Marion raised an eyebrow. "Don't linger or force her to eat more than she can. And most of all, don't start pestering her with questions."

"What?"

"I know you too well, Finn McAllister. You're probably itching to find out why she came to Maple Glen."

"I know," he muttered. "She needs to have some recovery time."

He picked up the tray, but when he reached the door, Marion added, "So remember that."

Finn stifled a sigh and headed upstairs. One drawback to living with a parent again was that there was no escaping these references to childhood habits. She *did* know him too well. When he reached the guest bedroom, he tapped lightly on the door. There wasn't an immediate response, and he was about to return to the kitchen but heard a faint "Come in."

Devon had turned on the bedside lamp and was sitting up against her pillows. The movement had shifted her leg farther down on the cushions. Finn set the tray on top of the chest of drawers.

"Want some help with that?" He gestured to her foot.

"Please." The word came out as a croak. She cleared her throat. "Thanks."

He set one hand beneath her calf and gently raised it while moving the cushion with the other hand, then carefully lowered the leg onto it. She winced and he asked, "How's the pain level?"

"Okay."

"Scale of one to ten?"

"Maybe six."

"Have some dinner then before more pain meds. Mom made chicken noodle soup, and there's one of her butter biscuits and a glass of water. We have juice, too, if you like."

Devon glanced over at the tray. "Sounds delicious."

"It is. You could probably use some hydration, so soup will help with that." Finn looked around the room. "I'll get another pillow or cushion for your lap to balance the tray." He paused. "Or I can help you with eating...or my mother, if you prefer."

She closed her eyes and groaned. "No, no," she mumbled. "I'm not at that place yet. I can manage."

Finn got it. Losing independence either through sickness or incapacity was stressful. He'd witnessed that in his father. "Okay, I'll get another pillow for you." His own room was two doors away and he quickly retrieved one from his bed.

"We should look for some kind of bell," he said as he placed the cushion on her lap and then settled the tray on top. He jiggled it a bit to make sure it was relatively stable. The tray had a good one-inch raised edge, so any spills would stay on it. As he finished making sure everything was okay, he noticed her looking up at him and realized she hadn't started eating. Waiting for some privacy, he thought. "All right, I'll leave you to it." But still he paused, almost reluctant to go. "Anything else I can do for you, before...uh... bedtime?"

"Would your mother be free to help me at some point?"

Her big blue eyes locked onto his and he felt heat rising up into his face. He cleared his throat. "Sure. Absolutely. I'll have her come up in about... what? Twenty minutes or so?"

She nodded and peered down at the tray.

Finn backed away, hesitating briefly at the door to say, "You'll be all right, Devon. Don't worry about anything." As he left the room, he figured she probably didn't need reassuring as much as she needed someone to wrap their arms around her and hold her tight. What was disconcerting was the unexpected image of *him* being that person.

FOR A MINUTE, Devon didn't know where she was. She turned her head to see sun streaming through the floral pattern of the curtains—shots of pink, blue and purple that teased a summer's day. Everything came back then, descending on her like a storm cloud. The snow, her fall and her ankle. She tried to wiggle it and winced, groaning as full awareness of her situation registered. There would be no memorial for Dan, at least not in the near future, and maybe not even a flight home on Saturday. *What was today?* She groaned again, closing her eyes against her new reality.

The light creak of a door got her attention, and she turned to see a small girl in pajamas tiptoeing across the room. She was looking down at the floor, concentrating on keeping quiet, and didn't notice Devon's smile until she was a few feet away from the bed. Then she whirled around and ran to the door to holler, "She's awake!"

There was murmuring from downstairs and soon, footsteps coming up.

"I didn't wake you, did I?"

Devon caught the slightly anxious tone in the question and was about to reassure her otherwise when Finn walked into the room, casting a quick frown at his niece. "Kaya?"

"I didn't wake her." She looked to Devon for support.

"She didn't."

He pursed his lips. "Good. And Grandma says your breakfast is ready."

"Can I come back again later? For a visit?"

"Of course," Devon said, noticing Finn give the girl another frown. She felt a bristle of annoyance. He'd rescued her from the storm, but she didn't need rescuing from a little girl.

Kaya gave a small wave and dashed out the door.

"She means well," he began.

"She's curious and a little girl," Devon added. His slight flush at the reminder pleased her a tiny bit. She hardly knew the man, but she was beginning to think he was used to being in charge. A sudden thought that Dan, too, had been like that at times caught her off guard and tears welled up again. She looked toward the window, blinking against the brightness. What was with all this crying? It wasn't like her, and she bit down on her lip until the dampness disappeared.

Swiveling to look at Finn, she saw him eyeing her with concern on his face. She felt intuitively that he was a kind man and that his need to be in charge stemmed from a sense of responsibility. But just as she'd resisted interference from her brother and had stood up against his tendency to run things, she could do the same with this man, a virtual stranger.

"How was your sleep?" he asked.

"Deep," she answered, smiling.

"Pain?"

"Only when I move it."

"Okay, that's good. Are you ready for breakfast, or...?"

"I think a visit to the bathroom first."

"Do you want my mother to come help you again, or can you manage with those?" He gestured to the crutches resting against the night table next to the bed. "Have you used crutches before?"

"Years ago, when I wasn't much older than Kaya. Same ankle, too, but a hairline fracture."

"Ah." He nodded. "Have you had problems with it since?"

"Not really. It was a long time ago."

Another nod. He seemed at a loss for words, keeping his dark brown eyes on hers. "Okay then, I'll tell Mom to bring some breakfast up and—"

"I'll come downstairs." When he furrowed his brow, she added, with a quick smile, "If I can't manage, I'll give a shout."

"Right." He started for the door, where he stopped to say, "The roads might be plowed today and, hopefully, we can make it into the clinic for that X-ray. Then we can…you know…make some decisions."

We? Devon bristled again until she realized whatever the outcome, she had no choice but to depend on this man and his family for now. She managed another smile and when he left, flung the duvet aside and slowly pivoted her right leg off the bed. She gasped at the sharp pain but kept moving until her left foot rested on the floor while her right dangled. Reaching forward, she grabbed the crutches.

As she'd told Finn, years had passed since her only other injury, but the memory refreshed as she placed her hands on the crossbar of each crutch and hoisted herself up off the bed, keeping her right foot hovering above the floor. There had been adults to help her then, too. Foster parents who'd been solicitous though not loving. For that—and support—she'd relied on Dan.

Hobbling across the room, she realized that as irksome as Finn's attention was, the softness in his face and warmth in his eyes when he looked at her made all the difference. She'd known him less than twenty-four hours but already knew she could depend on him. Even if that dependency came with disadvantages, she could handle them. Her impulsive trip to Maple Glen in mid-December had turned out to be a fiasco, but at worst, she wouldn't have to hang around for more than a few days longer. Her flight could be rescheduled, and she'd manage just fine with crutches or that boot thing the doctor had mentioned. She'd liked him—his calm presence and reassuring manner—and figured he must be an asset to a place as small as Maple Glen.

Yesterday when she'd set out on her ill-fated mission, she'd thought as pretty as the village was, she wouldn't want to spend more than a couple of days there. She snorted at that irony now as she limped out the bedroom door into the hallway. A faint murmur of voices from below caught her attention. Were they discussing what to do with her? Devon sighed. She'd been focusing on her own plight while ignoring theirs. They, too, had been caught up in the drama of her fall and were likely wondering how much longer they'd have to look after her.

She closed the bathroom door behind her, leaning against it to catch her breath. Using crutches took more energy than she'd thought, or perhaps her body was still recovering from the shock of the fall and the cold wait to be rescued. Dr. Danby had cautioned her not to push herself too much over the next few days, but what choice did she have? There were commitments and responsibilities awaiting her in Chicago, along with the task of fulfilling Dan's last wishes after probate of his will was finished. He had other bequests to carry out besides this memorial trip to the place where they'd been found twenty-five years ago. The fact that she might fail the most important of Dan's requests caused her eyes to well up yet again.

Devon shuffled to the mirror over the bathroom sink and stared at her ghostly white face, the dark circles beneath her eyes and the grim outline of her mouth. She propped the crutches against the sink and turned the hot water faucet. Water rushed into the basin, and she leaned against it, splashing some onto her face.

Depending on people she didn't know was contrary to her nature, but she would do whatever was necessary to keep her promise to Dan, even tolerating the well-intended intrusions of a family she had met by chance and the man in charge of it.

CHAPTER FOUR

"PANCAKES THE DAY after waffles?" Finn grinned at his mother, standing at the stove.

"In times like these, we need comfort food," his mother said with a shrug as she ladled more batter onto the grill. "Besides, Devon didn't eat much of the soup last night, and I bet she's hungry this morning."

"So the pancakes are for *her*?"

"I'm sure she won't be the only one eating them."

Finn heard the miffed tone in her reply and wrapped an arm across her shoulders. "I'm only teasing, Mom. Nurturing, especially through food, is your specialty and one we all love."

"There's a lot more to me than that, Finn." She looked from the grill to him.

After an awkward minute, he mumbled, "Okay, well, let me know if you want any help."

"I'm fine. Kaya is getting dressed, and I promised she could help me take breakfast up."

"Actually, Devon told me she'd try to come down for it, so unless she calls for help, assume she can manage."

"I'll figure it out," she said, her voice quiet but firm.

He backed out of the kitchen, feeling like he'd stumbled into quicksand. He had no idea how this casual conversation had taken such a sober turn. It was a sensation he'd been experiencing off and on for the past six months, living in a household of females, and he was perplexed by it. He was trying his best but often seemed to fall short of expectations.

As he headed into the hallway to get his phone, which he'd left on the small table near the front door, he heard the soft and uneven thuds of movement above. Devon using the crutches, perhaps, to freshen up in the bathroom. It was a good sign, that she was making an effort to get around on her own, but he hoped she wasn't pushing herself too much, just in case the X-ray showed something Theo might have missed.

Finn's phone lit up with a text notification. Theo, writing to say Route 7 had been cleared and he was heading into work at the clinic in Rutland.

Give me a ring if you decide to bring Devon in for that X-ray and I'll set aside time for it. Thinking business will be slow today anyway.

Good to know, Finn thought, as he texted back that he'd call when she was ready.

He'd checked the main street earlier, when he'd

first got up, but it hadn't been plowed out. The county was responsible for clearing the road leading from Route 7 into the Glen, but it seemed the village was always a last priority. The topic had generated a heated discussion at a recent village council meeting when some residents felt not enough was being done to address the problem. As a council member, Finn had left the meeting feeling both frustrated and disillusioned at the naivete of some of the villagers. Services required money and the Glen's population was small.

He was getting his jacket out of the hall closet when he heard the rumble of a snowplow and smiled. One less issue to deal with today. By the time he was outside, the plow was making a U-turn in front of the house, finishing the opposite side of the road as it headed out of the village. He waved at the driver, recognizing him as a retired firefighter from Wallingford. He knew a few men who'd taken early retirement the last couple of years and bolstered their pensions with part-time jobs. From the happy grin on the man's face as he waved back, Finn guessed there were no regrets. Personally, Finn loved his jobs—running the small fire department and volunteering for the conservancy—and couldn't imagine leaving either one.

He reached for the shovel leaning against one of the pillars supporting the veranda roof and headed for the driveway. Although he'd cleared the sidewalks yesterday morning and later in the day after Theo left, he hadn't bothered with the driveway, figuring no one would be using a vehicle for a bit. He opened the door of his pickup, which was parked to the right of the garage, to get the brush and scraper to sweep off the accumulated snow. His mother's car, which she seldom used in the winter, was in the garage, and when Roxanne returned, probably later in the day, she could park her car inside, too.

When Roxanne and Kaya had moved in six months ago, the constant shuffling of vehicles had irritated Finn, but now they'd come to a system that worked for the three of them. The fact that his pickup needed a clear exit to the road at all times in case of an emergency had finally registered with his sister. Once he finished with the concrete pad in front of the garage, he had to exchange the shovel for the snowblower to remove snow from the long gravel drive itself. The snowblower was old and unreliable. Finn had bought it for his father years ago, after the driveway—then only a grassy lane—had been refinished with gravel. Checking the time on his phone when he was done, he saw that he'd been working for almost an hour. He was starving and hoped there'd be leftover pancakes.

He stamped most of the snow off his boots before going into the house and was careful to stand on the thick mat his mother brought out every winter. It was showing its age, like everything in the house. Despite several small renovations and upgrades over the years, the Manor, as his great-grandparents had dubbed the family home, was falling apart. Finn had been thinking lately that the place needed serious work but had been reluctant to raise the issue with his mother. She had enough to worry about with her macular degeneration, his father's diagnosis and even Roxanne's move back home.

Finn carefully set his boots off to the side out of the way. He thought of his mother's remark while she was making breakfast, that there was more to her than nurturing, and felt bad that she'd interpreted what he'd intended as a compliment in a negative way. Of course, there was more to his mother than cooking! Marion McAllister was, and always had been, a vital force in the community. She had a busy social life with many friends. The murmur of voices from the kitchen took his mind away from family issues, which weren't going to be easily resolved and not that day. He smoothed his hair with his hands and walked down the hall.

His mother, Kaya and Devon were seated at the kitchen table littered with empty plates and remnants of pancakes and bacon. Momentarily unnoticed, Finn paused in the doorway to take in the scene. Kaya had obviously been entertaining them with some story, grinning broadly when the adults laughed. His mother gazed with adoration at her granddaughter and was about to pick up her coffee mug when she noticed Finn.

"We saved some for you," she said, tilting her head to the stove.

Truth be told, he was more interested in Devon than pancakes. She was sitting at a right angle to where he stood and had to turn slightly to see him. She was wearing a pale blue tracksuit that he thought was one of Roxanne's. It was a tad too big, and the sleeves were rolled up, but the color suited her, complementing the darker blue of her eyes. The smile she gave him was hard to decipher, though. Shy? Or guarded? Still, he was happy to see she'd made it downstairs for break-fast. He saw her crutches propped against a far counter, and he lowered his gaze, spotting her ankle resting atop a large cushion beneath the table. His mother was taking care of her.

"Did you come downstairs by yourself?" he asked.

"I watched from the bottom," his mother quickly said.

Finn bit his lip but said nothing. They'd worked it out without him, which was probably a good thing. But still…

When his mother started to get up for his break-fast, he said, "I'll get it, Mom." He felt all eyes on him as he went to the stove and had the uncom-fortable thought that he'd goofed. How, he wasn't quite sure. He took his usual place at the head of the table opposite his mother, where his father once sat, and a silence fell over the others. A quick memory took him back to his father, a loving man, but one whose word carried weight. Finn peered down at his pancakes until the moment passed. Then he began to eat, but somehow the pancakes weren't as satisfying as he'd expected.

"We thought we heard a snowplow," his mother said.

Finn swallowed a mouthful of pancake. "Yes. The road's clear here, and Theo texted to say Route 7 was open now, too."

"Will we be going to get my X-ray, then?"

He looked at Devon, sitting at his left. "Theo said the clinic wasn't busy, so we might as well, if you're up to it."

She shrugged as if she didn't have much choice. "I suppose it's best to make sure there's no fracture. Then I can make some plans about next steps."

Finn guessed those next steps would be when and how to leave Maple Glen. He nodded and forked another bite of pancake.

"Can I come, too?" Kaya piped up.

Finn looked at his mother, who instinctively came to his rescue. "Sweetie, we were going to make cookies this morning for your mother as a welcome home after the storm. Remember?"

Kaya frowned. "Oh, yeah."

For a second, she seemed to be mentally debating cookies or a drive to Rutland and a fast-food outlet she'd visited once with Finn. "Can we make chocolate chip ones?" she finally asked, turning to her grandmother.

"Of course." Marion winked at Finn.

"I should go upstairs and get ready," Devon said.

"Your clothes from yesterday will be dry now," Marion said. "Or you can just wear Roxanne's tracksuit."

Devon grasped hold of the table edge to stand up, then remembered her crutches, leaning against the counter behind Finn. "Oops!" she laughed.

Finn pushed his chair back and reached for the crutches as he got to his feet. Kaya swiveled off her chair and rushed to Devon's side while Marion stood poised to help if necessary. As he handed Devon the crutches, she murmured a quiet "Thanks," but her expression seemed more frustrated than grateful, he thought. Was she embarrassed by all the fuss?

"I'll follow you," he told her. "Stairs can be trickier going up than down."

She nodded and, taking hold of the crutches, pivoted slowly and started down the hall. Finn avoided his mother's gaze, thinking it might contain another warning about interfering too much. He ruffled Kaya's hair and said, "Save some cookies for me, shrimp."

"Maybe," she teased, giggling.

When he reached the bottom of the staircase,

Devon was partway up. She continued on without a backward glance, right hand on the banister and the other using one crutch as she levered herself up step by step. She'd figured out how to ascend and was doing so without any assistance. Finn grabbed the second crutch, which she'd left against the newel post. While he admired her independence, he wondered if she was the kind of person who never asked for help, the kind who sometimes got into trouble because of that stubbornness. A vision of her, snow-covered and lying against that tree yesterday, flashed in his mind. There was no option then about getting help or not. She needed rescuing and he'd been there to do it. End of discussion.

Finn exhaled and followed her up the stairs.

WAS HE ALWAYS RIGHT, or did he just think so? Devon sneaked a peek at Finn, his big hands gripping the steering wheel of his pickup. She'd offered to have him drive her rental car still parked at the B and B, but he'd said she'd need the extra leg room for her ankle, and the crutches would fit in the passenger side as well. And despite the fact that she wasn't tall and her legs weren't long, she conceded that the extra space was able to accommodate the large cushion for her ankle that Marion had insisted Finn place on the floor beneath the dashboard. Devon guessed from his expression as he accepted the cushion from his mother that he'd already thought of that, but he'd simply nodded at Marion.

The quiet exchange reminded her of breakfast, when he'd come into the kitchen as Kaya had finished recounting her story about the time Uncle Finn had taken her to Jake & Friends to ride a donkey. He'd bet her an ice-cream cone that he wasn't too big to ride one, too. When they got to the Stuart farm where the donkeys lived, the only available one was Matilda, and when he was up on the saddle, his feet were still touching the ground. He'd bent his knees to push his feet farther into the stirrups, and Matilda started bucking to get him off. Kaya wrapped up her story by announcing, "I made him buy me a double scoop and he did, but then he asked me for a bite."

"Did you give him one?" Devon asked.

"Yes. Even though I won the bet, he had a sad look on his face."

They were still laughing when Finn entered the kitchen, and for some reason, everyone fell silent. At first, she'd thought from his grim expression that he might have misinterpreted the scene. Now she was beginning to think there was an inner softness to the man, one he seemed to fight against, and the notion suddenly made him a lot more interesting. What path in his life had brought him to this household of three females? Was there a wife or ex-wife in the picture? For the first time, Devon was curious about her rescuer.

Yet she was content to let Finn do all the talking on the way to the clinic as he pointed out some of Maple Glen's highlights. She stared out the pickup window, thinking the town was smaller than any place she'd ever visited, and couldn't help but wonder at his enthusiasm. Had he lived only here all his life? If so, what made it so special to evoke such feeling? *More questions to add to my list*, she thought.

When they were leaving the clinic in Rutland an hour later, Devon realized she was going to have time to find some answers for her questions. She peered down at the compression bandage Theo had wrapped around her ankle. "No fracture," he'd assured her, "and when the swelling's gone, come back, and I'll fit you with something to keep your foot stable until it heals." He'd seen something in her face and added, "At least you won't need the crutches then. And maybe don't drive for a few days, at least not until the swelling's gone. Maybe not even then. The constant back and forth from gas to brake with your right foot, as well as the pressure, will put unnecessary stress on the ankle. The good news is that because this is a mild sprain with minor ligament damage, you should be good in a week or two. But until then, you'll need assistance getting around and maybe even with daily routines."

A couple of weeks! Then she'd shrugged, thinking she could recover at home in Chicago just as well as she could here. Two weeks in Maple Glen…she stifled a shudder. After Finn had helped her into the truck and was pulling out of the clinic parking lot, she said, "I suppose now I can make plans to return to Chicago."

A long minute passed before he replied, "Sure. That makes sense if you've got stuff to attend to there. Or you could rest up your ankle some more and consider getting back to your task." He looked over at her when she didn't answer. "The thing that brought you to Maple Glen."

Had she talked about why she was there? Perhaps in the initial aftermath of her discovery and rescue, when the cold and the pain in her ankle had made her memory of any communication a blur?

"No rush," he quickly added. "But we'd love to have you stay for a couple of days and show you some of the village. Then you can decide what you want to do…regarding your mission here, that is. It seems to be pretty important to you, and maybe I can even help you with it."

It was eerie, his use of the word *mission*, because that was exactly how she'd convinced herself to carry out Dan's request. She'd made a promise and taking it on had become her mission. She stared out the window. The drifts of snow from yesterday's downfall had begun to shrink from wind and sun. Shielding her eyes against the bright sky, she could see that the valley—the

Glen—was ringed by the Green Mountains ahead and the Taconic Mountains behind to the north. That information had been the extent of her research prior to arriving in Vermont.

Her ankle suddenly throbbed, reminding her that obviously she ought to have done more research—like when and how to hike the Long Trail. Mid-December hadn't been a wise choice, and Devon figured Dan would have been appalled at the idea. Thoughts of Dan intruded on the sunny day. If she left now, would she ever return? Even to keep her promise? She was beginning to doubt it. Perhaps Finn had a point about staying until she was able to follow through with her plan.

Driving through Wallingford, she turned to Finn. "Tell me about Maple Glen."

The surprise in his face inexplicably pleased her. She leaned against her seat's headrest and waited for him to begin.

CHAPTER FIVE

FINN HAD NEVER needed persuasion to talk about the Glen. Even as a kid, he'd been a passionate supporter of the small village. At school, his classmates had been bussed in from all over, but their stories about their own communities had never impressed him. Whatever he heard, nothing dissuaded him from believing that Maple Glen was the best place on earth to live.

"How did you get into firefighting?" Devon suddenly asked.

"Mom told you I was a firefighter?" Finn turned her way. He was sure he hadn't had a conversation with Devon about either his personal or professional life.

"Theo did while he was explaining my X-ray results. He said you were a volunteer search-and-rescue leader for the part of the trail near Maple Glen, but your full-time job was captain of the Wallingford Fire Department."

"Kind of a long story. I graduated from the Community College of Vermont with an associate degree in environmental science, thinking that the program would connect to the Appalachian Trail somehow." He sighed, thinking back to those days and his eventual realization that he was more interested in helping people than keeping data on Vermont's flora and fauna. "An impulsive visit to a job fair and a talk with a search-and-rescue guy, who was also a firefighter, inspired me to completely change direction. Instead of pursuing a bachelor's degree in science, I enrolled in the Vermont Fire Academy and never looked back." He looked at her again and grinned. "Or regretted the swerve in my career path."

"So, you've always lived and worked in this part of Vermont?"

"More or less." He'd have left it there but noticed her arched eyebrow.

"I'll take the more."

She was grinning but clearly wasn't going to let him leave it there. Well, he had nothing to hide. "I became friends with another recruit at the academy who hailed from Burlington. He introduced me to his sister, and we started dating." Finn paused, recalling the headiness of those early days and how impulsive he'd been.

"Marriage?" she prompted.

"Oh, yes. Way too soon. With the wisdom of hindsight, as the saying goes." He glanced at her again, the thoughtful expression on her face. "What about you?"

"Hmm?"

"Married? Divorced?" Did he really want to know? Couldn't he keep on imagining her as a solitary person? A waif lost in a storm?

"Neither," she finally said. "I came close once, but…"

"Long story?"

She smiled at him. "Kind of. Anyway, back to *your* story."

"After I graduated from the academy, I got a job in Burlington and moved there with my new wife."

"Happy times?" she asked when he fell silent.

"In the beginning." There was nothing to be gained by rehashing it. He'd left it all behind him four years ago.

"What brought you back here, then? I mean, leaving your job in Burlington and so on."

"Partly the divorce, but mostly because Mom was diagnosed with macular degeneration and my father with dementia. She couldn't look after him any longer."

There was a long silence until Devon murmured, "I'm sorry about your father. And your mom. She never mentioned it to me, and I never noticed she had an eye condition." After a pause, she said, "Too wrapped up in my own situation, I guess."

"Devon, you've been with us less than twenty-four hours. Go easy on yourself." He glanced at her, noticing her biting her lower lip. When she turned away to stare out the window, he figured she was struggling with some emotion. What was she feeling, though? And had he said something to trigger it?

They reached the turnoff from Route 7 to the county road that led to Maple Glen. Finn tapped the brakes as the truck hit a rut of snow left behind by the plow. The truck slid a few inches toward the ditch, but he quickly righted it. He glanced at Devon and saw that she was clenching the door handle with her fingers. *Is she ready to leap out?* he wondered.

"It's okay," he said. "I've had lots of experience driving these roads in all kinds of weather." Spotting the gas station and convenience store just ahead, he added, "Want something to eat or drink?" The distraction worked.

She smiled. "Thanks. Maybe a coffee, if they sell that."

"They do, but I can't attest to its quality." He pulled into the small parking area in front of the store. "Won't be long." Leaving the truck engine running, he got out and went inside, returning less than five minutes later with two Styrofoam coffee cups and a package of Twinkies.

"Don't get your hopes up," he warned as he clambered inside, handing her a cup and the package. "We probably should have waited until we reached the village bakery, but then it's so close to home, I might have suggested having my mom's coffee and the cookies she and Kaya are making."

"True, but now we can take our time, and you can tell me more about life in Maple Glen." She flashed a broad smile over the cup as she sipped her coffee.

"Okay, but when you've had enough, let me know." He swallowed some coffee and put the cup back in its holder. "One of my ancestors founded the Glen. That's the family history, but who knows? He settled here and farmed most of the land that comprises a large part of the village. Eventually other people arrived, and gradually, over a few generations, parcels of the original homestead were sold off. You won't have noticed, but there's a log cabin about half an acre behind our house that was built by my great-great-grandfather."

"What happened to the original home from the very first McAllister?"

"There was a fire, I think, and that's when some acreage was sold to pay for a new home. Then that, too, eventually disappeared—maybe torn down as the family grew. My father never knew the whole story. But we have photos of the Manor when it was being built by my great-grandfather in the early 1900s."

She was quiet for a long time. Then she said, her voice low and thoughtful, "I can't imagine knowing so much about one's family. Having a history, I mean."

The comment fit with her reply to his question about calling someone yesterday—*I don't have anyone*—and he was tempted to hear her own story but decided there'd be time enough for that later. When he spotted the first section of fence around the Stuart farm, he said, "See that place on my right?" He slowed down, easing to a stop across from the Jake & Friends sign.

She leaned forward to look out his side window.

"Maura, Theo's wife, owns it with her twin sister, Maddie." Finn noticed her quizzical expression. "It's a therapy riding business, but with donkeys instead of horses."

"Right," she said. "Kaya was telling us about it at breakfast. Specifically, the time the two of you went riding."

He felt his face heat up, recalling exactly the time she was referring to. "Yes, and...um...my one and only effort didn't end well."

He was grateful that a smile was her only response.

"So I assume Jake is one of the donkeys?"

"Yep. There are three or four others. Kaya rode one of them a couple of times last summer." Finn turned Devon's way and grinned. "That time she told you about was one. Fortunately, she took to it better than I did. She was having trouble adjusting to her new life here in the Glen, and my mother and sister thought she needed some distraction."

"Did the riding help her with what she was going through at the time?"

It was a fair question, and the fact that she'd posed it meant she was interested in Kaya, but Finn hesitated to get into the whole family situation from that time six months ago. He kept his answer brief. "It did. People can ride the donkeys just for fun, too. There's a charge but it isn't much." He took his foot off the brake and continued along the road, slowing again when they reached the Danby farm. He pointed to his left again.

"That's Theo's place, next door. He inherited it from his great-aunt and uncle and lives there with Maura now. They got married in September and are expecting their first child together, but Theo also has a thirteen-year-old son, Luke, who lives with them, though he also spends time during the year with his mother, who's on the West Coast." He noticed her frown at all the information. "If you stay long enough in Maple Glen, all these family configurations will be a lot clearer." He smiled at her and waited for some reply to his comment about staying long enough, but she just nodded and stared out the window again. He gave the truck some gas and continued toward the village proper.

She didn't speak the rest of the way, but he figured she might be tired.

Theo had taken him aside before they left the clinic to advise him to make sure she got lots of rest. *I've already spoken to Devon, but I want to let you know, too. Don't let her push herself too much too soon. There's no ligament damage to her ankle but if she tries using it too much before it's healed...*

Finn got it. He'd noticed her crane around to look at Bernie's B and B earlier on the way to Rutland and wondered if she was thinking she ought to return to her room. But he knew her best option was to continue to be looked after until the swelling was gone, and she was ready to be fitted for the boot that Theo had mentioned. Since she seemed to have no family members or close friends to rush to her aid, the McAllisters would have to do. At least, that's the story he was telling himself. Truth was, he really liked having her around.

As they approached the Shady Nook B and B, he said, "We can drop in to pick up your stuff if you like. No point in keeping the room if you don't need it." When she failed to answer right away, he wished he hadn't suggested the idea until she had a chance to process her next steps. That's what he'd normally advise members of his firefighting crew or people he'd helped on the trail. *Take the time to think everything through. Consider all the angles before making a decision*, he often told them.

Now he'd disregarded his own practice and rushed things, letting his personal desire to have her around the house a bit longer, get to know her better, dictate what he said. He could almost hear his mother's voice, reminding him to ease up. He was about to backtrack and let her know she didn't need to decide right then when she finally spoke.

"Okay, I guess that makes sense. Let's stop so I can pick up my things and check out."

Finn simply nodded but felt a small burst of elation.

DEVON HAD NEVER liked fuss or hubbub. Being the center of attention was not something she courted, but that was exactly where she found herself the minute she walked in the door. That is, the minute Finn carried her through the door.

As he'd turned onto the driveway leading up to the Manor, his loud sigh caught her attention even before she noticed the small car parked where his truck had been earlier that morning. She glimpsed his frown and his lips moving in a silent mutter as he aimed for a less convenient space on the far side of the car and switched off the truck engine.

"My sister, Roxanne, obviously made it back while we were at the clinic. She's supposed to park in that spot to the right of mine but probably thought I was on shift at the fire hall. She also could've moved it into the garage."

Devon didn't see the problem about the parking spot until she noticed an enormous snowdrift close to her side.

"Guess I should have shoveled that before we left," he mumbled. He managed a smile, but she saw that he was irritated. Maybe more at himself, she thought.

"I'll take you in first, then come back for your stuff." He had his door open and was climbing out before she could reply.

She saw him head around the back of the truck. Then he was at her side, opening the door, and Devon realized the only way she'd get through the drift and into the house was by being carried. Still, she hesitated, trying to think of other options.

"I promise not to drop you."

His smile was tight and she knew he felt bad, as if he thought she were embarrassed. But she wasn't, really, only hating her helplessness. The damsel-in-distress role wasn't one she'd ever considered taking on. But she didn't resist when one arm wrapped around her back and the other tucked beneath her legs. He pulled her closer to the open door, and in a quick, deft move, lifted her off the seat.

The snowdrift reached his knees, but he was tall. She'd have struggled to plow through it even with two working legs. When they got to the veranda steps, the front door was flung wide open, and a flurry of greetings from his mother and another woman, as well as apologies, took Devon's breath away. Finn could have set her down there but instead carried her into the entry hall, stamped his feet on the mat and continued on toward the kitchen where he gently set her down in a chair.

"I'll get your things and the crutches." Before he left, he brushed aside the cluster of curls that had fallen across her forehead. "Be right back."

He strode back along the hall, where Devon heard some murmurings followed by the front door closing shut and the sound of running footsteps.

Kaya burst into the kitchen. "My mommy's back and the cookies are delicious. Do you want one?"

Devon didn't have a chance to answer before Finn's mother rushed in, saying, "Kaya, let Devon have a chance to catch her breath."

Devon smiled, thinking she hadn't used any muscle power getting from the truck into the house and so had plenty of breath. Yet now that she was out of Finn's arms, she felt her heart pounding as if she'd jogged the short distance herself, and she *was* feeling a tad breathless.

A slender blonde woman came into the room with the crutches and propped them against a wall. "Hi, Devon. I'm Roxanne, Kaya's mom. Finn said to wait until he's back inside, and he'll help you get upstairs or wherever you want to go."

Devon's smile felt forced, and she hoped they wouldn't notice. They were being so kind and attentive while she simply wanted to retreat upstairs, close the door behind her and lie down. She cleared her throat and murmured, "Nice to meet you, Roxanne. And I'm fine. Really."

Still, as she unzipped her jacket and pulled her arms out, Roxanne swooped it from her and went to hang it up in the hall closet. Marion bent down to unlace the boot on Devon's good foot until she protested, "I'm fine. I can do that."

Marion must have heard the tension in her voice, because she moved aside as Devon untied her boot and pulled it off. The exertion triggered a throb in her sprained ankle, and she clenched her lips, keeping her head down a few seconds longer until the pain ebbed. When she sat up, everyone was staring at her with concern.

Devon exhaled. "I'd love a cookie now, Kaya."

She was sipping tea and eating a second cookie, with Kaya perched on her right and both Marion and Roxanne across from her at the table, when the front door slammed and she heard Finn stamping his feet in the hall.

Kaya jumped off the chair and ran to the kitchen doorway. "We're in here, Uncle Finn, having tea and cookies, 'cept I'm having hot chocolate. Come and join us."

The three women smiled at one another, and Marion stood to get another mug out of the cupboard. She was pouring tea into it when he appeared, his face and ears reddened from the cold.

"Just what I need," he said, rubbing his hands together. He pulled out the chair next to Devon and sat down, a rush of cold air from his movements wrapping around her.

"I guess you shoveled the other half of the drive," Marion said as she handed him his mug of tea.

Before he could reply, Roxanne said, "I'm sorry, Finn, but when I saw the truck wasn't there, I assumed you'd gone to work. Plus, the snowdrift—"

"Yeah," he interrupted. "I should have cleared it away before I took Devon to the clinic. Don't worry about it."

Devon saw his expression soften a little, but Roxanne's brow remained furrowed. *They've had this conversation before*, she thought.

"Tea and cookies and we haven't even had lunch yet!" Finn suddenly exclaimed, breaking the silence that had fallen over the room.

"Instead of lunch, we could have supper," Kaya said, giggling.

Finn pursed his lips, considering the idea. "Sure, but then that would mean your bedtime would be about two hours later, right? It's almost noon now, so instead of eight o'clock—" he craned he head around to check the clock on the wall behind him "—you'll be going to bed at two in the afternoon."

"I was just kidding!" Kaya cried. Everyone laughed, and when she realized he'd been kidding, too, she joined in.

Devon's head was spinning from the slight tension between Roxanne and Finn to the light-hearted teasing with Kaya.

Finn leaned in close, his warm breath brushing against her ear. "Do you want to stay down here for lunch or go upstairs for a bit of a rest first? Someone will bring you a bite to eat later, if you'd like."

He was reading her mind. "That sounds good," she said, nodding, and he got to his feet.

"I'll help Devon upstairs for a rest."

"I can help, too!" Kaya put in and started to climb off her chair.

Roxanne said, "You can help Grandma and me make some grilled cheese sandwiches for lunch."

Finn handed Devon the crutches, and on the way out of the kitchen, she heard Kaya chattering about what kind of cheese she wanted on her sandwich. Devon glanced up at Finn, who was grinning.

"One great thing about Kaya, she doesn't stay disappointed for long. There's always another interest to distract her."

"Were you like that, too, as a kid?" she asked as they walked down the hall.

"Not me, but Roxanne was." He paused, adding, "I was more…focused…I guess is the word I'm looking for."

"Serious?"

He thought that over as she handed him one of the crutches and began to start up the stairs. He didn't answer until she'd taken a couple of steps. "Kind of. But more like I just wanted everyone to be okay."

She stopped to turn around. His face was lost in thought. *Back to his childhood?* she wondered. Or perhaps a more recent time in his past?

"I think everyone's okay," she said.

"I hope so."

After he'd closed the bedroom door behind him, Devon lay on the bed, thinking how nice it would be to have someone—even just one person—worry that she was okay. That thought nestled in her mind until she fell asleep.

The muted sound of screaming awoke her much later. Where was it coming from? She held her breath, waiting for another crescendo. When it peaked again, she flung the duvet back and slowly got off the bed, reaching for the crutches propped up against the night table. The sound was coming from outside, she determined, as she hobbled to the window.

Rubbing some frost off a pane, she looked down onto the Manor's front lawn. Kaya was sitting cross-legged on a round plastic disc, which Finn was spinning and then releasing. Kaya screamed with glee as the disc shot across the packed snow and spun once more as it came to a stop.

Kaya shouted something that Devon couldn't hear, but she guessed it was a single word—"Again!"—as Finn trudged over to where she waited, a big smile on her face. Then she looked up and noticed Devon standing at the window. She waved and said something to Finn, who leaned back to peer up at Devon. He grinned and waved, then shrugged his shoulders as he pointed to Kaya.

What was he trying to tell her? That Kaya made him do it? Devon grinned back, waving until they started the game all over again.

As she limped away from the window, she spotted a tray on the dresser just to the right of the door. Drawing near, she saw a wrapped sandwich and a glass of water along with a glass of orange juice, and a plate of cookies. *Lunch.*

She leaned against the dresser and unwrapped the sandwich, biting into cheddar cheese and ham with a hint of mustard. A pickle sat on the edge of the plate. A few hours ago, she'd been annoyed by all the fuss these almost strangers bestowed on her. Now a bite of sandwich had to squeeze past a small lump in her throat. Devon ignored the prickle of tears and kept chewing, musing that people she'd known for less than forty-eight hours were taking care of her, and that wasn't such a bad thing after all.

CHAPTER SIX

FINN'S SHIFT AT the fire hall didn't start until the next day, but he received an alert that roused him from a dream featuring a raven-haired woman with big blue eyes, and he had to take a second to reorient himself. Then he picked up his phone and read the text.

Accident on Route 7 between Wallingford and Bennington. Two engines.

The department in Wallingford had a full-time crew of nine with a volunteer roster that could raise that number to eighteen or more, if necessary. As a captain, Finn was responsible for one of the three engines and the three-person crew that went with it. If two engines were needed, the accident had to be more than a slide into a ditch. He figured an ambulance would be dispatched from Rutland as well, but usually the engines were first on the scene, and any basic first aid was given by the firefighters.

He quickly dressed and took the stairs two at a time. Everyone was still asleep, so he scribbled a brief message on a Post-it, which he stuck on the fridge door for his mother. Then he texted the same information to Roxanne, who checked her cell phone more often than his mother did. As he got into his boots and jacket, he heard the first stirrings above. Probably Kaya, he thought. She was excited about going back to school today, now that the road was clear and the bus could get through.

He closed the door behind him and jogged to the pickup, which he'd moved to its usual spot yesterday after shoveling out Roxanne's side of the drive. Driving through the village at any time of day was easy, but at 6:00 a.m., it would be even better. Finn pressed hard on the accelerator once he reached the turnoff to Route 7.

He still remembered a serious accident at the junction of Route 7 and the county road when he'd been about eleven years old. Its impact on many village residents stayed with them for a long time. One man in particular, Walter Ingram, eventually took early retirement from the department. Though later, as an adult, Finn had learned there were other, more personal reasons for Ingram's withdrawal from the public eye.

Thoughts of the gentle man reminded Finn that Devon might be interested in meeting him and seeing his beekeeping operation on his property outside the Glen. She'd seemed interested in the area yesterday, and he decided showing her some of the sights and introducing her to a few locals might spur her to stay longer, beyond the week or two of rest Theo had recommended. Finn couldn't explain why, but he had this urge to show her a different kind of community from one in a city like Chicago, a place where she apparently had no one to contact about her fall on the trail.

As he passed the Tasty Delights bakery, he noticed lights on inside. Someone was prepping for the day's business. Fridays and weekends were always busy, but now, barely two weeks until Christmas, Sue and her team would be creating all the sweet and savory treats loved by the villagers, nearby farm residents and the few tourists who visited the valley in winter.

He suddenly remembered the gingerbread man cookie he'd bought Wednesday for Kaya. Devon's rescue that afternoon and subsequent arrival at the Manor had vanquished all thoughts of gingerbread men. Perhaps his mother had seen it on the counter and given it to Kaya. He hoped so. His young niece was a charming mix of cute and ornery. Lately, Finn had seen signs of a growing maturity, too, as she was learning to listen to other viewpoints and willing to make compromises more often.

Those were traits many adults themselves lacked and Finn was proud that he'd played a small part in Kaya's growing awareness. She'd definitely come a long way from the tempestuous child she'd been six months ago when she and Roxanne moved in, and Finn felt he and his mother had had much to do with that change. Roxanne had, too, but at the time, she was nursing her own emotional wounds from her marriage breakup.

Turning onto Route 7 from the county road, he saw that the snowplow hadn't passed by since yesterday when he'd driven Devon to the clinic. He muttered to himself, thinking of the drifts on both sides of the county road and Church Street in the village. Residents considered themselves fortunate to be plowed out at all, let alone twice. Route 7 was a state highway and had to be kept open, but many residents worked in other parts of the valley to the north or south of the Glen and needed the county road access to that main artery.

The fifteen-mile drive to Wallingford took him less than the usual time, as the highway was not only clear of snow but also of vehicles. Commuter traffic north to Rutland and south to Bennington wouldn't start for another hour. One engine was just pulling out of the parking lot in front of the fire hall when Finn arrived, and Finn's driver, Matt, was waiting behind the wheel of the second engine. Finn parked his truck and jumped out, running inside to change. His second-incommand, Brad, gave him the lowdown on the accident as he got into his gear.

"A two-car collision with one driver trapped in vehicle and the driver of the other car in shock. No fire, but gas fumes detected. Ambulance dispatched but not on scene yet. State police are on the way."

The two ran to the engine, and it roared out of the lot, siren blaring, the instant they were on board. Matt was an expert driver—fast but cautious, too. At that time in the morning, there were few drivers on the road who'd need the warning, but it was a good signal to any early commuters who might not notice the flashing lights. Fortunately, the shoulders of the highway were clear enough for people to move over if they had to.

The pumper whizzed past the cutoff to Maple Glen, and Finn wondered if his family and Devon were now awake and maybe enjoying a leisurely coffee around the kitchen table. Part of him wished he could be there, chatting about the day to come, but a bigger part was focused on what lay ahead. Adrenaline buzzed through him as he processed the little information he had—a driver trapped in a car and the smell of gas. The crew first on scene would search for any gas leaks and foam the area around the vehicles while Finn and his team would extract the driver stuck inside. They needed to work quickly at those two critical issues.

As the engine rolled to a stop at the site, Finn's first impression was that the cars had been traveling in opposite directions when one driver lost control and struck the oncoming car on the corner of its front end. The collision sent that car spinning around, and it ended up on the opposite shoulder of the highway and facing the opposite direction. Finn's gaze shot to the other side of the highway, where the car with the trapped driver had crashed into a utility pole.

Of course, the state police would begin their investigation as soon as they arrived, and judging from the distant sound of sirens, that was going to happen any second. Unless the siren was from the ambulance. Finn spotted the other team captain and pointed to the ground around the utility pole. They needed to apply plenty of foam around the car as well, before removing the driver. The other team was already advancing a hose line to the area while Finn and his team got the hydraulic rescue tools out of their pumper.

He was about to order one of his crew to assist the other driver—a middle-aged man sitting on the rear bumper of his SUV, a dazed expression on his face—when he saw the ambulance slowing down as it rounded the curve in the highway. Good timing. Now all of them could focus on extracting the trapped driver, who could be seriously injured, while the EMTs from the ambulance could begin treating the man in shock.

Finn raced to the driver's side of the crashed vehicle, followed by the two men with the hydraulic cutters. The driver's side door was jammed by the collision, and Finn's heart skipped a beat as he recognized the woman slumped over the discharged air bag, her face turned his way and her eyes closed. Betty Watson from Maple Glen. The mother of his search-and-rescue trainee, Scott.

DEVON SET THE book she was reading onto her lap and stared out the window for the umpteenth time. Then she picked up her phone to check the time. Almost noon. Only an hour had passed since she'd last looked, but it felt like much longer. She'd been lying half propped up on the living room sofa cushions for most of the morning, her right ankle elevated on two pillows and a colorful, crocheted afghan resting over the pajamas she hadn't bothered changing out of.

Yesterday, after seeing Theo at the clinic and accepting the fact that she wasn't going to make her flight back to Chicago on Saturday, Devon had canceled her booking. When asked if she wanted to reschedule, she'd hesitated before replying no. She still had most of the week she'd booked off ahead of her and figured she'd make final plans for her return closer to the time.

She should really check her business email and give her supervisor a heads-up that she might need extra time away from the office, but she had to admit that part of her wanted to hold on to the small bubble of comfort and tranquility that summed up the ambience of Finn's home and family.

A little before six that morning, she'd heard thudding steps along the hallway. *Finn?* She wondered where he was going in such a hurry. Last night when he'd brought a dinner tray up to her, he'd suggested they could go for a drive the next day if the roads were clear. She told him she'd like that. She'd slept most of the day yesterday, and when she wasn't sleeping, she was mentally replaying her fall in the woods. How incredibly lucky she'd been! Not only to be found on a day when she was the only hiker in the area but to be rescued by someone who knew what to do. Finn McAllister. She remembered how she'd read that surname on the mailbox and stared at the house before starting her hike. Then she'd seen the little girl—Kaya—waving from the window seconds before she crossed the bridge into the woods. Had everything since been mere coincidence? she wondered. Or fate? Or was it simply good luck?

Today felt different. The dark thoughts from yesterday—the whys of her decisions and her poor judgment to hike the trail in winter—had evaporated with the morning sunshine, and shortly after she heard Finn leave, she got up, washed and managed to get downstairs on her own. Marion was reading a note on the fridge and turned, surprised, to see Devon standing with her crutches in the doorway.

"There's been an accident on the highway and Finn's been called in to help."

The morning had rolled along from that moment, and Devon soon realized that the day's routine was the norm, unlike yesterday. It featured oatmeal, toast with peanut butter and jam, bananas, milk and coffee, along with brisk questions about Kaya's packed lunch, followed by a brief exchange about who would walk Kaya to the bus, and was Roxanne expected at work?

Devon's head was spinning. Her typical work mornings passed in complete silence unless she turned on the radio Dan had given her. *There's a world beyond what you read on your phone or laptop.* He'd been teasing, of course, but she'd gotten his point. The radio had added something missing from her morning routines—a human voice.

The McAllister family had plenty of voices, tumbling out at the same time and without any apparent direction. Yet Devon saw that messages were conveyed as Roxanne and Kaya rushed upstairs after eating to brush teeth before getting into winter clothes while Marion automatically poured a second cup of coffee for herself and Devon before loading the dishwasher.

"Is it always this busy in the morning?" she'd asked when Marion finally sat down.

"Oh, yes." Her sigh punctuated her answer. Then she'd insisted Devon elevate her foot and rest on the living room sofa until Finn returned, and that had been the first mention of him since Devon had entered the kitchen.

Now, some three or more hours later, Devon was still on the sofa. There'd been a slow trip to the downstairs bathroom at one point and a conversation about books with Marion, who brought her a few paperbacks. Then Roxanne announced she was going into work after all. Devon was intrigued by a hushed conversation between mother and daughter at the front door and the worried frown on Marion's face when she came back into the living room. She was tempted to ask if there was a problem but held back, knowing their problems were not hers, and besides, she'd personally hate being asked the same question. But she *could* ask about Finn.

"Have you heard from Finn? About the accident, I mean."

Marion shook her head. "No, but he might tell us about it, in his own time. He doesn't always like to talk about his work, especially if there's been an upsetting—or worse, tragic—event." She paused, her brow wrinkled in thought. "It would be good for him to share whatever he's feeling, but he's not that kind of person. Although he's always felt very deeply about what happens to people, he keeps his worries to himself." Then she smiled at Devon. "I'm going into the village. Would you like me to fetch anything for you before I go?"

Devon shook her head. "I'm good, but thanks."

"Okay, I won't be long. If you decide to go upstairs, take your time."

As she left the room, Devon couldn't help but wonder if this was what it was like to have a mother—someone to remind her not to do something she already knew she shouldn't. Throughout her life, the main person doing the reminding had been her brother because there had never been a mother figure. At least, not in Devon's memory.

When she heard Marion call out a goodbye and shut the door, Devon lay back down and closed her eyes, her mind going back as far as memory could take her. As hard as she tried, she could never get past that time when she was five. Lost, cold and frightened. Like the other day on the trail.

FINN RUBBED HIS EYES. If Kaya were here to prompt him, he'd have to bend down and kiss Sleeping Beauty in order for the magic to work. But Kaya was at school and the princess was a real person— a mystery woman named Devon, who was as beautiful as the fairy-tale sleeper. And he definitely was not on kissing terms with Devon. *Not yet*, was his wishful afterthought.

He cleared his throat a couple of times until her

eyelids fluttered open and her cobalt eyes stared with some disbelief at him. She smiled and some of the tension eased out of him.

"You're back." She pushed herself up to lean against the sofa cushions.

"Just now. Is my mother around?"

"She went into the village. I'm not sure when exactly."

Finn nodded. Then she'd probably heard the news about Betty Watson and had gone to see what she could do. He pulled a chair closer to the sofa, stifling a yawn as he sat down. Rubbing his eyes again, he waited for Devon to toss questions at him and, when none came, was grateful for her silence. But those blue eyes shone with curiosity, and he realized he *wanted* to tell her all about it. The accident. What he and his team had to do. The aftermath.

He cleared his throat again. "You know Bernie Watson, the owner of the Shady Nook B and B?"

She nodded.

"His sister-in-law, Betty, was in an accident out on Route 7 very early this morning. Apparently, she'd been driving to Bennington for an ultrasound at the hospital and now…well…now she's a patient there instead." He took a deep breath. "The good news is that her injuries aren't life-threatening, but she'll be in the hospital for several days at least. Maybe longer." He had to stop for a moment, reliving the shock of finding Betty

Watson in the car. Someone he'd known for years and the first person from Maple Glen he'd ever had to rescue.

Devon waited for him to continue, and he was grateful for the silent concern in her face. After a moment, he said, "The other driver was in shock, but he's okay now. Police are investigating. I don't know exactly what happened, but I have some thoughts." He paused, then quietly said, "The young fellow who was with me the other day when we found you on the trail, Scott. He's Betty's son." Her eyes widened and he knew she had a sense of what he'd experienced.

"Everyone is okay now, though? You and your… colleagues…you rescued them?" she finally asked.

"I guess you could say that. Betty was trapped inside her car for a bit." He didn't go into detail. They'd worked as speedily as possible, the fear of harming Betty while they pried her out and, worse, of a gas tank igniting while they used the hydraulic tools ever present in their minds.

"All of you saved a life today," she murmured.

They had. His gaze fixed on hers, and he felt the last of his energy drain out as he sagged against the chair. Folding her into his arms and letting her calm demeanor settle over him was precisely what he needed most right then. But they weren't on hugging terms. *Not yet*, he thought, smiling.

CHAPTER SEVEN

Once Kaya had finished eating and raced off to watch her one hour of TV before bed, dinner conversation focused on the accident and Betty Watson.

"After I left here to do some shopping in the village, I saw Bernie's car leaving the B and B parking lot in a big hurry," Marion began. "The B and B was closed—an unheard-of situation—so I knew right away something was wrong. When I walked into the bakery, Sue was talking with the new church deacon about the accident."

Devon was listening but kept her eyes on Finn the whole time. His face was impassive as he ate slowly but methodically, his attention split between his mother's account and the roast chicken on his plate. She noticed his tight grip on his knife and fork and the way he randomly picked at his food. Not really interested in it, but knowing he needed its nourishment.

"Myra said the Women's Social Club was meeting at the church to plan meals for the family,"

Marion went on, "and someone had gone to the Watsons' to stay with Ashley because Scott went with his father to the hospital."

"Have you heard how Betty's doing?" Roxanne asked.

Finn set his cutlery down on the table and pushed back his chair. "I'm going out to do some shoveling," he said. His voice was low and strained.

Devon saw Marion and Roxanne exchange glances, but no one said a word as he left the room.

"He needs some downtime," Marion explained to Devon. Then she looked at Roxanne. "Betty has broken ribs and damage to her spleen. A concussion from hitting the air bag so hard. Shock, of course. But all things considered, she's a very lucky woman."

No one spoke during the rest of the meal. Devon ate hers while looking occasionally at Finn's empty chair and half-eaten dinner. When Roxanne finished eating, she went upstairs to start Kaya's bathwater while Marion began clearing the table. She wrapped Finn's plate in cellophane and put it in the fridge.

"He can microwave it later if he wants," she murmured. Then glancing at Devon, she said, "I volunteered to make some phone calls, informing anyone who hasn't yet heard about the accident and to get volunteers for meals and, later, visits to Betty in the hospital. If she wants any, of course.

Ed—that's Betty's husband—may need relieving from his hospital visits."

"Is there anything I can do?" Devon felt obliged to make the offer, despite knowing her mobility issue would limit any useful assistance but was in awe of the outpouring of help from the community. What would it be like, she wondered, to have a whole village behind you?

"No, dear, but thanks for the offer. Though if Roxanne or I need to be somewhere tomorrow, perhaps you wouldn't mind keeping an eye on Kaya? It's just that Finn has a shift, and it's Saturday, so no school for Kaya. It wouldn't be for long," she rushed to add, "and one of us—Roxanne or I—will probably be around anyway, but just in case."

"That's fine, Marion. I'll definitely be here," Devon ended with a light laugh, gesturing to her crutches. Though inside, her stomach lurched. Her babysitting experience had been minimal.

"I appreciate it, thanks. Now, before I go make my calls, can I do anything for you?"

"I'm good and thanks for dinner, Marion. I don't often get home-cooked meals. Maybe I'll sit and read in the living room a bit before going upstairs. I like the book you lent me."

"Quite welcome, dear." Marion frowned. "How's your ankle doing? Has the swelling gone down any since early this morning?"

"Yes, it has, and I can wiggle my toes a bit without causing a lot of pain." Devon extended her right foot, encased in a very large loose woolen sock that she suspected belonged to Finn. She bent down to lower the upper part of the sock, revealing her ankle. The hard red swelling was receding to a purple-yellowish bruise.

"Oh, that does look better. Soon you'll be in that special boot, or whatever it is, and walking everywhere, more or less," Marion said.

"That's what I'm hoping. At least I should be able to go back to the B and B and let all of you return to your regular lives. Plus, I have some online work commitments, which I shouldn't put off any longer."

Marion patted Devon's shoulder. "Don't you worry about us. We love having you. Take your time." She looked at the kitchen wall clock. "Okay, I must get to those phone calls. When my son finishes whatever he's doing outside, get him to put a fire on in the living room. If you're still reading, that is. The room is so cozy when the fireplace is glowing." She paused. "Roxanne and I will be up in the family room."

As Marion left the kitchen, Devon pondered her last sentence. Was she telling Devon she'd have a chance to be alone with Finn? If so, why? Not that the idea wasn't appealing. She realized she wanted to know a lot more about her rescuer. She was on her way to the living room when the front door opened, sending in gust of cold air, as well as Finn.

"Hello," he said. "Are you on your way up-stairs?"

Devon shook her head. "I thought I'd read a bit more down here. I think I spent far too much time in my room yesterday," she added with a light laugh. She watched him unzip his jacket and brush snowflakes off the top of his head onto the mat. "Is it snowing again?"

He slung the jacket over the newel post at the bottom of the staircase. "Just lightly."

He stood quietly, looking at her as if he were coming to some decision. Devon hesitated, reluctant to speak and break a moment that seemed oddly intimate.

Finally, he asked, "Mind if I join you in there?" He tilted his head to the living room French doors. "I feel like warming up a bit. The temperature's dropped since this afternoon. I could put a fire on."

"That would be lovely." She pivoted on her crutches and followed him into the dimly lit room.

"Why don't you get comfortable there," he said, pointing to the sofa and the arrangement of cush-ions and pillows she'd been using that afternoon, "while I get the fire going. We haven't had one at all this winter. Don't know why. It seems we've spent a lot more time up in the family room since Kaya and Roxanne have been here."

Yet another mysterious situation, Devon thought. Why had Roxanne moved back to her family home? Perhaps Devon would find out eventually. Right now, she was more interested in being alone with Finn. Who knows? The chance to ask some questions might arise. She hobbled to the sofa and sat down, placed the crutches against the end table and swung her legs up and onto the pillows.

He knelt in front of the fireplace, a large stone structure that was clearly as old as the house. A large copper bucket filled with various shapes of wood sat on the floor next to it, and a wicker basket beside the bucket contained a small stack of folded newspapers. Devon watched him crumple some of the paper and then carefully choose kindling and larger pieces of wood from the bucket, setting them in some kind of order onto the metal grate in the hearth. There seemed to be an art to setting a fire and he was good at it. Ironic, she thought, considering his profession. As the first flames shot upward into the flue, he stood up, holding his hands out to the warmth as he stared into the fire.

Lost in his memory of the day? Devon wondered.

When he turned around, though, he was smiling. "I hope your day was better than mine."

She guessed he was making light of whatever he was feeling and recalled Marion's comments about his tendency to hide worries or serious thoughts. She could have dismissed the opener by describing her rather boring day but opted not to. "It *had* to be better than yours."

He grimaced as he pulled the armchair closer to the sofa and sat down, extending his long legs toward the fireplace. Then he ran his fingers through his damp hair, leaving a trail of sandy-brown spikes. "Everything went well," he began, "despite a couple of obstacles that could have been very serious."

When he didn't elaborate, Devon said, "But you and your team overcame those obstacles."

"We did, but normally I wouldn't have this… this sickening feeling in my gut." He shifted his gaze from her to the fire.

"Because the person you helped was someone you knew." Her quiet comment echoed in the room.

A long sigh was his response. When he looked at her, his face was drawn. "Almost five years ago, I was on a house fire call. This was in Burlington. When I was still married." He looked at the fire again.

Devon waited.

"It was a bad fire, out of control, but we still managed to get most of the family out." He stopped, staring at his feet this time. "Someone shouted that there was an older man—the grandfather—in a basement apartment. The chances of saving him were so minimal…" He took a breath, exhaling loudly. "I was with my buddy—Jim—and he pointed down the stairs, indicating we should at least try. So we did."

She knew from his voice it hadn't ended well.

"We were on our way out. The man was unconscious, and it took the two of us. But before we made it to the door, there was a flashover." He turned toward Devon. "That happens when there's a sudden ignition that's out of control. A piece of furniture in the adjacent living room ignited, and the entire room, including the hallway where we were standing, went *poof*." He snapped his fingers.

Devon shuddered at the horrifying mental image that simple gesture had created.

"I managed to drag the grandfather out, but Jim didn't make it. He was trapped by a falling ceiling beam." Finn stopped, gazing into the fireplace again. "Funny how a fire can be both beautiful and deadly at the same time." After a long moment, during which the only sound in the room was the crackling fire, he said, "At the time, it seemed like everything in my personal life went downhill from that night on."

Devon waited for him to continue, but he was lost in the past. "Today wasn't a tragedy, though," she said.

He shifted his gaze to her, the lines in his face relaxed now. "No, thank goodness. But it was the first time since Burlington that someone I knew was in danger. A big part of me feared that—"

"You might fail?" she ventured.

"Yes. That's it exactly. How could I face everyone here in the Glen—and my family—if I couldn't save her?"

Devon reached over, placing her hand on his arm at the break in his voice. "But you did, Finn. You and the others *did* save her."

He didn't speak for a long time. Then he looked at her, the pain in his face slowly easing. "Yeah, we did." He turned back to the fire and sighed.

Devon wished she knew him well enough to say the words he needed—wanted—to hear. She sank back onto the pillows and stared up at the ceiling. Light from the fire flickered across it, casting strange shadows in the dark room. She closed her eyes, letting herself drift into the peace and quiet of the room. When Finn didn't speak again, she murmured, "I should get up to bed. Marion asked me to pitch in with Kaya tomorrow, and I have a feeling I'll need a lot of energy."

Finn turned her way and smiled. "That you will."

He watched silently as she levered herself off the sofa and reached for her crutches. Devon was relieved that he wasn't rushing to help. She could manage on her own now. He was getting out of his chair as she got to her feet. His hesitation prompted her to say, "I'm fine. I'll put the stairway light on."

He nodded, but before she reached the French doors leading into the hall, he said, "Thanks, Devon. For listening."

What could she say to this man she'd known a little more than forty-eight hours? She wanted more than anything to hug him, but they were almost strangers, really. Not even friends. She needed to remember that she had a life far away from him, as wonderful as he was.

Her eyes stayed with his a moment longer. "Anytime, Finn." Then she swung around to head upstairs.

DEVON ROLLED OVER in bed and looked out the window. Sunlight streamed in, which was a good sign for the day, she figured, melting any snow or ice that had been clinging to sidewalks and roads. Finn's talk last night had kept her awake longer than she'd expected. She'd replayed his account of the fire that had killed his friend and wondered if the trauma of that tragedy had contributed to the breakup of his marriage.

The real question, though, had been, Why had he opened up to her at all? Given what Marion had said about his tendency to hide his emotions? Then she reminded herself that her experience as a social worker had taught her that people often revealed their inner feelings more easily with strangers than with family or good friends. *That's what this is all about*, she told herself as she shifted to lower her legs and feet to the floor. A stranger confidence. Still, it was good for him to get it out.

The sounds of movement on the stairs and below hustled her along. She picked up her phone to see that it was already nine o'clock. She'd slept for more than ten hours, which was longer and better than any sleep in Chicago. Her condo was downtown, and the nights were always punctuated with sirens, horns and the hum of traffic. Everything was so quiet here and she wasn't sure if she liked that or not. For some reason, familiar sounds and noises had always been a comfort to her. *And you know why, Devon, so don't kid yourself.*

She limped to her backpack resting on top of a large cedar chest across the room and rummaged for clean underwear and socks. The sweatshirt and track pants from yesterday would have to do, and she realized she should ask Marion if she could do some laundry. It was doubtful that the B and B would have a guest facility for that. The thought of moving back to the Shady Nook made her pause. Finn had mentioned the place was closed yesterday, that the woman involved in the accident—Betty?—was related to Bernie. His sister-in-law, Devon recalled. If the place remained closed, she'd have to adjust her plans about returning there, and that aroused mixed feelings in her. The comfort of the McAllister household was enticing, but she would inevitably be returning to her real life soon, where the only person she had to rely on was herself.

For now, there was breakfast, and after that, possibly spending time with Kaya. She hoped there were plenty of art supplies and books on hand. Those items were her mainstay when she worked with troubled children. But only for an hour or so, not a whole day. She sighed and headed for the door and the kitchen below.

Everyone had finished breakfast. Marion was loading the dishwasher while Roxanne was speaking quietly to Kaya in the corner of the room nearest the door leading to the mudroom. Judging from Kaya's face, Devon guessed the little girl was either unhappy about something or was being given a talking to, as Devon's foster mother used to say. Often to her.

Marion looked up and smiled when Devon came into the kitchen. "Sleep well?"

"Too well. I don't remember ever sleeping in so late."

"That country air," Marion said. Then she looked across the room where Kaya and Roxanne were whispering. "Kaya, honey, why don't you get dressed while Devon has her breakfast? Then maybe we can rustle up that activity set your uncle gave you for your birthday. I'm sure it's in a closet or drawer somewhere."

Kaya mumbled an "Okay" and headed for the door followed by Roxanne, who shot her mother a grateful smile on the way out.

After they left, Marion said, "Kaya's unhappy about her mother going to Bennington this morning. She had a last-minute appointment with her lawyer and had promised to play with Kaya until we leave for the community center." Then she quickly added, "Goodness, dear, have a seat. I made some muffins earlier before Finn left. He's taken some to the fire hall with him, and I've set aside a dozen for the Watson family, and of course, a few for us, too. Would you like one with your coffee, or maybe something more substantial, like an egg?"

"Coffee and a muffin would be wonderful, thanks." Devon leaned her crutches against the wall next to her chair and sat down. "What time was Finn's shift? I didn't hear anyone moving around until after I woke up."

"He had to be there by eight. It's a twelve-hour shift, so he won't be home until after we've eaten tonight." Marion set the dishwasher going and poured coffee into a mug, which she handed to Devon. "Thank goodness for microwave ovens! I've reheated many meals for him over the last four years." She took the lid off a plastic food container and pulled out two muffins, which she set on a plate and brought to the table. "There's butter in that dish, Devon, and I have some jams in the fridge if you want some of that, too."

Devon eyed the muffins stuffed with raspberries. "They definitely don't need any jam."

"The berries are from our raspberry canes out behind the house. We had a bumper crop last summer, and I put up several bags of them for the freezer." She sat across from Devon and picked up a coffee mug on the table in front of her. Taking a sip, she pulled a face. "Ugh! Cold."

"Is there any left?" Devon asked. "Would you like some of mine?"

"Thanks, but I've already had two cups, so I better not. I wanted to have lots of energy for this morning. Some of us are meeting at the community center to use the kitchen there to make meals for the Watsons. A friend of mine who's one of those super-organized types has already printed out recipes for casseroles and soups. We figured comfort food, you know?"

Devon nodded. She could relate to comfort food, though her preferences were for takeout Indian curries or Thai noodles. *Not much of that in Maple Glen*, she thought. "When do you have to be there?"

"Soon." She checked the clock. "I should move along now, but before I go, I want to make sure you're still okay looking after Kaya."

"Of course." Devon spread butter on her muffin and bit into a burst of summer sweetness.

"Wonderful. Our Plan B was to drive Kaya to a school friend in Wallingford, but staying here would be more convenient for all of us, especially since Roxanne will be going south to Bennington."

Right. The lawyer. "You mentioned an activity set?" Devon asked.

"So I did!" Marion scrambled to her feet. "I'll go look for it right now. Roxanne will be down any minute with Kaya, so take advantage of the next five minutes of calm." Marion laughed as she hurried out of the kitchen.

CHAPTER EIGHT

DEVON WAS ALREADY EXHAUSTED, and noon—the time Marion promised to return—was more than an hour away. Kaya had tired of her new activity set shortly after the box of art projects had been spread out over the dining room table and, instead, began to pepper Devon with probing questions ranging from "Why did you come to Maple Glen?" and "What's Chicago like?" to more basic ones: "How old are you?" and "Were you born with curly hair?"

Of course, Devon's work experience had taught her patience as well as insight, though most of the children and teens she'd worked with in her career had been withdrawn and reluctant to speak at all. She'd been the one asking probing questions disguised as innocuous small talk. So she didn't really mind the inquisition but wished she could elicit information from Kaya, too. Like *Where is your father? Why did you and your mother come to Maple Glen? What do you like best about your uncle?*

A phone call from Theo Danby was a welcome

break that morning. He'd procured something more appropriate for her ankle than the boot he'd mentioned previously, a kind of brace, and if she could get to the clinic that day, he'd fit it for her. Devon explained the situation at the Manor, and he'd replied that if someone was free to drive her to his farm the next morning, he'd show her how to adjust it and so on. Devon was happy to get rid of the crutches, and the device Theo had would give her more mobility. She'd be free to move around on her own and free to return to Chicago. That realization didn't excite her as much as she'd expected. Besides, there was still the matter of her promise to Dan, and leaving Maple Glen without fulfilling it would realistically mean she never would.

"Devon?" Kaya was standing on the second-floor landing. She'd gone up to her room to look for her treasure box. "Should I bring it down or can you come up to see it?"

Devon had been waiting for Kaya at the foot of the staircase when Theo phoned, and now, eyeing the large wooden box sitting at her feet on the landing, said, "I'll come up to see it."

"Okay." Kaya stooped to pick up the box. "Let's go through it in your room. Mine is kind of messy."

Devon rolled her eyes. Kaya had been itching to explore Devon's room and belongings since Finn had come back from the B and B with her backpack but had been warned off by Roxanne, who'd said, *Devon has a right to privacy. You're not allowed in her room without an invitation.*

"Sure," Devon said now, giving in to the inevitable, and began the slow walk up. *How much easier this trip will be when I'm not using crutches anymore!* Her second thought was that her days making the climb up the stairs in the Manor were limited.

Kaya flashed a big smile when she reached the landing. "Wait till you see all my treasures, and then you can show me yours, too." Catching Devon's frown, she quickly added, "If you have any with you, of course."

When they reached Devon's room, Kaya sat cross-legged on the carpet and opened the large wooden box. Devon hobbled to the armchair that Finn had deposited in the room's bay window after their trip to the medical clinic on Thursday. *So you can look out from here, and not have to go down to the living room.* It had been a thoughtful gesture, but at the time, she was hoping her stay with the family would be a short one. With her improved mobility from the device Theo had for her, that hope was about to be realized.

Thinking about when she could organize her return to Chicago, Devon was only half attentive as Kaya proudly held up items from her treasure chest while giving a brief history of each object. The girl's reference to Uncle Finn caught her interest, though.

"And this is a special stone Uncle Finn gave me. He said it might bring me good luck and even if it doesn't, he said it will always remind me of Maple Glen, no matter where I am." She held up a nondescript gray stone. "Wanna see it?"

"Sure." Kaya passed her the stone, and Devon turned it over and over in her palm. It was a flat piece of shale with tiny markings on it. Small fossils or possible cuttings from some ancient person. "That's very cool," she said, handing it back to Kaya.

"He said he found it on the trail. You know, Maple Glen is close to the App... *Applay-shun* Trail, Uncle Finn said, which is a special place, and so it makes sense that this stone is special, too." She studied Devon a second longer. "That's where he found you, too, isn't it?"

Devon nodded.

After another brief silence, Kaya said, "Even though Uncle Finn doesn't have this stone anymore, it still brought him luck, didn't it? 'Cause he found you. That's what he told me the other day."

Devon cleared her throat. "Um, yes, and that was lucky for me as well." The memory of that moment only days ago brought an unexpected rush of emotion. "And he told you *he* was lucky to find *me*, did he?"

"Yes."

Devon kept her head bent, studying the stone long enough for the unexpected well of tears to ebb. Then she passed the stone back to Kaya, who placed it in the wooden box. "Shall we go down to the kitchen and have a snack?"

"Sure." But without missing a beat, Kaya asked, "What about your treasures?"

Devon saw the expectation in the girl's face as she stared at Devon's backpack on the cedar chest. The small cloth pouch containing the items she'd intended to bury on the trail was inside—the compass Dan had taken that day, her tiny stuffed rabbit and the old photo of the house they once lived in, when they had a family. A time Devon didn't even remember because she'd only been a toddler. She hesitated but thought, *What harm could come from showing them to her?*

"Aw, he's so cute!" Kaya exclaimed, hugging the tattered bunny, stained from years of being held by Devon's sticky fingers. She set the rabbit onto the cedar chest and picked up the compass, which didn't convey the same interest. "Uncle Finn has one of these, but it's bigger and newer."

It was a toy compass, really. Her brother had bought it prior to the trip to White Rocks National Recreation Area all those years ago. She didn't realize he'd planned the whole thing—their escape—until she was in her teens. Gazing at it now, she felt the familiar stir of loss. Not only for Dan but for the anniversary trek to the trail they'd never made together. "How about that snack?"

she asked when Kaya put the compass next to the rabbit.

"Sure," Kaya mumbled, but her attention was on the photograph crinkled by years of being folded over and over again. "What's this a picture of?" She held up the photo.

Devon resisted snatching it out of Kaya's fingers. This was her most treasured item of all, because it represented a time of childhood happiness. Not that she actually remembered any of it, but Dan's few stories had created a false memory in her mind. "Oh, that's where I used to live. When I was a baby," she said.

"Was it in Chicago?"

"No, near a city called Boston."

"Oh, I've heard of that." Kaya stared at it a long moment, then flipped it over. "What's that name on the back here?"

Devon leaned over to look. She'd forgotten that surname was there. "Um, it's a family name. Morrison."

Kaya nodded thoughtfully, then said, "That house looks old."

"It was, but I don't really remember much about it." Devon instantly regretted the comment, knowing it could lead to questions she didn't want to answer. Fortunately, Kaya had a different response.

"I wish I had a picture of where me and my mommy and daddy used to live."

"Oh? Where was that?"

"In New Jersey. But we didn't have a house. We lived in a very big apartment building. I had a nice bedroom." When she looked up at Devon, her eyes were glistening. "I kind of miss my bedroom, but that's a secret, so don't tell anyone."

"I promise," Devon said. "But why is it a secret?"

"Mommy says if we talk about New Jersey too much, it'll make Granny and Uncle Finn feel sad."

"Why is that?" She kept her voice as casual as possible.

"Because they might think we don't like it here in Maple Glen. And we do, but sometimes I miss my bedroom and my friends there." She sighed. "I can hardly remember them anymore, except for Jeanie, my very best friend."

"It's good to have nice memories."

Kaya nodded. "Especially when bad ones pop into your head."

"Bad ones?"

"Like when my mommy and daddy were shouting at each other, and my mommy was always crying."

Devon dwelled on that answer a long moment. Then she said, "Let's go downstairs and have that snack. I'm starving!"

"Me too," Kaya cried, her face clearing into a big smile.

"But first," Devon added, "how about a hug?" She bent to wrap her arms around Kaya. "I'm glad you live here now," she murmured, "because if you didn't, I wouldn't have met you."

Kaya squeezed her tighter.

ON SUNDAY MORNING, Finn stretched out, prolonging the inevitable. At some point he'd have to get out of bed, but for now, he wanted to luxuriate in a rare sleep-in. One of his men, Matt, owed him a shift and was taking it today. Finn hoped his colleague's shift was as uneventful as his own had been yesterday. Despite that fact, Finn had been exhausted when he finally got home. *Definitely better than Friday, though*, he told himself. The adrenaline surge and inexhaustible energy of emergency calls got him through the events, but after a busy shift, he often felt emotionally drained and on the verge of physical collapse.

When he'd moved back home four years ago, he'd decided not to burden his mother with these feelings. She had enough to deal with, coping with her eye condition and, most of all, the devastating loss of the man her husband had once been. Fortunately, Marion's macular degeneration was the most common type, and its progress was slow. Lewis wasn't so lucky. The last time Finn had visited his father, he'd had to introduce himself. The experience had almost been humorous, as Lewis had scrunched up his face and said, "Finn McAllister? That's a familiar name."

Roxanne had smiled when Finn told her about it, but then both brother and sister had fallen silent for a long moment, remembering the father they'd had. Finn was grateful for the rare occasions when snippets of his dad's personality reappeared, even if briefly.

When he'd arrived home last night, the house was in darkness except for the lights on the veranda and in the front hall. Everyone had gone to bed, and he'd felt a little disappointed that Devon wasn't sitting by a fire in the living room as she had been the other night.

He'd heard at the fire hall that many people in the village had gathered at the community center to make meals for the Watsons, and he figured his mother would have been there. Devon's task had been to hang out with Kaya, and he'd wondered throughout the day how that was going. He'd phoned the house landline once, and Kaya had answered and given him a breathless summary of the day. When Devon got on the line, he'd heard some fatigue in her voice, but she'd seemed happy enough. She'd told him about the new ankle support that Theo had to give her tomorrow, and when Finn had informed her that he had the day off and would drive her to get it, she'd sounded almost as excited as Kaya.

"That's great, Finn. Thank you! I can hardly wait to ditch these crutches and get walking on my own." He'd been at a loss for words then, because he knew better mobility also meant a higher chance of her returning to Chicago sooner.

When he heard people moving around downstairs, Finn got up. Before he'd fallen asleep last night, he'd made some plans for him and Devon, which included not only picking up the special device at the Danby farm but also a tour of Maple Glen. Perhaps she'd be interested in seeing the main entrance to White Rocks outside Wallingford. He still didn't know why she'd picked an unusual route like the Glen access to hike or why she'd come in the middle of winter. But he hoped today would lead to a clearer picture of who Devon Fairchild was.

Finn quickly dressed and, peering through his bedroom door, checked to see if the bathroom was in use. The door was open, so he headed that way. He passed his mother's room and saw her bed was already made. He figured she was whipping up pancakes or waffles or some other Sunday breakfast special. While he shaved, he heard the thump of crutches on the stairs and smiled. Soon, Devon's comings and goings would sound the same as others in the household. The thought took him back to minutes ago when he'd imagined her leaving the Glen. Finn stared at his reflection and sighed. *Don't go there today. Just take advantage of the time she's here.* And resolving to follow his own good advice, Finn walked downstairs to the kitchen.

Marion looked up from the stove where she was tending to something in a frying pan. "This is a lovely surprise, having you for breakfast today."

"You got my text yesterday, didn't you? That

Matt owed me a shift and wanted to pay me back today?"

"I did, dear, but didn't read it until I went to bed. Such a busy day."

Finn stifled his irritation. What was the point of text messages if people waited for hours to read them? What if there was an emergency?

As if sensing what he might be thinking, Marion patted his cheek on her way to the table with a platter of French toast. "It's all right, dear. Roxanne read her message and told me."

Finn forced a smile and speared two slices onto his plate. He was tempted to say that Roxanne wouldn't always be around to pass on texts to his mother but immediately thought, maybe she would be. As much as he loved his sister and especially his niece, living permanently at the Manor wouldn't be good for any of them. His spirits lifted when he heard Devon coming down the stairs. Soon she was beaming a smile from the kitchen doorway, and the day brightened.

"French toast!" she enthused. "My favorite!"

Marion shot Finn a triumphant look. *Someone appreciates me* was the message, but he only had eyes for Devon. Her standard wardrobe of track pants and sweatshirt had been replaced by form-fitting black jeans and a bright-colored top that complemented her raven hair and blue eyes. *Chicago clothes?* he wondered.

"I figured we were entitled to a hearty breakfast, considering our light supper last night," Marion said. Turning to Finn, she explained, "We were all exhausted by a long day and had hamburgers for supper followed by an early bedtime."

"Amazing what a long night's sleep can do," Devon said as she crutched toward the table.

Finn quickly got to his feet and pulled out a chair for her. As she sat down, a light floral scent wafted around him, and he gazed down at her damp hair, tempted to brush aside a strand of curls that pressed against the nape of her neck. Instead, he paused a second longer, thinking a gesture like that was meant for other people, not a man and woman who'd known each other less than a week.

"I think we're all going to be in better moods today," Marion was saying. She caught Finn's frown and explained. "Kaya was feeling the effects of being cooped up inside most of the day."

Devon said, "I sat outside on the veranda while she played in the snow for a bit, but she really wanted to visit a school friend—"

"In Wallingford," Marion interjected.

"It was only at the end of the day that she started to exhibit signs of boredom and frustration." Devon laughed. "Sorry, that's my social worker jargon coming through. She was great, really, for most of the day."

Marion set a plate in front of Devon and sat opposite Finn with her own breakfast. "Roxanne will appreciate hearing that," she said. "Something set Kaya off right after supper. She was talking to Roxanne at the bottom of the stairs just before they went up to get ready for bed. Whatever it was, Roxanne wasn't happy about it, because I heard her sharp response, and she's always so patient with Kaya."

Finn's thoughts raced back to late June when his sister and niece first arrived in Maple Glen. Kaya seemed to have meltdowns every other day, and Roxanne had struggled to cope with them, hiding her own tears from Kaya but not from Marion or Finn. He refrained from reminding his mother about those days, but casting a quick glance at Devon's thoughtful expression, he guessed that she might have a different take on the incident. The sounds of excitement down the hallway reassured Finn that moods were definitely lighter today.

Kaya rushed into the kitchen, followed by her mother. "This day is getting better and better," she burbled, checking out the food on the table. "French toast and a playdate with my best friend in Maple Glen—Shelley."

Finn noticed that Roxanne's smile was wan, but her eyes gleamed lovingly at her daughter. He gazed around the table, thinking that despite all their ups and downs, they were family. That was precious, something to be protected. As he picked up his mug of coffee, he saw Devon smile and wink. Something unspoken passed between them, but he failed to identify it.

A kind of awareness? he asked himself. Not likely. People who had known each other less than a week didn't have that kind of empathic connection... *Did they?*

CHAPTER NINE

DEVON LEANED AGAINST the headrest of the passenger seat in Finn's pickup. The hearty breakfast of French toast, bacon and orange slices had left her drowsily satisfied, but she thought her sense of well-being had more to do with the man sitting next to her than food. He'd insisted on carrying her out to the truck again, although the sidewalk and drive area were clear of snow. "Too risky with crutches," he'd said, and she knew she wasn't going to protest.

The village had been quiet that morning as they drove through it. Recovering from yesterday's cooking marathon, Devon guessed, as they passed the community center. She noted that Bernie's B and B was still in darkness even though it was almost eleven. Finn had mentioned at breakfast that the prognosis for Betty Watson was good, but she'd be in the hospital a bit longer, maybe even for Christmas. He told her the community would rally to support the family in every way.

A few cars were pulling into the parking area

beside the church. Marion had announced that she and Roxanne were meeting there after the service with other members to finalize plans for the church bazaar, an annual event the week of Christmas. "There's always something unusual or creative at the bazaar," Marion had said as she finished cleaning up after breakfast. Finn had gone upstairs to do some scheduling on his computer, and Roxanne was helping Kaya get ready for her playdate in Wallingford.

"Betty Watson's arts and crafts always raise a lot of money for the church. Obviously, she won't be there herself, but I'm sure someone in the family will attend on her behalf." She'd paused. "Perhaps you'll still be here, too, Devon. I think you'd really like it."

Devon had simply smiled. Once she knew how the device that Theo had for her ankle was going to work, she'd be able to make some plans. For now, she didn't want to disappoint the generous woman who'd just served up a wonderful breakfast.

She was still lost in thought when she sensed the truck slowing down to turn into a long drive leading to a farmhouse. Theo's house, she knew from the day they drove to the clinic. She craned her neck to look beyond the house to the farm farther on. The donkey riding place, run by Theo's wife and her sister. Their names had popped up in conversation a couple of times. Both names started with *M*, but she couldn't remember which one was married to Theo. Of course, those first two days at the Manor had been a blur of pain, with people coming into her room to ask how she was and if she needed anything.

Except for Finn. He seemed to intuitively know what she wanted or needed, or else told her what he *thought* she needed. She sneaked a peek at him as he steered the truck toward an empty spot next to an SUV. His face was serious, deep in thought. *Wondering what this foot device will mean for my staying longer?* She didn't know yet herself, but at least now she had options.

As Finn set her down on the porch, a very pretty red-haired woman opened the door.

"Hey, Finn!" Her smile extended to Devon. "You must be Devon. I'm Maura. Theo told me about your accident. So lucky you were found by someone who knew what he was doing!"

Finn shuffled a tad impatiently next to Devon.

"Come in, you two. I've just made coffee." She ushered them into a dark hallway and gestured to a doorway off to her left. "Go on into the living room—or 'the parlor' as Theo's aunt called it. Theo's on the phone upstairs with his ex. Their son, Luke," she explained to Devon, "is supposed to go to his mother's on the West Coast for part of the holidays, and Luke wants to make it the second week, leading into New Year's. Anyway,

Theo won't be long. So, coffee?" She looked expectantly at both Finn and Devon.

"Sure," Finn said.

Devon nodded, still taking in all that Maura had said. Finn signaled for her to go ahead, and she hobbled into the room, decorated with the chintz and dark wood of another era.

Finn must have noticed her expression because he smiled and said, "They plan to completely renovate this place because they've got a baby coming, and Luke has decided to live in the Glen full time. He's in eighth grade in Wallingford and will go to high school next year in Rutland."

Devon immediately thought of a troubled teen she'd once worked with whose life was upended by her parents' divorce. "Will that be okay with Luke's mother?"

"Seems so. She's also expecting a baby, and soon. I guess, either way, Luke has some adjusting to do. At least he'll be in the Glen, where he's already found a place for himself in the community. He's quite a kid. I think you'd like him."

Devon preferred to make her own judgments about people but liked the fact that Finn spoke well of Luke. Some adults were quick to stereotype all teenagers, and so far, she hadn't seen that flaw in Finn.

"Devon," Finn said, breaking into her thoughts, "why don't you sit in that chair with the ottoman to support your ankle?"

It was a sensible suggestion, yet part of her bristled, mainly because she'd already decided on the chair and was on her way to it. For a quick second, she considered taking another one, but knew that was childish. She'd no sooner sat down than Theo bustled into the room carrying a box under one arm.

"Maura says to tell you coffee's on the way." He set the box down on a table, fumbling with the lid as he opened it up.

He seemed a bit flustered, and Devon wondered if the phone conversation with his ex was responsible. But he quickly rallied and walked over to bend down next to the ottoman where Devon's right foot was resting. "Okay, let me have a look at this first before deciding the next step." He removed the large woolen sock that covered the compressor bandage. "I think I've seen this sock before," he said, grinning, "but on a much bigger foot." He looked pointedly at Finn.

Devon watched him unwrap the bandage, careful not to press down on her foot—especially the ankle—as he removed it and dropped it onto the floor. He worked quietly, and she knew instinctively not to make small talk as he gently lifted her foot up off the ottoman and very slowly manipulated her ankle. One movement caused a light gasp, and he raised his head to her.

"Okay?"

She bit her lip but nodded. Out of the corner of

her eye, she thought she saw Finn start toward her, then take a step back. *Making sure I'm all right*, she thought, and felt a rush of warmth for him.

"Say stop when you've had enough of my poking and prodding." Theo smiled, but his eyes fixed on hers, concerned and reassuring at the same time.

"I'm fine," was all she said.

Finally, he set her foot back down. "The swelling's mostly gone, and I think that twinge of pain you felt was from the bruising around the joint. You haven't been putting weight on the ankle, have you?"

She shook her head.

"Good. Don't do that unless you're wearing the brace I have for you." He stood up and went to the box, pulling out a length of black fabric that puzzled Devon at first until he opened a Velcro tab and began to wind the material around her ankle. "This is an ankle brace. It's a strap, basically, that athletes often use to quell swelling from inflammation and to stabilize the foot and the ankle. Your sprain is a moderate one, so I decided against the walking boot I'd mentioned the other day. This will give you a lot more flexibility, and you should be able to wear it with ordinary shoes or boots—any kind of footwear that isn't constricting or inflexible. Even sneakers would be fine, as long as they have arch and ankle supports."

Devon thought of her hiking boots with their hard leather and thick laces and the fashionable, low-heeled ankle boots she'd worn traveling to Maple Glen. Neither seemed suitable for the brace, but that was a minor problem, she decided.

Just as Theo was finishing strapping the Velcro tab on, Maura came into the room carrying a tray of coffee mugs and a plate of cookies. "Ready for a break?" she asked, then burst into a giggle. "Oops, excuse that blunder."

Devon caught the adoring look from Theo to Maura and saw that Finn had, too. When he glanced at Devon, she thought his expression was a bit wistful.

"Yes. Thanks, Maura," Theo said, his smile deepening as she set the tray down on the coffee table in front of the sofa. Then turning back to Devon, he said, "Wear the brace only in daytime and no more than two hours at a time in the beginning. Then remove it for an hour and use the crutches if you need to. Then back on for another two hours. Keep doing that the first few days until your foot and ankle adjust to the brace. If swelling reoccurs, take it off, ice and elevate. Like you did before." He cocked his head at Finn. "I'm sure this guy will remind you about that. And if any serious pain develops, call me or come to the clinic. Whichever is fastest. Otherwise, I think you'll be just fine. Your healing is progressing as it should, as far as I can see."

"Can I drive now? With this?" She pointed to the brace.

Theo frowned. "Best hold off a couple more days until you're accustomed to it. See how well you can walk wearing it with some appropriate footwear."

So maybe not driving to the airport just yet, she thought, accepting a mug of coffee and a cookie from Maura. Devon also thought that Finn seemed more relaxed now after hearing Theo's advice about driving.

She bit into the cookie and chewed, listening to the three of them talk about Betty Watson and her family. For a brief moment, she felt apart from them, an outsider knowing something about their topic but without the emotional involvement. What was it like, she wondered, to have a sense of belonging to something larger than yourself?

Less than an hour later, Finn was escorting her to the pickup. She was wearing the brace with Finn's sock over it because she had no other footwear. He'd offered to carry her over the snow-covered gravel drive, but Theo and Maura were waving goodbye from the front door, and Devon knew she'd be embarrassed. The chivalrous gesture looked too much like a marriage tradition. She and Finn were as far away from that as...as the earth is from the sun, she thought. She managed the short distance with the crutches and felt a sense of triumph. Another step toward independence.

After Finn turned over the truck engine, he said, "There's a new mall this side of Rutland. If you want, we could go look for some footwear that will work with that brace."

"Yes! That would be great. I'm eager to start walking on my own again, even if that involves this brace for a while."

Finn simply nodded and shifted into Drive. The truck pulled out onto the county road and headed north toward Route 7 and Rutland. Passing the adjacent farm with its Jake & Friends sign, Devon noticed a few vehicles parked along its long driveway. "A lot of cars there. Is the place open for business throughout the winter?"

"It is and looks like it's doing well. A few months ago, the business was getting a bit stretched financially, but Maura and Maddie managed to make it all come together. They hosted the village annual Fourth of July Festival and a lot of people outside the Glen came for that, got to see the donkeys and find out about the therapy program. Mom told me the sisters have hired a full-time instructor with lots of experience working with therapy animals and the clients."

"How did they get into that business? Maura and Maddie."

"They inherited the farm from their father, who passed away...um...maybe two years ago. He was ill for a while, and Maura moved back home to take care of him. He already had a couple of donkeys—one was given to him by a local man who was selling his property and couldn't look after him. That was Jake. Then one day, Maura's dad came home to find another donkey had been dropped off at the farm by some anonymous donor." Finn looked across at her, grinning. "I think that was Matilda."

"So, does Maddie still live there? And when did Maura meet Theo?"

Finn shook his head. "Long story about Maura and Theo, going back to their teens. And, yes, Maddie lives there with her partner, Shawn Harrison. That's another long story."

"Local history?"

"Yep. We call it the Glen grapevine. My father used to say, 'Almost everybody knows almost everything about everyone almost all the time in Maple Glen.'" Finn mimicked a drawl, grinning at her. "I guess you haven't experienced much of that in Chicago."

"Only in the workplace, but in a different way." Devon sighed. "I can't imagine what that's like, people in your neighborhood knowing so much about your personal life."

"Yeah, it can be problematic for sure. But there are also positive aspects to small-town grapevines. You don't have to ask for help because people know when you need it."

Devon had mixed feelings about office grapevines, recalling an incident at her own place of work a couple of years ago when a coworker's personal problems had circulated around the office, leading to her emotional resignation. The event had confirmed Devon's longtime vow to keep her personal life even more private. "I wouldn't like that," she finally murmured, staring out the window as the Welcome to Wallingford sign came into view.

When she turned his way again, his face was impassive as he looked at the road ahead, but the muscles around his jaw were tight and clenched.

No ONE DID Sunday roast better than his mother, Finn was thinking, as he pushed back his chair and began to help carry empty plates into the kitchen. The meal more than made up for the gloomy pall that had fallen over him after Devon's comment about the Glen grapevine on the drive to Rutland. He'd stewed about it during the entire shopping expedition for footwear that would accommodate her ankle brace.

Not that they were in the new mall long, definitely no longer than absolutely necessary because Finn hated shopping, almost as much as he hated the large multistore complexes where, in his opinion, people wandered aimlessly simply to fill their time. Roxanne had teased him about that a few months ago when the family had taken

Kaya to the opening of the new ice cream chain in the same mall.

"You're too young to be so grumpy!" Roxanne had exclaimed, and Kaya had giggled, which made Finn even grouchier.

Fortunately for him, Devon was quick, making a purchase of winter-duty sneakers and boots that, in Finn's limited fashion know-how, even his mother wouldn't wear. But she clearly knew what she was doing, because her foot, encased in the ankle brace, slipped easily into both. She kept the boots on and handed him the crutches. He admired the determination in her face as she took the first step, gingerly setting her right foot in its brace onto the mall floor. A slight wince was the only sign of pain, but he forced himself not to rush to her side. Another step, and then she reached for his hand, which he quickly clasped around hers. She walked slowly and carefully, pausing every now and then to let Christmas shoppers pass by, grasping his one hand while he held on to the crutches with the other. Finn counted fifteen paces before she asked for the crutches back and used them to aid her walking, keeping her right foot off the ground.

He'd reminded her that Theo said to take her time, and she'd summoned a wan smile for him. Then she insisted on treating him to ice cream at the place he'd been to months before with his family, and as they enjoyed the cones sitting on a bench festooned with large red bows, they'd laughed at the absurdity of eating ice cream cones in the middle of winter, even if they were inside a mall. His mood had lifted from earlier, when he'd heard her response to the Glen grapevine. Yet once they were heading back home, Finn's mood dipped again. Maple Glen wasn't the kind of place a big-city woman like Devon would be drawn to. What would it take to overcome her obvious bias against small-town culture?

He carried the plates into the kitchen where his mother had begun stacking the dishwasher. "I'll take over in here," he said. "You go on into the living room with Roxanne, Kaya and Devon. Roxanne's making a fire before she takes Kaya upstairs for her bath."

Marion smiled. "That's sweet of you, dear, and I'd take you up on that, but I know which pieces of my china shouldn't go into the machine. Besides, I thought Devon seemed a bit withdrawn after your shopping trip. Maybe she could use some cheering up."

Finn thought he was the last person Devon would want cheering her up, but he made his way to the living room, where she was half reclining on the sofa, staring into the fire. She turned at his approach, and her welcome smile encouraged him to drag the armchair closer to both her and the fireplace.

"Roxanne's getting Kaya ready for bed, I assume?" he asked.

"She is. Apparently, the playdate went so well that Kaya can hardly wait to go to school tomorrow and see her new best friend."

"Aw, that's good. Kaya had a hard time making new friends when they first arrived here. She started school just before it let out at the end of June, so…"

"Hard to make friends at the end of a term," Devon filled in.

He wondered from the tone in her voice if she'd had a similar experience as a child. He really needed to learn more about this woman.

"Thanks for today," she went on to say. "For the drive to Theo's to pick up the brace and for taking me to the shopping mall. I gathered malls aren't your favorite place, and to be honest, they're not mine, either. But I needed the shoes and boots, and it seems Maple Glen isn't known for its shopping opportunities as much as—"

"Its grapevine?"

Her head turned sharply his way, and she smiled at his grin. "I was going to say 'hiking trails,' but 'grapevine' works, too," she quipped.

He felt the buzz of a connection—two like-minded people finding common ground. "I'm on nights this week, starting Tuesday, but are you up for a tour of the area tomorrow? Not just the Glen, but more of Otter Valley itself?"

Her face lit up. "I'd love that."

He impulsively reached for her hand and squeezed it. Her eyes met his, unflinching and aglow with something more than the reflection of flames from the fireplace. Finn wanted to draw her nearer to the edge of the sofa, within kissing distance of his chair. Then footsteps sounded from the staircase, heading their way.

"It's a deal, then," he murmured, his voice low in the quiet room. He pressed her fingers gently against his and let go of her hand. Tomorrow, he'd show her there was a lot more to Maple Glen than grapevines and hiking trails.

CHAPTER TEN

"A ROAD TRIP? Can I come?"

Everyone in the kitchen laughed. "It's Monday, sweetheart. You have school," Roxanne said as she handed Kaya her lunch box. "Now, put this in your backpack and then go upstairs to brush your teeth. We've got ten minutes till the bus comes."

For the first time since she'd been staying with the family, Devon felt a part of the morning routine. She already knew that Kaya would take too long upstairs and that her mother would have to call her to move it—*quickly!* Marion would sigh and smile at Devon. And Finn? She sneaked a peek.

His expression ranged from exasperation to bemused resignation. She wondered if he was still adjusting to the shift in the household since last June, when his sister and niece had arrived in Maple Glen. From personal experience, she knew sometimes people didn't adjust at all. They either moved on or they moved out. But she refused to let memories intrude on her road trip today.

She was looking forward to a day away from the house and, especially, time spent alone with Finn.

There'd been a moment last night when she was sitting in the living room absorbed in thoughts of the day and questions about what lay ahead when Finn had briefly clasped her hand, and she'd felt that everything was going to be okay. That reassurance of his strong warm hand pressing hers was exactly what her spirits had needed right then. For a second, though, she'd also thought he was going to lean closer and kiss her. The spell was broken when Roxanne came down after putting Kaya to bed, and despite the instant letdown, Devon knew the timing had been in her favor. A romantic entanglement with the man who'd rescued her was the stuff of novels, not real life, which was full of commitments and duties—like carrying out the promise to her brother. Now that commitment had yet to be fulfilled, postponed by her fall on the Long Trail. She'd only taken a few days off from work, thinking her mission would be carried out by the weekend. Today was Monday, and she was expected in the office on Wednesday. That definitely wasn't going to happen. She stifled a sigh, thinking of the request for more time off she'd have to make. The real world was closing in, despite her efforts to push it aside.

She watched Finn get up and help Marion clear the breakfast dishes. Here was a man who would never shirk a commitment or a duty. A good son, a tolerant brother and a caring uncle. What would he be like, she wondered, as a husband? Or a father? Would he look at his wife the way Theo had yesterday at Maura? That question instantly begged another: Would she herself ever be on the receiving end of such adoration?

"Devon?"

She blinked, realizing at once that the man in her head was standing in front of her, a light smile on his face. She flushed, as if he'd had access to her thoughts seconds ago.

"I asked if you could be ready to leave in, say, ten minutes."

She nodded.

"Great. I'm just going to send off a couple of emails, so if you want a hand going upstairs…"

Emails. Perhaps this was the best time to fire one off to her supervisor, explaining her situation and booking some sick leave.

"I'm good, but thanks." She'd managed the stairs without crutches when she'd come down for breakfast, holding on to the banister while carefully setting her right foot, wrapped inside the brace, onto each step, one by one. That had been another bit of advice from Theo—*Going upstairs, lead with your good foot, and going down, lead with your injured one, holding on to the railing all the time.* But because he'd also told her to wear the brace for two hours at a time, she decided to take the crutches on the road trip to alternate with the brace.

Once she'd quickly sent off the message to her boss, she changed into the same outfit as yesterday with the down jacket she'd worn on the flight to Rutland, plus the new boots and brace. A bit more than ten minutes later, she was waiting in the hall entry, watching him take the stairs two at a time.

"Sorry," he said. "Ed Watson phoned to thank the crew for everything we did for Betty."

"How is his wife doing?"

"Okay, but it'll be a slow recovery."

Devon thought he was downplaying his own role as leader of the rescue team but liked him for that. "And the investigation?" she asked.

"It's ongoing. I heard they got a statement from the man involved, the one heading north, but I don't know what he said." He took his jacket out of the hall closet and put it on as he was talking. "I have a feeling one of them was distracted and maybe hit a patch of black ice." He zipped up the jacket and smiled. "All set?"

Devon beamed at his obvious anticipation and felt a surge of excitement, too. She handed him one of her crutches, using the other as a cane to stabilize her while walking with the brace. She found she was getting used to the brace already, its support easing her weight on the ankle, but was mindful of every step she took, careful not to twist or turn the foot. *Don't pivot on it and avoid crossing the ankle over top of the other foot when you're sitting*, Theo had said. As soon as they reached the veranda steps, Devon saw that Finn had shoveled a clear path all around his pickup. There'd be no need for him to carry her, and for a nanosecond she felt disappointed.

He waited at the passenger-side door while she slowly climbed onto her seat, then stowed the crutches in the rear compartment and closed her door. Devon tracked his movement around the back of the truck, noticing him check the tires as he went. He was thorough and careful in everything he did, she thought. *Which makes him a good firefighter and volunteer rescue guy.*

She herself took pride in similar traits, earning her a reputation as a dependable, insightful and intuitive social worker. Or so her last performance review had indicated. When she'd shown the report to Dan, he'd remarked that the woman who'd been their own social worker twenty-five years ago would likewise have been proud. Devon had almost forgotten the kind woman who'd gone beyond professional obligations to ensure that she and her brother were well taken care of. She couldn't recall her name but guessed some record of it would be in the file Dan received when he turned eighteen. The file was now in a box in her condo storage unit among Dan's other papers, which she hadn't yet mustered the courage to peruse.

The wrench of the driver door opening shifted

her to the present as Finn got behind the wheel. "A great day for a drive," he said, starting the engine. "Sunny, with no sign of bad weather."

"Like the morning I set out for the trail."

He shot her a quick look as he shifted into Reverse to make his U-turn. "But snow was in the forecast then."

Her sigh filled the truck. "Yeah, the sun and the puffy white clouds fooled me."

"Well, you probably weren't the only person to be fooled that day, if it's any consolation."

"Bernie did try to warn me."

"Bernie's lived here his whole life. He knows how weather changes in the valley."

"Was the B and B his original home?"

"No, the Harrisons used to live there until their son—Shawn—went off to college and moved away from the Glen. Bernie managed the gas station and convenience store at the junction of Route 7 and the county road. We passed it on our way to Rutland yesterday."

"Oh, right." She'd been more aware of the man sitting next to her and whatever was on his mind than the scenery outside her window.

"When the Harrisons put their house up for sale, Bernie bought it and turned it into a B and B," Finn went on to say.

"Is he married? Just that I didn't notice a woman around the night I stayed there."

"A lifelong bachelor, though I've no idea if he had a romance in his youth."

Devon pushed aside the instant thought of a life without romance. She was only thirty! There was plenty of time. But another of Dan's pleas in his last days flashed again—*Have the family we never had.* So far, she hadn't met anyone who came close to qualifying for the role of partner in her personal life. There'd always been some trait in the few men she'd dated long term that had prompted her to move on.

She glanced at Finn as he turned onto Church Street. Could he be the one to change her mind about a permanent relationship? He ticked all the right boxes, but she'd known him less than a week. Hardly enough time to gauge a person's true character. Especially the sides people tended to keep private or hidden.

"Our first stop," he announced, bringing her back to the moment, "is Tasty Delights bakery where we'll pick up a coffee and, of course, a tasty delight."

"We just ate breakfast," she pointed out.

"Cereal?" he scoffed. "We need some hearty nourishment for the road ahead."

She laughed, but as Finn parked in front of the bakery, she mentally ticked off the first box, debating between *impulsive* or *adventurous* as a label. She could live with either one, she decided, as they got out of the truck. Finn handed her one crutch for support, and they headed into the bakery.

FINN KNEW HIS face was red and there wasn't a single thing he could do about it other than pretend to be looking at the selection of bagged cookies on a rack adjacent to the counter. Being the center of attention had never appealed to him, and right now, too many pairs of eyes were aimed at his back as he stooped to choose a bag of chocolate chip cookies for Kaya.

There was a fraction of a lull and then Devon got the hint. "Well, we should go. Thanks, Sue, and very nice to meet you."

If there wasn't already a lot to attract him to her, that sentence alone would have made the case. He took the bag to the counter, still aware of those eyes but not minding them so much now that they were leaving. "Guess I should get Kaya something, too," he mumbled, digging into his jacket pocket for his wallet.

Sue waved a dismissing hand. "Take them. A small thank-you for helping Betty."

"Yes," someone behind him cried out and someone else clapped lightly.

Heat rose up into his face again, and he nodded, turned and, as quickly as possible, made his way around the line of people to the door. He was in the truck before he realized he'd left Devon behind, not only with one of her crutches, but the tray of coffees and bag of pastries. Muttering, he climbed out again and was about to cross the road when he saw a man he didn't recognize hold the door open for Devon as she exited the bakery, the crutch under one arm and the pastries balanced on top of the coffee tray.

She didn't say a word as she handed him the tray and rounded the truck to get in on her side. But she smiled, and Finn wanted to hug her more than anything. They took a minute, silently sipping the brew and munching on the pastry still warm from the oven.

"What does *kringle* mean anyway?" Devon asked around a mouthful of pastry, and Finn wondered for a second what she was saying.

"Sue once told me it's an old Danish word, meaning 'circle' or 'oval.' Her mother was Danish and brought the recipe with her when she moved here with Sue's father. It's only made at Christmas, so we try to get our fill of it while we can."

"It's delicious…buttery with lots of dried fruits and nuts."

Finn watched her lick her fingers before picking up her coffee cup for another sip. He liked the fact that she enjoyed food and guessed his mother did, too, because ever since Devon had been staying at the Manor, Marion had been baking and cooking far more than usual. Of course, it was the Christmas season, which is why Sue's bakery was featuring kringle, along with other seasonal treats. But Finn also suspected his mother's motivation for cooking seriously took off once she knew Devon appreciated her efforts. Roxanne's appetite was only recently picking up since moving back home. Stress did that, Finn knew. Kaya always welcomed sweets but was picky about everything else. Finn ate basically everything but usually on the run. "Sit and enjoy it. Take your time," his mother pleaded in vain.

Funny, he thought, as they were finishing their kringle and coffee, how they'd all been eating their meals together these last few days. Kaya would be prattling on and Roxanne and Mom would be itemizing things needed for the bazaar or the cookie exchange or whatever was coming up in the Glen before Christmas. None of that interested him very much, of course. What held his attention through every meal was Devon and the range of expressions that flitted across her face as she listened, too. Interest was there, but so was curiosity and occasionally, puzzlement. He had the feeling that the whole "sit down for a meal with your family" thing was completely alien to her. Why that was, he didn't know, but he'd do his best to find out.

"Now where?" Devon heaved a loud satisfied sigh. She was rubbing her hands together, shaking tiny crumbs onto her lap and gazing at him with the expectation of someone ready for an adventure.

"I figure that since we've had our second

breakfast, we could work off some of that extra energy. Are you up for a different kind of ride?" The truck engine rumbled into life. "I'm thinking about riding a four-legged animal," he hinted at her frown. "Jake & Friends?" he clarified as her frown deepened.

"Donkey riding?"

He laughed at the disbelief in her voice. "Well, we could give it a try. Kaya loves it."

"Oh, well, it's a done deal then, if Kaya loves it."

"She told me I should try it again," he added, glancing quickly at her before steering the truck back onto the road.

"Uh-huh. Right now, I'm trying very hard to picture you sitting astride a donkey." She raised a single teasing eyebrow and grinned.

"Don't underestimate my talents," he said in a mocking scold. "I have many talents you have yet to see. Hidden ones." He focused on the road ahead then, and when a quipped reply didn't sound, he looked her way again.

Her eyes were shining, fixed on his with an expression that set his heart racing. He reached across the console for her hand, holding it as long as safe driving permitted.

When he let go a few seconds later, she said, "If the donkey riding isn't enough recreation, I know that Kaya has a new activity set at home we could check out."

"I think I can come up with something more exciting than that," Finn said, casting one more smile her way. He turned back to his driving, squinting against the sun's glare. The day was going to be just fine, he thought, and felt a surge of new energy that had nothing to do with the kringle pastry.

MADDIE STUART LOOKED nothing like her sister, Maura. Devon vaguely recalled someone at the Manor mentioning the sisters were twins. *Obviously nonidentical ones* was her first thought when the farmhouse side door opened. Maddie was about the same height as her twin, but that was the only similarity. Her black shoulder-length hair set off pale skin and dark eyes. She cocked her head slightly, grinning at Finn.

"Hey, Finn! You've missed breakfast—sorry about that." Then, looking at Devon, she said, "And you must be Devon. Maura told me a bit about your accident on the trail. Luckily for you, this guy found you, even in a snowstorm."

The whole village must have heard her story by now, Devon figured. She wasn't sure if she liked that or not.

"We haven't come for breakfast, having just enjoyed a kringle pastry at the bakery," Finn said. "Though I admit your coffee is on a par with Sue's."

Devon saw the corners of his mouth lift in a tease. Was this an ongoing joke between them?

"I thought Devon might be interested in seeing the donkeys. Maybe even riding one."

Maddie immediately looked down at Devon's foot. "Are you up for that?" she asked.

Was she? Tossing aside all caution, Devon quickly nodded. She seriously wanted to ride a donkey.

"Okay, well, why don't you two head to the barn, and I'll join you in a few minutes?"

"Is Shawn around?" Finn asked.

"He's upstairs on the computer, catching up on his work email. I'll tell him you're here."

When the door closed, Finn held on to Devon's elbow, guiding her along a muddy path to the barn. She was grateful for her warm and sturdy new boots—fake leather and washable. Exactly what was needed for walking around on a farm in the winter. They might even be useful in Chicago, for the days when snow turned into mucky slush. Then she reminded herself that city sidewalks were usually cleared.

When they reached the open barn door, Devon paused on the threshold, taking in the pungent aromas of animals and fresh hay. Except for an elementary school field trip, she'd never been on a farm. Once Dan had mentioned selling his company and taking early retirement in the country—*Maybe a farm*, he'd said with a laugh—but they both knew that would never happen. They were city people.

Finn led the way down the central aisle with a number of stalls on either side. There were a couple of shovels leaning against one of the stalls and a few empty buckets sitting on the barn floor. As she moved farther inside, she heard the shuffling of hooves and saw the silhouettes of big heads and twitching ears. Suddenly, from out of nowhere, a small black-and-white dog ran toward them barking. Devon automatically edged closer to Finn, who placed a reassuring arm around her shoulders.

"Don't worry," he said, as the dog reached them. "This is Shep, and he's just telling us this is his territory. Plus, Roger's his best friend and he's checking me out." He nodded his head toward the donkey in the nearest stall and bent to pat the dog, now wagging his tail and sniffing Finn's hand. "You know me, don't you, fella?" Standing again, Finn said, "Hold out your hand and let him have a sniff. Then, the next time we come, he'll recognize both of us."

The dog's wet nose traced a path across her opened palm and fingers, and Devon giggled at the sensation.

As the dog moved off, trotting toward the end of the aisle, Finn asked, "Have you ever had a dog as a pet?"

She shook her head. There had been a dog at one of the foster homes she and Dan had lived at for a brief time, but it was a guard dog, chained up in the backyard. All of the kids in the home had been afraid of it, except for Dan. *He's like that because of how he's been treated*, he'd tried to explain.

Devon took a deep breath, waiting for the instant memory to disappear. "Let's go look at those donkeys."

CHAPTER ELEVEN

FINN SMILED AT the delight in Devon's face as she ran her hand along the donkey's snout.

"The fur is so thick and coarse, not like a horse's at all."

"I think Matilda's the best choice for you, Devon. She's mild-mannered and pretty docile." Maddie unlatched the stall door and went in to get Matilda ready for riding, fastening the bridle on first and then the saddle before leading her out of the stall.

Devon immediately stepped back, bumping into Finn, who set his hands on her shoulders to steady her. "She's bigger up close!" she exclaimed.

"Bulkier than a horse but not as tall. See?" Maddie led the donkey closer. "You're actually taller than she is." She grinned expectantly at Finn. "Well? You going, too, or not? If so, I may have to get my camera."

Finn shrugged, dismissing her tease. His one-time attempt at donkey riding had been in the summer, when he'd taken Kaya for a lesson. He'd ridden Matilda then and was far too tall for her.

She bucked, and Finn had slipped off onto the barn floor.

"I'm game."

"Lizzie?" Maddie's grin widened.

"No way!" He looked at Devon and said, "Lizzie's ornery as anything and she sometimes bites."

"How about Roger?"

"Sure," he agreed. He'd heard from Kaya that Roger was a slow-moving animal, the oldest donkey on the farm.

"All right. Here—" she handed him Matilda's lead "—you hang on to her while I get Roger."

Devon edged closer to Matilda, stroking her head and mane. When she stopped, Matilda craned around to nuzzle her shoulder. "She likes me! I think she's telling me not to stop."

That moment alone compensated for his having to ride a donkey again, Finn thought. Seeing Roger plodding toward him, already saddled up, he knew he couldn't back down.

"I think you both should mount them inside. The ring is pretty muddy," Maddie said as she saddled up Matilda. "You first, Devon. And I suggest you use this little step." She walked a few paces to an adjacent empty stall and returned with a wooden block, setting it down at Matilda's side.

Finn was about to move forward to assist Devon, but she gave a slight headshake. He scarcely heard Maddie's instructions to Devon, watching her every move in case she needed help. She followed Maddie's directions, grasping hold of the pommel, stepping onto the block with her left foot, then swinging her right leg over and, finally, settling into the saddle. He hoped he'd do as well.

"Finn? Ready? You won't need the block, but remember that Roger's right eye is blind, so you'd best get up on his left side while I hold on to him. He hasn't been ridden in a while and may be skittish." She stood in front of Roger, one hand tightly clasping his reins.

Now she tells me, he thought. Mindful of Devon's eyes on him, he moved with purpose and determination to Roger's left side. He reached for the pommel and placed his left foot in the stirrup. As he hefted his weight onto his foot and began to rise up, Roger snorted and stepped backward. Maddie quickly calmed him, producing a piece of something from her shirt pocket and offering it to Roger as Finn followed through onto the saddle.

"Some kind of magic potion?" Finn quipped.

"Just a slice of apple."

He noticed Maddie and Devon smiling at each other but didn't mind. He'd learned long ago that the ability to laugh at oneself—or at least to recognize the humor in a given situation—was a great way to diminish embarrassment. When he saw Devon wink, he felt a rush of warmth for her.

"All set?" Maddie asked, and without waiting

for a reply added, "I'll lead Matilda, so you'll have to handle Roger on your own, Finn. You okay with that?"

He nodded but wasn't so sure. There was no way he was going to reverse that plan, however, and leave Devon managing Matilda by herself. Besides, if he extended his legs, he could touch the ground. Surely that would slow Roger down. "All right. Let's do this!" he whooped as Maddie took Matilda's lead and headed for the rear barn door and the riding ring outside.

Maddie opened the gate and took Matilda and Devon through. The bright sun had melted any residual snow in the oval-shaped riding ring, producing even more mud. Finn raised his bent knees more, pushing his feet as far onto the stirrups as possible. He noticed that Devon, who was much shorter than he was, had no problem keeping her feet well away from the ground. Donkeys were cute, but horses definitely made for easier riding. He just hoped Maddie wouldn't make any more than one or two circuits of the ring.

Roger seemed content with Finn on his back. He was the largest of the Stuart donkeys and, despite his blind eye, easily followed Maddie with Matilda and Devon. But Roger was also slow, and Finn wanted to catch up with the trio ahead. He wasn't certain how to do that other than to dig the stirrups into Roger's side. Not wanting to alarm the donkey, he gave a slight push with his heels.

Other than a slight uplifting of his head and a snort, Roger's response was low-key. Watching Devon and Maddie chatting as if they'd known each other forever, Finn's patience waned. He wanted to be part of whatever conversation they were clearly enjoying.

As the trio ahead arrived back at the gate, completing the first lap around the ring, Finn decided to be more assertive in his effort to get Roger to pick up the pace. He dug in his heels harder and pulled back the reins. Roger brayed and came to a dead stop. Right then, a black-and-white streak of motion charged through the open gate toward Roger and Finn.

Finn saw Maddie swing around, annoyance in her face as she hollered, "Shep, stay!" But Shep was only interested in making sure that Roger was okay. He circled the donkey, barking furiously at the rider on Roger's back.

Finn pulled harder on the reins, thinking he could control Roger. Instead, Roger reared his head back and shifted more weight onto his hind legs. *He's going to buck and tilt me off.* Finn instinctively lowered his legs, and as his feet hit the ground, Roger decided he'd had enough. He was about to shake Finn off when Maddie dropped Matilda's lead and ran toward Roger.

The rescue played out in slow motion. Another slice of apple distracted Roger as Maddie reached for his bridle. Shep appeared to sense that his best friend was okay and stopped barking. Finn managed to get his feet onto the muddy ground and stay upright after swinging off Roger's back.

Finn saw that Maddie was trying hard to hide a grin as she said, "Why don't you lead Matilda and Devon back to the barn while I take Roger?" She peered down at Finn's mud-covered hiking boots. "Too late for those now anyway."

As Finn squelched toward Devon, perched calmly on Matilda's back, he knew his face was red. When he reached for Matilda's bridle, Devon smiled and said, "At least the rest of you is mud-free."

He laughed, letting go of his frustration. "So much for donkey riding," he said.

"Thanks for this, Finn. Not for what just happened—though it will make a great story—but for giving me the chance to ride Matilda. I loved it." Her eyes sparkled.

Finn could only nod, filled with gratitude and something more. Affection? As he led Matilda and Devon out of the ring, he figured his boots might be ruined, but not the day.

DEVON COULDN'T TAKE her eyes off Finn. They were sitting around the farmhouse kitchen drinking coffee, and Shawn had just joined them. He wanted to know why Finn had been in the mudroom off the kitchen cleaning his boots, and Maddie recounted the whole story. Devon barely listened, her attention focused on the man across the table from her. He'd given a good-natured grin when Shawn teased him, though his face had reddened slightly. She figured that was because he felt her eyes on him. So far, twice that day he'd been the center of attention—at the bakery and here at the farm. He'd handled both situations with an easy, casual grace that Devon envied. She doubted she'd be as accepting about the teasing. Despite the efforts she'd made over the years to dismiss embarrassment or shrug off teasing, now and again she found herself wanting to lash out.

When she was being teased mercilessly at their last foster home, it had been her brother who'd suggested she take a few deep breaths and count to ten. *When you get mad, they'll only tease you more. You're giving them what they want—a reaction.* He'd proven to be right about that, as he had so many other times over the years. Though Devon found counting to ten had never been enough.

When Maddie stood up and offered another round of coffee, Finn glanced at Devon, his eyes signaling a message that she got at once. *He's ready to leave*, she thought. It was almost noon, and she knew there were other sights in the valley he wanted to show her.

As they were saying goodbye, Maddie suddenly hugged Devon. "Come back anytime for a visit or a ride. Bring Kaya the next time—*she* loves riding."

Finn gave an exaggerated cough at the implication that made everyone laugh.

On the way to the truck, Devon impulsively said, "I'd offer to carry you over this mud now that your boots are clean, but you're a tad too big for me."

He gave her a sheepish smile, wrapped an arm around her shoulders and tucked her close against his side. "I have to say, you aced donkey riding."

She laughed aloud. "I didn't do a thing. I just sat on Matilda's back."

"Maybe so, but at least you *stayed* on her back." He opened the truck passenger door, holding it as she climbed up onto the seat.

When he got behind the wheel, she said, "Thanks again, Finn. It's hard to explain, but I felt so peaceful sitting on Matilda, feeling her slow, gentle sway beneath me. It was like...um—" she frowned, searching for the right words "—my body felt every movement, but my head was in another place."

He nodded thoughtfully. "That's why it's called riding therapy," he murmured, fixing his eyes on hers. After a long minute, he turned over the engine and shifted into Reverse. "How about some lunch in Wallingford before the second leg of our tour?"

"Sounds good," she said. "And no mud involved anywhere, I hope?"

He arched an eyebrow. "Well," he drawled, "I

can't promise you that on a day like today. And your boots are still a bit pristine."

Devon laughed. As the truck rumbled down the drive and turned onto the county road leading out of Maple Glen, the contentment that flowed through her was similar to the feeling she'd had circling the ring as she sat on Matilda. *Riding therapy*, she thought. *It really does work.* When she was back in Chicago, she'd search for a riding stable that offered a similar program. But would she feel the same thrill there as she did here at Jake & Friends? Somehow, she doubted it.

DEVON WAS HARD-PRESSED to recall what she ate for lunch as Finn pulled away from Wallingford town center. While he'd eaten with gusto, she'd chewed bread and swallowed some kind of soup. Her interest had definitely not been on food but on Finn. She decided that her initial image of Finn as simply a man who wanted to take charge had been wrong. Of course he had elements of that trait. When she was mounting Matilda, she'd seen him struggling not to help her. Now she was realizing there was much more to Finn McAllister, and she wanted to learn as much about him as she could before leaving Maple Glen.

That inevitability was closer than she'd thought yesterday and, certainly, closer than Finn probably realized. She'd managed perfectly fine with the brace so far, and other than a twinge of an ache now and then, her ankle was okay. The knowledge that her time here was coming to an end saddened her. She couldn't explain why, but she was beginning to think she'd rather stay in the village than return to Chicago.

The city had little to offer now that Dan was gone. Her job and the small cactus garden in her apartment weren't as compelling a draw for her as spending time in Finn's company. She sighed and peered out the window as the truck wound its way through the back streets of Wallingford, mentally listing the pros and cons of a life in Maple Glen—or Chicago. A pointless exercise, she knew, given that the real draw in Maple Glen was Finn, and he hadn't actually made a pitch for her to stay. And if he did, what then? Would he be enough reason to quit her job and move her whole life here?

"If I had a penny, I'd offer it to you," Finn commented, looking across at her.

"Hmm?"

"For your thoughts."

"Oh…not even worth a penny," she laughed, evading a reply. "I liked Maddie and her sister. They seem to be genuine, down-to-earth people. So, how did Maddie and Shawn meet? You said there was a long story there."

"Shawn Harrison was Maddie's senior high school crush. I actually haven't heard the whole story. Shawn's not the talkative type, especially when it comes to affairs of the heart, so to speak."

Like most men I've known, Devon thought. "And what about Maura and Theo? You said they were high school sweethearts, too?"

"More like summer ones. Theo's not originally from the Glen. He came every summer to stay at his aunt and uncle's farm—where he and Maura are living now—and he, Maddie and Maura were a regular trio of mischief and adventure when they were young. As teenagers, things changed for them."

"Complications arising from adolescent crushes?"

"You said it." He turned from driving to look at her. "Luckily, it worked out for them. How about you?"

"What about me?" She sensed where he was going with the question and was already thinking of a credible yet neutral reply.

"Teenage crushes?"

"The usual one or two. Nothing serious, like what the Stuart sisters had." She glanced out the window again, avoiding his gaze. "Where to now?"

"Some place you might like to keep in mind for future visits to Maple Glen and, especially, the Long Trail," he said, steering the truck onto another road and then making a right into a large parking area. The lot was empty but for one other vehicle. He parked and turned off the engine.

A vast forest lay at the far end of the lot. Devon leaned forward to stare beyond the acres of trees to the looming mountains. A sense of unease crept up her spine. "What is this place?" She saw at once that the tone of her question had signaled something to him. He looked disconcerted, unsure what was on her mind.

"Um, well this is White Rocks National Recreation Area and it's one of the main jumping off places on the Long Trail. I wanted to show you how convenient it is, compared to the of section you attempted in the Glen. I mean—" his voice faltered "—if you want to try hiking the trail again sometime—when your ankle is strong enough—this is the best place. Most novice hikers start here."

Devon barely heard what he'd said. She opened the passenger door and started to climb out.

"Hey, wait a sec. What's up?" Finn was scrambling out his side, moving quickly around the truck to clasp her by the arm. "Are you okay? You look pale, like you've seen a ghost."

Devon struggled to express what she was feeling. "Seeing a ghost" was closer to the mark than Finn could possibly know. A surge of dizziness mixed with nausea roiled up and she inhaled rapid breaths that almost had her hyperventilating.

Finn held her a long moment before moving her back onto the passenger seat where she tried desperately to catch her breath and stop the memories. When she was breathing regularly, he climbed back inside the truck and turned over the engine. Before shifting into gear, he looked across at her and said, "Take your time. I'm not going to ask you what just happened because I know you'll tell me eventually. At least, I hope you will, Devon, because I care about you. I care about what you're feeling and thinking right now, and I know it's not my place to probe, but I think you realize you need to talk to someone. And I also think I'm the best person for that." He reached across to stroke the side of her cheek with the back of his hand.

He *was* the right person to talk to. Devon knew that the moment he held her in his arms, waiting for her to breathe normally. The shivering that threatened to take control vanished as the warmth of his body pressed against hers. His calm reassurance soon brought her back from the past she'd spent her entire life trying to forget.

CHAPTER TWELVE

SHE WAS QUIET all the way back to the Glen. Finn canceled his plan to walk around the conservation area after her panic attack. That's what it was, he figured. Something triggered a negative reaction. Although she had yet to say a word about what happened, his gut told him it had something to do with the parking area and entrance to the Long Trail. He couldn't imagine why.

Every now and then, he sneaked a peek at her. She was focused on the countryside, staring out her window, but her hands were clasped tightly together, the fingers nervously wriggling. *Like mine*, he suddenly realized, noting the way his right index finger tapped lightly on the steering wheel.

When he turned off Route 7 to the county road and passed the donkey farm and Theo's place, he decided to break the silence. "We could go straight back to the house, or if you like, we could drive some more. Whatever feels good for you."

She didn't answer for a long moment, but when

the church came into view, she finally said, "I guess home, but I'd like to be alone for a bit...if that's okay."

Of course it's okay, he thought, feeling frustrated. What he really preferred was to continue the drive, give her a chance to talk. *This isn't about you*, he reminded himself then. It was only midafternoon. Roxanne would still be at work and Kaya at school, which left his mother to greet them, and Finn knew she'd be eager to hear all about their road trip.

He turned into the driveway and parked the truck in its usual spot. The garage door was down, which meant his mother was probably home. He switched off the engine and looked at Devon. "It's just my mom at home right now. I'll explain that your ankle is bothering you and you need some rest and elevation. She might even be in the kitchen, and you can sneak upstairs as soon as we get inside."

"Ah, Finn, that's both sweet and funny. Let me handle this, though. I'm quite capable."

There's the Devon I know, he thought, as he got out of the truck. He reached into the rear to get the crutches as she climbed out the other side. "Want these to get inside?"

"Yes, actually, I could use them now. Too much sitting and my ankle is protesting."

"I could carry you."

Her laugh was reassuring. Perhaps she'd recovered from whatever bad memory had surfaced at the recreation area.

"No, but thanks for the offer."

He handed her the crutches and let her take the lead, following close enough to steady her if necessary. He noticed right away that she was favoring her right leg and ankle. *Likely more swelling again*, he thought. At least his suggested cover story for an escape up to her room was legitimate.

When Devon stepped onto the veranda, he moved around her to open the front door. The radio was playing in the kitchen, which meant that his mother might be prepping something for dinner. He helped Devon with her jacket, placed it over the newel post and stooped to unzip her boots.

"I can do that," she said.

"It's no problem." He wanted to check her ankle and slipped off the right boot first before she could object. He could feel a slight swelling around the edges of the brace under her sock. "Elevate your ankle on those extra pillows in your room, and I'll come up with an ice pack in a few minutes." Still crouching at her feet, he took off the left boot.

She nodded and began the slow ascent to her room. When she reached the landing, Finn removed his jacket and, retrieving hers from the newel post, hung them both in the hall closet. Then he headed for the kitchen and the onslaught of questions he feared would follow. But his mother surprised him.

She was standing at the counter nearest the stove dicing vegetables. "Hello, dear," she said, looking up with a smile. "I thought I'd make a hearty beef stew for dinner and my butter biscuits. What do you think?"

"Sounds great, Mom. Uh, is that gel pack still in the freezer?"

"I think so." She frowned. "Did you have a nice time? Is everything okay?"

Finn patted her shoulder. "Yep. Just that Devon's tired and her ankle has swelled up a bit. Too much sitting I think."

"Poor thing. You take her the ice pack and I'll put the kettle on for tea."

Finn smiled. *Tea, the McAllister cure for any ailment.* He got the cold gel pack, found a cloth towel to wrap around it and headed upstairs. Devon's bedroom door was closed, and he gave a light tap. After a few seconds, he heard a soft "Come in" and let himself inside. She was lying on top of the bed with her right leg and foot resting on two large pillows. Her sock and the brace were off, lying next to the pillows.

"How does it feel?" He peered down at the puffiness around her ankle bone.

"No pain unless I push on the swelling."

"Well, better not do that then," he teased. He sat on the edge of the bed. "Mind if I have a closer look at it?" When she shrugged, he carefully picked up her foot and ran his fingers around the swollen area. It wasn't hot—a good sign—nor was the swelling hard. "I think some elevating and cooling will do the trick, but if you want, I can call Theo."

"It's fine, really." But the flicker of a smile in her pale face didn't reach her eyes.

As much as he wanted to discuss what had happened at the recreation area, he figured she wanted to be alone. He got to his feet, feeling awkward at her silence.

"Later, Finn," she murmured. "We'll talk—only later."

"Sure. Uh, Mom's making tea, so I'll bring you a cup when it's ready. Okay?"

Her nod was barely perceptible. He stood a minute longer before quietly leaving the room. When he returned fifteen minutes later, she was sleeping. He set the tea and plate of cookies onto the bedside table, then got the afghan from the armchair in front of the window and carefully tucked it around her.

IT WAS DARK when Devon awoke. For a second, she didn't know where she was. Her sleep had been deep and enmeshed in the past. She sat up, switched on the lamp next to the bed and saw the cup of tea and cookies Finn must have delivered. Hours ago, she decided, judging by the tea's temperature. Still, she sipped a bit and nibbled at a cookie. He'd covered her with the afghan, too, and once again she thought how considerate he was, how he thought of everything a person might need or want.

She remembered telling him they would talk later, and now she was regretting that. He would be the best person to recount her life story to, but she was having second thoughts. If her time in Maple Glen was coming to a close, she didn't want the cold hard facts of her past wedged between them. The lighthearted, fun parts of the day were what she wanted to hold on to. She especially didn't want to see even a glimmer of pity in his eyes—not ever.

Tossing off the blanket, she examined her ankle still propped on the pillows. The swelling had gone down, so she replaced the brace and put on her sock. A quick check of her phone showed the time as 5:45 p.m. If she went down for supper rather than waiting for Finn to bring it up to her, she might be able to postpone any talk about her past. For now, at least.

After a trip to the bathroom to refresh herself, she was descending to the first floor. The lights were on in the hallway and living room, and she followed the voices coming from the kitchen. Mouthwatering aromas greeted her, as well as three smiling faces. Roxanne was sitting next to Kaya, while Marion was at the stove ladling something hot into bowls. Finn stood at the opposite counter preparing a tray. *For her.* She thought she saw a hint of disappointment in his face as she entered the room.

"You're just in time for dinner, with Granny's butter biscuits."

Kaya's enthusiasm brought smiles, though not from Finn. He stopped what he was doing and moved quickly to pull out a chair for her. As he bent down, he whispered in her ear, "Feeling better?"

She nodded, aware of the interested expressions around her while trying to ignore the shiver from Finn's warm breath.

Marion set bowls of stew in front of everyone and brought a plate of biscuits to the table, where she sat in her customary place, at the head. Between mouthfuls of biscuit, Kaya announced that the coming Friday was the last day of school before the holidays. She had plans for sleepovers and playdates with her new best friend, Shelley, in Wallingford, and was everyone coming to her school's Christmas pageant on Thursday night?

Devon exchanged smiles with Roxanne, who interrupted Kaya's monologue. "Focus on your supper, Kaya, and I've marked the pageant on the calendar."

"What role do you have in the pageant?" Devon asked.

"I'm an angel!" Kaya exclaimed. "But I don't have any speaking lines. I hold up my arms, like this." She leaped off her chair to demonstrate, raising her arms in a circle above her head. "And, Granny, do you have my costume ready?"

"I do, darling, and tomorrow we'll have a fitting when you get home from school."

"Will you come, too, Devon?"

All eyes turned her way, and Devon felt her face heat up. "If I'm invited I will."

"You're definitely invited," Kaya said solemnly.

The room was quiet, then as everyone resumed eating. Devon watched Finn get up to help himself to seconds. Except for his whisper moments ago, he'd said nothing during the meal, and Devon guessed he had a lot on his mind. Like finding out what had happened to her at the recreation parking area.

She wished she could explain that herself. There'd been a sudden flood of emotion, as if she were drowning in the past. That was how she thought of it in the privacy of her room.

When Roxanne started clearing away the empty bowls and plates, Finn got out up to help but suddenly stopped midway to the sink to ask, "Want to go out for a bit, Devon? See some stars from the veranda?" He was smiling, but his eyes carried a message.

Marion and Roxanne looked her way, and Kaya leaped up. "Can I come?"

"School night, remember? And you haven't looked over your spelling words for tomorrow yet," Roxanne swiftly put in.

"I'll finish up here, Roxanne, while you and Kaya get the homework done," Marion said. She patted Finn's hand as she took the used cutlery from him. "Let me know if the sky's clear enough to see the Big Dipper, and I'll come join you," she said.

From the smile she cast her way, Devon knew she was teasing. Minutes later, she was standing on the veranda shivering in her jacket while Finn stepped down onto the sidewalk. He made a slow 360-degree turn, looking up at the night sky. *Searching for the Big Dipper?* "You don't have to pretend anymore," she said.

He spun around, facing her. "Huh?"

"I think looking at the stars was a pretext to get me out here alone." Her heart skipped a beat as he slowly climbed the steps, standing so close she could feel his breath warming her cold cheeks.

"You're way too clever for me, Devon Fairchild," he murmured. He inched closer and placed his hands on her shoulders. "I know you said you were going to talk later and explain what happened at the recreation area," he murmured, shifting his hands to the small of her back, pulling her against him. "But I figured I'd rather be doing this outside on a cold winter night with the stars sparkling above us," he whispered, drawing a finger across her cheek down to her lips and then lowered his mouth onto hers.

Devon wrapped her arms around him, holding

on for what seemed an eternity until she gradually eased out of his embrace, her heart pounding so hard she was certain he could hear. She gazed up into his eyes that seemed to reflect all the constellations above them. Then she moved back into his arms.

FINN SLEPT IN, an event that raised eyebrows from his mother and sister as he entered the kitchen.

Kaya gawked. "I thought you were at work, Uncle Finn."

"Tonight," he said, his voice cracking. He cleared his throat. "And a good night's sleep has given me an appetite. What's for breakfast?" He registered Devon's empty chair as he sat at the other end of the table opposite his mother.

"Since it's a Tuesday, the usual. Help yourself to cereal or toast," Marion said dryly.

Finn decided from her pointed glance where Devon usually sat that she'd done some math that morning. Put two and two together, given that he and Devon had lingered on the veranda until most of the lights inside were out and the cold finally forced them indoors. His mother had always been intuitive that way, something his teenaged self had rebelled against. But he assumed some nonchalance as he reached for the box of cereal.

"Mom, will you be home around four when Kaya's bus arrives?" Roxanne asked. "It's just that my appointment in Bennington is at three, and in case I don't get back in time…"

"I have some shopping to do in Rutland—" Marion looked briefly at Kaya, then at Roxanne "—but should be back in time. Though maybe Finn will be around or Devon." Her gaze drifted to Finn.

There seemed to be a lot of messages in that answer, Finn thought, as he poured milk over the cereal in the bowl in front of him, and he debated getting drawn into whatever his mother was hinting at. Instead, he turned to Roxanne. "Your lawyer?" he asked in a low voice.

She nodded, tilting her head at Kaya, who was on her second bowl of Cheerios.

"I'll be here," he said, before spooning cereal into his mouth. He knew not to say anything more in front of Kaya. Roxanne filed for divorce in the summer, but her ex—Leo—was trying to reopen the divorce settlement, even suggesting he'd be willing to move to Vermont from New Jersey to facilitate his chances of getting joint custody. *No way*, Finn had said when Roxanne confided in him three weeks ago. *That's not going to happen.* But her expression had told him she wasn't so certain. Like many scam artists, Leo had an irresistible charming side. Once upon a time, he'd even pulled Finn into his orbit.

Roxanne was mouthing a thank-you when Kaya loudly uttered, "Hi, Devon! You slept in, too, like Uncle Finn."

She stood red-faced in the doorway. Finn tried to shift the attention from her to him. "Everyone's entitled to sleep in once in a while, Kaya."

"I guess so, but Granny said you almost never do."

"Only because it's true," Marion tutted, sheepishly. "Coffee, Devon?" She started to get up when Devon stopped her.

"I'll get it, thanks, Marion." She was holding on to one crutch, using it as a cane, and moved slowly to the coffee maker on the counter.

Judging from the glow in her cheeks, Finn guessed she, too, had slept well. When they'd kissed again at the bottom of the staircase before she went up to her room, Finn had forced himself to let go. As if he'd known instinctively that the end of the evening would be a snapshot of memory—a picture he might never see again except in his mind. Now, in the glare of the morning sunlight, last night was already fading.

Devon carried her coffee mug to the table. Her hand shook slightly as she set it down, and Finn bit his lower lip, fighting the urge to reach out and clasp it, bring it up to his mouth for another kiss. Did she have the same dreams as he had? He hoped so, and judging from the serene expression on her face, still pink from Kaya's greeting, he figured she had.

"I'm shopping in Rutland today, Devon, if you'd like to come with me," his mother said.

"Are you going to the new mall? Can I come and see Santa?" Kaya blurted.

"School, Kaya. Remember?" Roxanne said, grinning.

Devon propped her crutch against her side of the table and sat down. "That's nice of you to think of me, Marion, but I have some business emails to attend to. Then I think Finn planned to show me some more of Wallingford today, before he has to go to work." She gazed calmly at him as she sipped some coffee.

His admiration for her quick thinking was shadowed by her mention of business emails, yet another reminder that she had a life beyond Maple Glen, one he knew almost nothing about. *Today would be the day to change all that.*

Soon the morning's schedule took over, with Roxanne ushering Kaya up to brush her teeth and Marion clearing dishes.

Finn quickly stepped in. "I'll finish up here, Mom. You get ready for your Christmas shopping trip, and if you see the mall's Santa Claus—"

"I plan to make an appointment for Kaya to see him, dear."

As always, his mother was one step ahead of him. He grinned, and she patted his cheek as she left the room. He let the silence go on another minute before quipping, "Wallingford? Again?"

She barely smiled. "To the recreation area car park. To tell you my story."

CHAPTER THIRTEEN

THERE WAS NO impromptu stop at Tasty Delights bakery this time. Devon guessed Finn wanted to hear what she had to tell him as soon as possible, before she could change her mind. And she wanted to, badly. She'd made the decision to tell him her life story in the wee hours of the morning after replaying the kisses they'd shared the night before—the comfort of Finn's arms mixed with her need to tell him about Dan and the memories he had recounted to her over the years. Now her brother was gone, and there was no other person who knew the whole story.

Finn didn't speak until they reached the turn-off to Wallingford. "Sure you want to do this? Go back to the recreation area, I mean?"

Not really, she thought, but she knew she had to follow through with her decision. "Yes," she lied.

He nodded. When they reached Wallingford, he drove through the town center, heading for the road that would take them to the recreation area. Devon's heart rate accelerated, and her hands felt clammy. She tugged her gloves out of her jacket pocket and put them on.

"Want me to turn up the heat?" he asked, looking her way.

"Please. Just a bit."

He reached for the temperature gauge on the display panel. "You don't have to do this, you know."

But she did. He deserved to know her story, at least some of it. He and the rest of his family had been so discreet, never probing, giving her time and space to fill in the blanks about why she'd come to Maple Glen. She guessed they'd realized she wasn't an experienced hiker, which made her decision to walk the trail in winter perplexing.

She planned to tell him an edited version of what happened twenty-five years ago. She hoped it would be enough to satisfy his curiosity, but would it be enough to account for her extreme reaction yesterday?

An image of her brother flashed in her mind. He wouldn't approve; he would want her to tell Finn all of it. The whole unfiltered story. *I want you to have the family we never had.* But there was no guarantee that Finn was the man she could have a family with. She was getting ahead of herself; she had only known him for days. Besides, marrying Finn would mean living in Maple Glen, a village smaller in population than her condo building. What would she do all day while Finn was working shifts at the fire hall? Where could she resume her social work career, if at all? What if this newly paired version of Finn McAllister and Devon Fairchild simply didn't work out? Her heart sank at the thought. Her solitary life in Chicago suddenly seemed so much safer.

"Want to get out and walk around or stay in the truck?"

She realized Finn had been staring at her. "Um, maybe get out and walk a bit. I'll take the crutch."

He nodded and got out, opened the rear door and reached for the single crutch she'd decided to bring. "We're not going into the woods," he said as he stood waiting for her to climb out. "Too risky for you right now. There's a rest area near the entrance to the trail, and we can walk around there or just sit for a bit."

She saw where he was pointing and took the crutch he held, tucked it under her left arm and started walking. On the way, he said, "Might as well buy you a real cane rather than using one crutch all the time. We can make a quick stop in Rutland before going home."

Making small talk to break the silence? she wondered.

The rest area consisted of a collection of benches, picnic tables and a little playground enclosure for children that Devon thought hadn't been there twenty-five years ago. Another addition was a wood-framed building not much bigger than a double garage with signs for women's and men's washrooms.

"It's probably locked for the winter," Finn said, noting where she was looking.

"I don't think it was here the last time I was," she murmured.

"Which was?"

He was trying to sound casual, she thought. "Twenty-five years ago," she replied, heading for a bench. She was sitting, the crutch propped against the end of the bench, when he joined her.

"The sun will keep us warm for a bit," he said as he sat next to her.

He's letting me take my time, showing me he can be patient, as well as considerate. There's so much to like about this man. "I came to Maple Glen to keep a promise I made to my brother, Dan, who passed away in September," she began. "We basically grew up in foster homes because our mother died when I was about three and Dan about eight. I barely remember her, and the vague memories I have were probably implanted by Dan. He was only eight, so the little he could recall was likely a combination of real and false memory. You know?"

Finn nodded. He clasped her hand in his, and the warmth reassured her. "I think finding foster parents willing to take two children was difficult back then," she went on. "As a social worker, I know that even now, finding a home for a three-year-old and an eight-year-old who've just lost their only parent might be a challenge."

"And your father?" he asked.

"He left my mother when I was two, or so Dan told me. I have no memory of him at all, and Dan's was sketchy. He recalled a lot of arguments." She stopped for a moment, looking across the large parking area at the backdrop of mountains, their snowy tops gleaming in the bright sun. The scene was breathtaking but its beauty deceptive. Devon knew that potential dangers lurked in the shadows of those majestic trees, and she suspected that Finn, as a search-and-rescue volunteer, did, too.

"Anyway, unfortunately we ended up with foster parents who were only in it for the money. They weren't abusive," she quickly added, "but neglectful. They had some addictions—drinking, gambling maybe. I have no idea why they decided to come here, but they rented a camper van and we went on a long road trip. Maybe to escape creditors." She paused, laughing lightly. "Not the kind of road trip we had yesterday. Dan told me there were lots of stops and long days cooped inside while they were sleeping off a bender. We were left to ourselves, and Dan soon became a pseudo parent, looking out for me as well as entertaining me. They were happy to let him take charge."

"Did you have a social worker at the time?"

"Probably. I don't recall ever meeting one, though I was only five when we came here."

"And what happened here?"

Devon took a long, deep breath. How much to tell? All of it or the short version? She and Dan had spent the rest of their lives after that September perfecting new identities and new memories. Was she ready to give up that hard-earned privacy, even to someone as trustworthy as Finn?

"Not very much, really. We spent the entire day hanging out right here in this little area. Then some curious person wondered why two youngsters were wandering around a car park in the late afternoon when most people were leaving. The police were called, and Dan took them to the camper van where our foster parents were still sleeping. I suppose there was a discussion, and next thing we knew, someone came to take us away. Social Services probably or the equivalent."

Another hand squeeze. "And then?" His voice was low and calm, almost neutral. Keeping his thoughts to himself.

"We were returned to our home state, Massachusetts, and soon ended up in a very nice foster home, where we spent the rest of our childhoods. When Dan turned eighteen, he became my legal guardian, and two years later, when he was working and making money, I went to live with him." She looked at Finn for the first time since she'd begun talking and smiled. "We had the blessing of our foster parents, Ellen and Ted. They had other foster children, too, and a couple of their own, so our leaving was a benefit in a way. For all of us." After a minute, she said, "That's my story."

Finn tucked her against him, holding her for a long time. Finally, he murmured, "Shall we go for a quick cup of coffee or hot chocolate at the Wallingford diner before heading back?"

"Yes," she whispered, nestling against him a bit longer until he stood and held out his hand.

By the time they reached the truck, she'd convinced herself that not revealing everything had been the right decision. This version of her life was the best option for now.

SOMETHING DIDN'T ADD UP. Finn had gone over and over Devon's story the rest of the day and well into his night shift at the fire hall. It had been a sad tale that ended well for them but, in his opinion, not the kind of gut-wrenching experience that would lead to the kind of panic attack Devon had yesterday. He was convinced there was more to it but couldn't explain why she'd keep part of it a secret. His hope was that if she stayed long enough in the Glen to feel as if she could fully trust him, he'd eventually learn the rest.

He'd done all the talking as they sipped hot chocolate at the diner in Wallingford, filling her in a little bit about why his sister and niece had moved back home. She'd surprised him by saying Kaya had told her about living in New Jersey.

"It was the day I looked after her. She was in my room and had seen an old photograph that Dan gave me years ago of the house we'd once lived in, before our parents split up. She said she used to live in an apartment building in New Jersey. I gathered she missed her friends there from what she said."

Then, after a slight pause, Devon had added, "She told me there was a lot of shouting and arguing between her parents but that Roxanne had told her not to tell you or your mother that she missed New Jersey in case it would make you sad."

That revelation had floored him and had been on his mind all day, too, along with Devon's story. He'd known the reasons for his sister leaving Leo but didn't understand why she'd told Kaya not to talk about her unhappiness. How could that be good for a child caught in the middle of a parental divorce? And why couldn't Roxanne trust that Finn would respond appropriately to such information? Didn't she realize when he and his mother welcomed them back to the Manor, they did so happily, with no conditions? He was determined to confront his sister about Kaya's confiding to Devon as soon as he had an opportunity.

Fortunately, his shift had been noneventful, because his mind had been preoccupied with all of that. Then two reminders appeared on his cell phone of commitments he'd made and forgotten about with everything that had been going on at the Manor: Scott Watson's next training session was tomorrow, exactly a week after he and Finn had discovered Devon on the trail; plus, he'd promised to take Luke Danby on a hike that coming weekend. It was time he got back to the real world of work and commitments instead of spending all his time driving around the valley with a beautiful, mysterious woman.

It was still dark when he arrived home shortly after six in the morning. Despite his fatigue, Finn was too wired to head right to bed. He wanted to make himself a coffee and sit in the darkness of the living room with his thoughts, but he knew his mother or Kaya or Roxanne would hear him stirring below and come downstairs to start their day. Instead, he poured a glass of water, which he took with him upstairs, hesitating outside Devon's closed door in case she might be awake and moving about. After a second, he tiptoed along to his own room and bed.

"DID YOU KNOW that Christmas is only one week away?" Kaya asked Devon the minute she entered the kitchen. "And starting this Friday, I'm off school for two whole weeks!" Kaya's fist shot upward with excitement.

The news startled Devon. She and Dan had never made a big deal out of Christmas. *That's for families*, he'd often told her. Yet there'd been a modest version of the holiday when they were living with Ellen and Ted. Not the kind of commercial extravaganza pictured in movies or stores, but a low-key event with a couple of gifts and a nice meal. Although Marion and Roxanne had spoken last night about taking Kaya to see Santa Claus on Saturday, and there was going to be a Christmas cookie exchange on Friday at the community center, which Marion insisted Devon should attend with her, the actual arrival of the special day had completely eluded her.

"Wow," she said, a bit unenthusiastically, drawing a quick look from Marion. "I guess I forgot," she mumbled as she went to the counter to pour her coffee. When she turned around, she almost giggled at the stupefaction in Kaya's face. Roxanne and Marion exchanged looks then, and Devon wondered if they'd been discussing her before she came down for breakfast. Or perhaps she was being overly sensitive due to a lack of sleep.

Before Finn left for his shift last night, he'd come up to her room. She'd been reading one of Marion's romance novels in the armchair in front of the bay window, but her attention kept drifting to the recreation area and Finn's quiet acceptance of her tale. Was it guilt that had her tossing and turning all night? Not that she had actually lied, but she had omitted specific details that would have accounted for her emotional reaction at the park the day before.

That realization was confirmed when Finn had said, "Tomorrow let's find some time to go over what you told me today. Kind of a debriefing."

Debriefing? What were they, business partners? Secret agents? Still, she felt a pang of guilt at the revised edition of her story.

As she sat at the table with her coffee, Roxanne said, "Would you like to come with me when I take Kaya to see Santa on Saturday morning?"

Devon promptly said, "Sure," and knew that was guilt talking, again.

"Yay!" exclaimed Kaya, rushing from her chair to Devon and hugging her.

Both Marion and Roxanne were smiling as Devon patted Kaya on the back, a fact that demonstrated how challenging it was to maintain a bad mood in the Manor. Back home in Chicago, Devon could go a whole week feeling indignant, if not outright cranky.

Roxanne rushed Kaya through the rest of the morning routine and walked her to the bus before heading for her own job, while Marion excused herself to make phone call reminders about the cookie exchange. Devon was alone in the kitchen making herself another piece of toast and enjoying the quiet when Finn appeared.

He scanned the room and Devon grinned at

his disbelief. "Apparently it's only a week until Christmas and there's a lot to do."

He sat down, rubbing his face and yawning.

"Rough night?"

"Not at work," he said, his red-rimmed eyes on hers.

"It's pretty early still," she said. "Why don't you go back to bed?"

He shrugged. "I'm up now. Maybe I'll catch a nap later on."

A hush of expectation fell over the room. *He wants to talk more*, Devon thought, *while I can hardly remember what I've already told him.*

"Roxanne's invited me to go with her and Kaya to see Santa on Saturday. And your mother's asked me to participate in Friday's cookie exchange. We're baking tomorrow. Plus, there's the school Christmas pageant tomorrow night." She stopped at the grin on his face.

"You sound just like Kaya."

Devon smiled. Nervousness had led to her rambling, but she wasn't going to admit that to Finn. "I guess after being here a whole week, I've begun to imitate your family's mannerisms. The tics of communication."

A thoughtful expression settled over him. "Has it really been only a week?"

"As Kaya herself reminded me at breakfast."

"I feel like I've known you much longer."

The intensity of his gaze was unnerving. Devon

got to her feet and went to the counter. "Would you like some toast? Coffee?"

When she turned to look at him, he was shaking his head. "Not yet. Right now I'm happy just to be alone with you." He held out a beckoning hand.

She moved toward him, grasping his hand as he pulled her onto his lap.

"This is what I want," he whispered, tucking her head into the crook of his neck.

For a few precious seconds Devon sank into his arms, listening to the steady thud of his heart, forgetting the half-truths of yesterday's story and imagining this man was hers. Then she heard Marion walking around upstairs. Finn relaxed his hold and she leaned away from him.

"Later?" he said in a low voice as she got up from his lap.

That single word had many meanings, Devon thought, as she returned to the counter to pour his coffee. Later for hugs and kisses? Or for the debriefing? Either way, the day had begun—again.

CHAPTER FOURTEEN

FINN LIKED ROUTINES because they were predictable. He'd mastered the art of creating good routines through his years of firefighting, a profession that depended on safe, clear procedures that everyone understood and followed. When Roxanne and Kaya moved into the Manor six months ago, Finn saw the routines that he and his mother had established slowly erode. There were days when he'd felt that his love for his family as well as his need for routine were at odds. Which is why Devon's revelation that Roxanne had told her daughter not to mention her feelings about leaving New Jersey rankled him. He was hurt that Roxanne couldn't discuss the issue with him and their mother, and he decided to confront his sister when she came home from work that day.

When Marion returned from making her phone calls, Devon had excused herself to answer some work emails. Finn wondered what the business emails pertained to. Now that he had her personal story, he was curious about her professional one.

Would her career be a serious obstacle to her staying on in Maple Glen, not just for the short term but, he hoped, permanently?

"You're looking very thoughtful this morning," Marion piped up as she poured herself another cup of coffee. "Want seconds?" she asked, turning toward Finn.

"Um, no thanks, Mom." He rubbed his face again, this time steeling himself for what he needed to tell her.

She sat opposite him, setting her coffee mug and the notebook in her hand onto the table. "The cookie exchange is all set for Friday, but there's a minor glitch about the bazaar."

"Oh, what's that?" he asked, his interest centered on what he was about to say rather than the annual Christmas event.

"It was going to be held Saturday at the church, as usual, but Reverend Higgins has asked the committee if we could move it to the community center instead. Apparently, he's had a last-minute request to conduct a wedding in the church that afternoon."

"Oh? Well, I guess the change in venue is okay, isn't it?"

Marion sighed. "True, but now the bazaar will have to be on Sunday at the community center because there's a youth club Ping-Pong tournament there on Saturday, and kids are coming from all over the county. We'll have to make signs advising of the change in day and location."

"The problem is all settled, then?" He was itching to get to his own news.

"Yes, thank goodness. What are your plans for the day? You look like you could use a bit more sleep, though. Was there a callout last night?"

"No, it was a quiet one. I even managed to get schedules organized for the full-time crews, as well as the volunteers."

"Then why are you down here at nine in the morning when you've only been in bed since six thirty?"

He shrugged. "Couldn't sleep."

"Too much on your mind?" She leaned forward, her eyes intent on his.

There was a hint of a smile in them, Finn thought. *She thinks my mind's been on Devon and is eager to hear all about it. And she's on the right track, but there's more to my sleeplessness.*

"Yesterday Devon told me that Kaya confided she sometimes feels unhappy here. Not seriously unhappy," he quickly clarified at his mother's expression, "but she misses her friends and her bedroom in New Jersey."

"That's understandable, don't you think? Remember her moods those first few weeks?"

"Of course, but the thing is, Roxanne told Kaya not to mention how she was feeling to us."

Marion frowned. "To you and me? Why not?"

"Because we might feel sad. I intend to ask Roxanne about it when she gets home from work."

There was a long minute of silence. "Maybe we should just stay out of it," Marion said.

"Can't we ask Roxanne why she couldn't talk to us about Kaya being unhappy? And is Roxanne unhappy, too?"

"I think she might be still, a little bit. But she's nowhere near as unhappy as she was six months ago, Finn, when she and Kaya first arrived here. Her life was pretty much shattered last spring by Leo's infidelity."

"And his gambling debts," Finn muttered, thinking how Marion had cashed in some of her savings to help out. And he'd helped his mother take care of Kaya as much as possible to let Roxanne have time to herself.

After a moment, Marion got up. "I have a meeting at the community center now to sort out the changed plans for the bazaar. If you insist on confronting your sister, remember that she's been through a lot. There's probably a simple explanation for this." She patted his cheek and left the room.

Finn sat for a long time, contemplating the future, an exercise in futility he knew, because the basic routines that once governed life in the Manor—before Roxanne and Kaya—wouldn't likely return. Plus, the last couple of days, his vision of his future had included Devon Fairchild, and he had no idea at all how that could work. When he realized there were no easy answers, he decided to go back to bed.

DEVON SET HER phone down on the bedside table and leaned against the headboard, shutting her eyes against the brief glimpse of her life beyond Maple Glen. Her work supervisor had sounded a tad peeved about the request for extra leave she'd sent a couple of days ago. *Can't you travel with a sprained ankle?* she'd asked, but when Devon had offered to get a doctor's note, her boss had backed down. Devon loved working with kids, but not so much with bureaucracy.

Still, her supervisor had a point. She probably could travel now that her ankle was improving with the brace, but was torn by the reality of leaving Maple Glen. Compared to her life in Chicago, there was so much more happening in the village, a fact she'd never contemplated a few days ago. Despite her indifference to Christmas events in general, she found she was looking forward to the cookie exchange, even the baking tomorrow. There was the pageant, which would be sweet, and the bazaar, which could be interesting. She'd never attended one, but Kaya had assured her there were lots of things to buy. *Especially home-made things, like fudge and cupcakes*, she'd enthused at supper last night. But Devon's thoughts had mainly been on Finn, wondering if he was also thinking of that moment on the bench at the recreation area, when he'd held her in his arms after she'd told him her story?

Her story. Devon got up off the bed and wandered to the bay window, gazing down on a scene that, a week ago today, she'd viewed from a completely different perspective. Seconds before she'd crossed the bridge and entered the woods, she'd looked at the Manor, admiring its old-world majesty and had seen a child waving from the front window. How different the village, the Manor and especially the little girl all seemed today! There was a significance to them now that completely altered her viewpoint from last Wednesday. Although she'd negotiated a return to work after the Christmas holiday, Devon still had another decision to make.

When Dan died, he'd left Devon his 50 percent share in the start-up company he and his friend and partner had nurtured from ground floor to the stock market. *Your retirement fund*, he'd said. She had no real interest in the company but thought Dan would be pleased if she followed its growth. Three weeks ago, his partner, Mike, advised her he wanted to sell the company in a once-in-a-lifetime opportunity, as he'd put it. *A win-win for both of us and our investors, Devon. But you have to be on board. They want all of it.*

She'd been living in a bubble the past week, drawn into the kind of family life she'd never personally experienced. Mike's new email was a good reminder of her commitments and career in Chicago. The real world outside Maple Glen was pressing in, and Devon knew she could no longer dismiss it. However, there was one promise she had yet to fulfill, and there was only one person she'd want to help her with it: Finn McAllister. Once that mission was accomplished, she'd decide what to do with her share of Dan's company.

She left her room to look for Finn but, spotting his closed bedroom door, guessed he'd gone back to bed. He had another shift at suppertime, and from his appearance at breakfast, he clearly needed the sleep. Marion was closing the front door as Devon descended the stairs and glanced up at her.

"Devon? Do you have a minute?"

The oddly formal tone in her voice alerted Devon. *A serious talk?* She followed Marion into the living room, where they sat opposite one another, Marion on the sofa and Devon in the armchair.

"Finn told me what Kaya revealed the other day when you were babysitting her. About missing her home and friends."

Devon nodded.

"Did she also say why she and her mother left New Jersey?"

"Only that her parents were arguing." She omitted the girl's actual words, wishing now that she hadn't confided in Finn. She understood why he might have wanted to speak to his mother, but she also worried that Kaya might be brought into the discussion, along with Roxanne. Devon's lapse was leading to something she'd never intended or wanted.

Marion's sigh echoed in the quiet room. "Finn and I knew that they were unhappy when they first got here, and I understand why Roxanne didn't want to worry us any more than we already were." Another loud sigh. "That's a big issue with families, isn't it?" She looked across at Devon. "Miscommunication. Making assumptions that can lead to hurt feelings. Right?"

Devon could only nod in agreement. Her own experience with families was a world away from Marion's, but those issues prevailed in foster homes, too.

"Finn wants to talk to Roxanne about this when she comes home, but I'm trying to convince him not to. She might take it the wrong way, and she's just beginning to resemble the daughter my husband and I raised. I don't want her to go back to the Roxanne who appeared on our doorstep last June." Marion stood up. "Thanks, dear. I wanted a clearer picture of what Kaya had confided, and I'm glad that she felt comfortable enough with you to say what she did."

Devon sat in the armchair after Marion left the room, thinking how an innocent remark from

Kaya to her and then to Finn had taken on a complicated significance. For the first time since she'd moved into the Manor, she saw how a person could get pulled into a family without really understanding the dynamics or knowing the house rules. She thought about what Marion had said about Finn's tendency to help others. The last thing she wanted was to be another rescue project for Finn McAllister. *Perhaps it's time for me to go back to the B and B, if it's open. Neutral territory.*

Knocking roused Finn. He reached for his phone and saw that it was almost three.

"Coming," he mumbled, his voice thick with sleep. He flung open the door to see Devon, an apologetic smile on her face.

"Sorry, but someone's come to see you. Scott Watson."

Finn swore silently. He'd forgotten to reschedule the training session today with Scott, thinking the kid might be needed at home. He took a deep breath and beamed a smile at the woman of his dreams, all too aware of his sleep T-shirt barely covering his boxer shorts. "Um, thanks, Devon. Can you ask him to step inside?"

"I did. He's waiting at the bottom of the stairs."

"Thanks, and...uh...is my mother around?"

"She had a meeting at the community center."

"Okay. Tell Scott I'll be right there." He closed

the door as she left and quickly got dressed. It was too late to take Scott out on the trail because of his shift starting at six. He'd meant to mention that to Scott last week after their hike, but then they'd found Devon and so much had happened since. He'd lost his focus.

He found Scott pacing the small entryway and was about to apologize when the young man beat him to it. "Sorry, Finn. I should have come round earlier, but Dad and I moved Mom back home from the hospital, and I had a list of items to buy in Rutland for her convalescence and totally forgot we were hiking this afternoon."

Finn smiled. "Aw, no problem. How is she?"

"Good. The doctor's happy and so are all of us. It will just take some time for everything to heal. Plus, she needs help getting in and out of bed and so on. But at least she'll be home for Christmas."

A shadow fell across his face and Finn guessed what the young man was thinking. Betty Watson, normally a dynamo of creativity and cooking, wouldn't be her usual self this year. Finn knew the church social committee was organizing a Christmas dinner to deliver to the family but thought that might be a surprise.

"I'm guessing you're going to be around for the whole holiday?"

"Yep. Now for certain," Scott said.

"Okay, well, we can reschedule your training, then, and I was also wondering if you'd like to take someone out for a short hike yourself. You know Luke Danby? Dr. Danby's son? I promised to take him out this weekend, but to tell you the truth, there's too much going on right now. I'll have to postpone our walk, but can I suggest you might be free to take him? That is, only if you feel comfortable doing so. And probably only to the white blaze cutoff."

"About where we found Devon last Wednesday?"

Scott tilted his head to the living room and Finn saw her sitting on the sofa, reading. "Yeah," Finn said.

"Uh, sure, Finn. No problem." Scott opened the front door and stepped onto the veranda. "I'm not supposed to say anything, but Mom and Dad are buying Christmas treats for all the crew at the fire hall. She's sorry she can't bake them herself, but they placed an order with Mrs. Giordano, and it's going to be delivered on Monday, so everyone— the regulars and volunteers—will get a chance to have some."

Finn was touched. "Thanks for letting me know, Scott. I'll be sure everyone gets to enjoy. And I'll text you about walking with Luke after I've arranged things with him."

He closed the door and stood for a moment in the foyer, thinking how much he loved his community, with people like the Watsons thinking of others despite their own troubles. His next thought was a wish that Devon could learn to love the Glen as much as he did.

She looked up when he went into the living room and smiled. Finn thought it was a tentative smile and he hesitated, unsure if she wanted his company or not. Perhaps she was worried about rehashing the story from yesterday and now he was sorry he'd brought it up at breakfast. So what if it seemed there were a few holes in it? Couldn't he simply let it go?

"I should buy Scott a present," she said, "for helping to carry me out last week."

Finn realized she'd overheard Scott telling him about the gifts for the fire crews. "Nah," he said. "Scott would be embarrassed. He was doing his job. Well, doing what he's been training to do. Same as what the fire crews were doing when they helped Betty. No one expects gifts for that."

"But the family is sending baked goods."

"Yeah, I know. Because they want to show their support and to let us know they appreciate our efforts. And because the crews and the Watsons are all part of the same community, kind of. The broader community of the Glen and Wallingford." He sat in the armchair across from her. "I've worked in bigger communities, like Burlington, when I started out in firefighting. There's a similar kind of togetherness in those places and even in big cities like Chicago, isn't there?" When she shrugged, Finn began to wonder what was on her mind.

Then she set the book in her hand onto the sofa and leaned forward. "Finn, I—"

"Look," he interrupted. "I'm sorry I bugged you about going over your story again." When she frowned, he added, "Last night, before I went to work?"

Her smile picked up some strength. "Oh, you mean the debriefing?"

He felt his face redden. Had he actually used that word? "Yeah. Poor choice of language. I know telling me about your past took some courage. It's not my business to probe any further."

She was silent long enough for him to wonder if he'd goofed again. Then she dropped a bombshell. "Your mother spoke to me about that thing with Kaya and Roxanne. She said you were going to confront Roxanne about it."

Finn tensed, guessing where the conversation was headed. He was about to offer an explanation for why he wanted to clarify things with his sister, but a small part of him nagged, *Why?* Why did he need to account for saying anything to his sister to someone he'd known only a week? *But this is Devon*, he reminded himself. *No longer a stranger. The woman you've been dreaming about these last few nights.*

"I'm asking you not to speak to Roxanne," she went on to say. "She has enough on her mind and shouldn't feel guilty about telling her daughter not to upset you and your mother unnecessarily. How Kaya feels is Roxanne's business and her problem to deal with. Not mine or yours or your mother's. One thing I've learned as a social worker is that life transitions can be challenging, even painful. But eventually, time and patient understanding will resolve many situations." She fell back against the sofa as if exhausted.

Finn was searching for the appropriate words to assure her that he understood, that even if he wasn't totally convinced she was right, he wouldn't say anything since she'd asked him not to. But her next statement left him speechless.

"I've been thinking," she began, turning her head slightly so she wasn't looking directly at him. "It may be best for me to go back to the B and B. I called Bernie and he has a vacancy." Then she suddenly smiled. "But I'd still like to take part in the cookie exchange and go to Kaya's pageant and maybe even get to the bazaar. If that's okay?"

He tried to stifle the disappointment and hurt that surged through him. "Of course," he mumbled.

But it wasn't okay at all.

CHAPTER FIFTEEN

IT WAS THE kiss more than anything. All the fuss about Kaya's revelation had been her rationale for leaving the Manor, but the kiss that morning when she and Finn were alone in the kitchen was what really spurred Devon to realize she needed some distance from Finn. Being rescued by the man was one thing; falling in love with him was a much more complicated scenario.

After she'd told him she intended to move back to the B and B, he hadn't said a word, but she'd seen a whole range of emotions cross his face. The hurt she saw there bothered her the most, but she knew she was making the right decision. Spending so much time with him under the same roof and feeling what she had when he'd kissed her could lead to heartbreak for both of them. He was tied to his family and his village, and she had a career she was proud of, with commitments and responsibilities in Chicago that she could no longer put off. Leaving the McAllister home would give her the perspective she needed.

She was up in her room packing when she heard the front door close. Looking out the bedroom window, she saw Finn backing out of the driveway. He still had a couple of hours before his six o'clock shift, but she figured he wanted to be alone. Either that or he was avoiding her. *Just as well*, she thought. If he begged her to stay, she knew she would. But Finn McAllister wasn't the kind of man who'd beg. She was carrying her backpack downstairs when Marion came out from the kitchen.

"Devon?" She eyed the backpack. "What's happening?"

"I thought maybe it's time I returned to the B and B. All of you have been wonderful, but I... I've encroached on your generosity long enough. I plan to stay through the weekend so I can help with the cookie exchange and maybe even the bazaar. I'd especially love to go to Kaya's pageant tomorrow night. Is that okay?"

"Of course it's okay, Devon. But why leave? We have lots of room and you've settled in so well." She frowned. "Does this move have something to do with all the kerfuffle over Kaya and Roxanne? Because these misunderstandings happen, and they're forgotten very quickly." She smiled. "Trust me, I know."

Except I don't know much about a typical family, Devon thought. She'd witnessed and been part of many misunderstandings in her foster home experience but had never felt overly affected by them. Of course, Dan had been with her to talk her through the tough times.

"No, it's not that, Marion. Though I know I had no right to interfere in a family matter, and I apologize for that."

"Then—" Marion's face cleared as she had another thought "—has something happened between you and Finn? Because I've noticed—"

"No!" Devon interrupted. She wasn't about to have a heart-to-heart talk about Finn with his mother. "I've simply realized my commitments in Chicago can no longer be deferred. This past week in Maple Glen has been wonderful, and I'll never forget how all of you welcomed me and made me feel like I was part of the family. I promise to keep in touch," she added, thinking at the same time that she probably wouldn't. She saw from Marion's expression that she wasn't convinced.

"Let's sit for a moment, okay?" Marion suggested, gesturing toward the living room.

Devon nodded and followed her into the room, thinking this was going to be a replay of their talk earlier that day.

"The thing is," Marion began once they were seated, "when Finn came back home four years ago to help me with his father, he was still suffering the loss of his best friend in that fire in Burlington. I'm sure he's told you about it?"

Devon nodded.

"The loss of his marriage wasn't as emotional. I'd seen the early signs myself, though it took Finn a bit longer." Marion smiled. "I'm not sure when or how it came about that Finn assumed the role of protector for our family, but I do know he was a very serious teenager who kept his passions and emotions in check. Long before Lewis's decline into dementia, Finn took on responsibilities that, frankly, no one ever asked him to. When Roxanne came home from college with Leo, her ex, it was Finn who tried to persuade her to take things slowly and get to know Leo better. Unfortunately, she was smitten and they eloped." Marion sighed. "Still, when she turned up on our doorstep last June, Finn supported her unconditionally and never once took the 'I told you so' stance. The problem is, he also became her big brother again, as if he and Roxanne were teens."

"How has Roxanne responded to that?" Devon asked.

"She understands why he does it but is frustrated that he can't seem to see that she's very capable of sorting out her problems. That's why I didn't want him to talk to her about Kaya's feelings about the move from New Jersey."

"I didn't intend for it to blow up into this big—"

"Deal?" Marion nodded. "Precisely. It's Finn's rescue syndrome, as I call it. His desire to be responsible and help shadows his own needs. He constantly suppresses his own wants to keep us all happy. I think you see that," she said, smiling. After a pause, she added, "Perhaps you want to assert your independence before you're drawn into something more serious with Finn?"

She was on the right track, Devon thought, but seemed to be fishing for information that she wasn't going to confide. "My commitments in Chicago have brought me back to earth, so to speak. Maple Glen..." Devon paused, stuck for words.

Marion nodded. "There's an irresistible draw to the Glen, certainly. Almost a magnetism. I didn't grow up here, but in Montpelier. I met Lewis in college, and the first time he brought me here to meet his family, I was hooked." She kept her gaze on Devon a minute longer. "Take your time to think everything through, Devon. I know nothing about your personal life, other than you're a social worker. I'd love it if you trusted me enough to tell me more but understand if you prefer not to." She stood up. "I should do some dinner prep. I noticed that Finn's truck isn't here, so I assume he went into work early. Did he say why?"

"Um, no. He left when I was upstairs."

"Oh?" She raised an eyebrow. "I see. Well, this is his last shift before the holidays, so maybe he has work to finish up before he's off. Can you manage to get to the B and B on your own, or would you like a ride?"

"I can manage, Marion. The brace has made a huge difference and I can walk without any difficulty now. Thanks again. For everything." Devon impulsively hugged her.

They smiled at one another for a moment, long enough that Devon was tempted to change her mind. But Finn would be home for good in the morning and she'd be pulled back into the irresistible comfort of his arms, her obligations beyond Maple Glen swept aside again.

"Our door is always open to you, Devon," Marion murmured. "Now, I have something on the stove in the kitchen. I'll see you about nine tomorrow morning? To bake our cookies?"

"I wouldn't miss it," Devon said. When Marion left the room, Devon wiped her eyes with the back of her hand before retrieving her backpack from the hallway floor. Then she walked out the door and, closing it behind her, wondered if she was making a mistake she might never be able to fix.

FOR A MOMENT, Finn thought he was a teen again, tugged from bed by mouthwatering aromas drifting up from the kitchen. *Christmas baking.* Sweets weren't normally his thing, except at Christmas, when the seasonal treats like kringle or his mother's shortbread made their brief appearance. The first Christmas following his father's admission to the care home, Finn's mother decided to buy all their holiday baked goods. Finn understood. His father had enjoyed her baking, and his mother must have figured *Why bother?* if he couldn't be there. But her friends in the community got together and included her in the annual cookie exchange, despite the fact that she'd chosen not to participate. Marion—and hence Finn—had received dozens of cookies that lasted through Roxanne and Leo's arrival for the holiday and beyond. Marion's decision to take some of those cookies to his father's care home staff and patients became a new tradition, and every year since, they had set aside a day for baking cookies in the Manor.

Devon was coming back to help with the baking—or so she'd said yesterday—to soften the blow of her departure. She hoped to still take part in the pre-Christmas events before she left. *If that's okay.* That phrase had bothered him all night long. Had she understood so little of his family and how they worked that she'd had to add that sentence? He'd been on the verge of pleading with her to stay—and begging was not his style—when she'd uttered those words. He could barely see for the dampness in his eyes and speaking was impossible, so he just walked away.

There was work to do at the fire hall prior to starting his holiday leave, and that was how he rationalized a reaction that he knew was immature. He hoped that Devon was able to understand and forgive him, now that he was off shift and they'd be together at some, if not all, of the pre-Christmas events. While he was working, he even dared to hope that she might change her mind about staying at the B and B, but when he'd gotten home at daybreak and seen her bedroom door wide open, the bed stripped of sheets, his disappointment gnawed at him until he finally fell asleep.

He quickly dressed and made for the kitchen, where he found Devon and his mother hovering over the open oven door. "They look ready," his mother was saying as Finn walked in.

"You're the expert," Devon said, and she looked up in surprise at Finn.

"What do you think, Finn?" His mother stood aside as he leaned in.

"Um, I could try one to find out."

Marion closed the oven door. "I'll add an extra two minutes." After resetting the timer, she said, "I need to call Lewis's care home to confirm the best time to deliver these. Devon, I'll trust you to stand guard while I'm gone."

"How will I know if they're done?" Devon managed to ask before Marion left.

"Finn will know," Marion said as she left the room.

"I'll only be able to tell by biting into one," Finn quipped.

"I may have to test that theory myself," Devon added.

Her sudden grin sent his heart racing, but there was an awkward minute until she said, "There's some coffee left and, well, cereal." She pointed to the boxes on the table.

"Okay. I'm glad you didn't eat all the cereal." His face warmed at the inane joke, but her smile encouraged him to ask, "Have you had breakfast yet?"

"At the B and B."

Of course. Bernie's legendary breakfasts. He felt even more ridiculous.

"Your mom said you were on Christmas vacation now."

"Yep." She seemed about to say something, so he waited.

"Well," she finally said, "I was wondering, if you're not busy, would you be interested in going for a short walk along the trail?"

"Of course!" The day was suddenly looking a tad brighter. "When do you think you might be finished with the baking?"

The oven timer dinged then, and she laughed. "Right now?"

The sky was a brilliant blue, with no clouds in sight. Weather similar to the day, a little more than a week ago, that Bernie Watson had warned could end in a storm. She'd only been there nine days, Devon mused, as she followed Finn across the Otter Creek bridge. How was that possible?

She stared at Finn's back and the small daypack slung nonchalantly across his broad shoulders. His long stride took him to the other side before she was halfway across, and he waited with a broad smile as she joined up with him.

That smile had been on his face since mid-morning when she'd asked him to walk part of the Long Trail with her. Despite his obvious dis-appointment yesterday at her decision to leave the Manor, he hadn't reproached her or even asked if she might change her mind and move back in with the family. She liked that. In fact, she'd been so sure he'd agree to take her that she'd worn her Gore-Tex jacket and waterproof snow pants when she'd arrived to bake cookies with Marion, who had made no comment on her outfit, which Devon also liked.

"Why don't you take the lead now?" Finn sug-gested. "Stop when and where you want."

All she'd told him before leaving the house was that she had to fulfill a promise she'd made to her brother before he died. He hadn't asked what that promise was, just nodded and went to tell his mother where they were going. But now she had to get some crucial information. "I need to bury something, if possible. Three small items. Will there be a spot we can do that along the way?"

Except for a tiny flicker of surprise in his face, he barely reacted. "The ground is frozen, but there may be a place. Will these items fit in my hand?"

She nodded. They were small, but she felt their weight in her backpack.

"Okay. I have an idea, and you can decide when we get there."

"Should I still go first, then?"

"Yep. I'll stop you when I see what I'm looking for."

She stepped into the thicket of trees and was assailed at once by the same sensations she'd felt nine days ago. The silence struck first, and then gradually, the sounds of the forest chimed in— the rustling of small mammals, the wind shifting tree branches and, when she stopped to catch her breath, the drip of melting snow from those branches. But unlike the first time she entered these dark woods, she had Finn at her back.

"How's your ankle holding up?" he quietly asked.

She turned his way and managed a confident smile. "It's fine."

"Don't push it. Stop when you need to."

"I promise." She continued on, assured by his presence as well as his silence. *At least if I fall again, he'll catch me*, she thought.

They'd just reached the junction of blue and white blazes when Finn stopped her. "Would this place work for you? To bury those items?"

She looked around but couldn't decide. There was no hope of finding the exact same spot. Even if Dan were with her, she doubted they'd be able to find it after twenty-five years. They'd only been kids.

"Um, I suppose. Why here?"

"The trail goes higher, and there'll be more ice once we're out of the sun's reach. We're almost where you fell last week."

She took a deep breath. *This will have to do. You can't carry those things around with you for the rest of your life.* "Yes," she said. "This will do."

As soon as she replied, he moved around her and headed off the path toward a tree a few yards away. Devon couldn't see exactly what he was doing, but he walked back to her and said, "Come with me."

He held out his hand and she clasped it, letting him lead her off the path across a jumble of fallen branches and strewn rocks to the tree. Up close, she saw a hole in the trunk.

"There was an owl living in this tree last summer," Finn said. "I think it would make a nice dry place for your…items. And it's not far from the path or from the Glen. You could always come back and—you know—check on them. If you wanted to, that is."

What she wanted was to fling her arms around him and hold him tight. "This is perfect, Finn," she said instead. "Thank you." She set her daypack on the ground and unzipped a side pocket. The treasures she'd promised Dan to bury were wrapped in the same piece of cloth she'd used for years to hide them from the other foster kids at Ellen and Ted's place. She took out the package and unfolded the cloth.

Finn didn't lean forward until she held them out to him.

"This little bunny was my favorite since I was a toddler. Dan kept it safe for me until I was old enough to do that." She held up the miniature stuffed rabbit, and Finn smiled. Then she held up the compass. "I don't know where or when Dan bought this, but he had it with him the day we were at the recreation area."

She saw that Finn was recalling her story from the other day, about hanging out there the whole day until someone called the police. It was time to set the record straight.

"He had it so he could guide us through the woods after we left our foster parents' camper van. When he decided we were going to run away."

A question crossed his face, but Finn only nodded, waiting for her to go on.

Finally, she held up the wrinkled photograph. "This is the house we once lived in, when our parents were still together."

She handed him the photo and he stared at it for a long time, then he flipped it over and saw the word written on the back. "Morrison?" he asked.

"Morrison. My birth name was Chloe Morrison. And Dan's was Billy Morrison. We disappeared in these woods for two whole days and nights twenty-five years ago, until someone found us."

He kept his eyes on the photograph a long time until he finally raised his head. His face was sober with thought.

There were many comments he might have made, but Devon never expected to hear him finally say, "I know who found you."

CHAPTER SIXTEEN

AFTER DEVON REACHED up to tuck the three mementos into the tree hollow, Finn waited quietly while she stood, head bowed, as if she were saying a prayer. He guessed she was sending a message to her brother, or perhaps simply thinking of him and those two days twenty-five years ago.

His own thoughts were as muddled and strewn as the white rocks tumbling down the mountain looming over them. Now the reason for Devon Fairchild, aka Chloe Morrison, to appear in Maple Glen to honor a significant anniversary was clear. That was no coincidence, really. But what if she hadn't fallen that day? She could have carried out her promise, returned to the B and B and left for Chicago without ever encountering him. That what-if frightened him. He had come so close to never meeting Devon at all.

He pushed aside the awful thought when she turned his way, a tentative smile on her face. She was feeling relief at accomplishing her mission. But she still hadn't asked for the name of their rescuer that day. "I know where there's a nice log to sit on, and it might even be in a patch of sun by now. Plus—" he held aloft his daypack "—I've got a thermos of hot chocolate in here."

"Lovely," she said quietly.

He reached for her hand and led her back to the path. When she waited for him to go ahead, he said, "No, you first. I'll let you know when we've reached that log." If she tripped or lost her balance, he'd be right there, ready to catch her. Twenty minutes of walking took them to a small clearing and the log perched on the side of the path facing White Rocks Mountain. "Okay, this is it," he said.

He brushed some snow that hadn't yet melted off the log, and setting their backpacks on the ground, they sat down. Just then, a shaft of sunlight broke through the trees and beamed onto the log. Finn took this as a good omen, but he wasn't going to push his luck. Devon needed some time to process what she'd done, hiding the treasures she and her brother had salvaged from their childhood. He could wait. Waiting was a skill he'd mastered long ago.

She sipped from the thermos cup he handed her and closed her eyes. "This moment," she murmured. "I'll remember this moment the rest of my life. The warmth of the sun against my cold cheeks and this delicious hot chocolate. The light feeling flowing through me now that I've done what Dan asked me to." She passed Finn the empty cup and smiled. "Thanks for this, Finn." Then she gave a light laugh and said, "For bringing me. The hot chocolate was a wonderful bonus." She gazed up at the sky, lost in thought.

Finn poured his hot chocolate and waited.

"The media had it all wrong at first," she began. "Our foster parents said we'd gone exploring and were lost. The story headlined newspapers for the two days we were missing. A fundraising campaign was set up in case…you know…there might be a need for a funeral. Our foster parents got money for an exclusive to some tabloid. Volunteer searchers came from all over the state, and they used helicopters and dogs to look for us. I still don't know why the dogs didn't pick up our scent, but Dan took us on such a meandering path off the main trail, that could have thrown them off."

She paused, reflecting, Finn guessed, on those two days and nights. He downed his hot chocolate and reached for her hand.

"Dan had granola bars and cookies. Even some of those cheese sticks—you know the kind—that he must have taken from the camper van. He thought to bring a bottle of water." She squeezed Finn's hand, smiling. "You'd have liked Dan. You share similar traits. He was always well organized, a planner. That's why his company is so successful."

Finn thought he would have liked Dan. He was about to speak when Devon went on with her story.

"The nights were the worst. I can only recall feeling super scared. All the sounds. Dan wrapped his arms around me, hushing me when I started to cry. He was so gentle with me. Never got angry or frustrated."

"You were lucky to have him for a brother," Finn said.

"I was." She stared across the long valley separating them from White Rocks Mountain. Finally, she turned his way. "You said you know who found us. Tell me that part."

"I was eleven that September, and all of us in Maple Glen were following the story because we were so close to where it was taking place. I heard the missing boy was almost my age, and I felt kind of a connection to him because I knew how frightening it must have been to be lost out here for two days and nights. Of course, a lot of people in the Glen volunteered to search, but it was the Wallingford fire chief who found you. His name is Walter Ingram and he's retired now, but he still lives in the area. Right outside the Glen, actually."

Finn knew he'd never forget the wonder in Devon's face right then. She was speechless, her hand clenched tightly in his. He thought maybe her mind was racing back to the past, trying to match a face to the name she now had.

"We were huddled under some branches, and I think I'd sneezed," she said. "That's what Dan told me later anyway. I don't remember much about this Walter Ingram. He was big and strong, but his voice was soft and gentle. He told us we were safe and that everything would be okay. When I think of it now, I guess his smile was meant to be reassuring. But I do remember Dan crying and begging him not to take us back to the camper van. That's when he told…Walter…that we had run away and were afraid to go back to our foster parents. We weren't lost at all."

Finn felt his jaw tighten, picturing two scared kids. One of them this beautiful woman sitting next to him holding his hand. He couldn't speak.

"Anyway, everything was a blur after that. I know now that a couple of people came from social services. We never saw our foster parents again, and other than some feeble protests, they basically went off the radar—with a lot of money, probably. We were taken back to the Boston area and placed with a wonderful social worker who was with us until Dan turned eighteen. Then he became my legal guardian, and the first thing he did was legally change our names."

"Because…?"

"Have you heard the term 'media frenzy'? That's what it was then, especially when the truth behind story broke. We were swiftly ushered away from the public eye into Ellen and Ted's home, as I've told you. So we finally got some good parenting, but…"

"Not attention devoted just to you both?"

"That's it. We were cared for and felt safe, but never loved the way...you know...people in families are loved. I mean, it was a version of a family, and there was attention and caring and counseling. But it wasn't like what you have, or what Theo and Maura have, or the Watsons."

He could see that, which made him even more determined to convince her that good families, in his opinion, were the norm. But he sensed from her thoughtful expression that she wasn't quite finished telling him what she wanted to. *Needed to.*

"We were lucky, Dan and I. Our sad story had a happy ending after all." She looked at Finn, her eyes glimmering in the sunlight.

Or with tears, he realized, and he put his arm around her.

"The only reason Dan wanted to make this trek at the twenty-five-year mark was to finally lay it all to rest. He said, 'We've gone on with our new lives, and when we get rid of these last three objects, we can finally break loose from the past.' He said that two months before he learned his cancer was terminal."

She began to weep then, and Finn held her close, thinking he never wanted to let her go.

THEY TOOK THEIR time going back and barely spoke the whole way. Devon was exhausted from talking, and she guessed Finn was still digesting it all, trying to connect little Chloe Morrison to Devon Fairchild, a persona dreamed up by both her and Dan when he was eighteen. The name had seemed exotic to her thirteen-year-old self, but not quite real until she received her official new ID.

When they were almost at the bridge, Finn stopped. "I assume you want to keep all this between us," he said.

She nodded. Although she'd finally told someone her story for the first time in her life, she realized the minute she stepped off that bridge, she'd be back in the real world. A world where she was Devon Fairchild, but also a world where someone, someday, could discover Chloe Morrison. The lightness that had been flowing through her since she hid her treasures and then told her story began to dissipate.

"The other thing is," Finn was saying, "that you wanted to go to Kaya's Christmas pageant tonight and my mom said to invite you to have dinner with us before we go...if you'd like to."

Devon's heart swelled at the hesitance in his face, uncertain about what she wanted and protective at the same time. No pressure, his voice was implying.

"I'd like that," she said, and then stepped onto the bridge.

FOR THE FIRST time in a long time, Finn was grateful for the usual hubbub at supper. Kaya was high on the excitement of one more day of school plus the pageant. Roxanne was rushing around ironing a costume and coaxing Kaya to eat something while his mother served the meal. "You get ready, Finn, while Devon relaxes in the living room."

Devon had made a quick stop at the B and B to change her clothes while Finn had texted his mother to tell her they'd be home soon. Life resumed its usual pace the instant they stepped off the Otter Creek bridge, but Finn knew things would never be the same again. With or without Devon Fairchild in it; his life was changing, and there wasn't a thing he could do about it. Though he had some thoughts and ideas, one of which he suggested before they returned to the Manor.

"I want to take you to meet Walter Ingram," he'd said when they left the B and B, where Devon had changed into black jeans and a sweater. Finn had been waiting in what Bernie Watson called the parlor, all too aware of the man's interested face when they'd arrived together. Another item for the Glen grapevine, Finn guessed.

"Yes," she'd said. "Soon."

He'd contact Walter and arrange a meeting for the next day, if possible. Then she'd reminded him of the cookie exchange in the morning, and Finn had realized they were both getting swept up in the tsunami of Christmas in Maple Glen. So long as Devon was with him, he didn't mind at all.

When he and Devon arrived for supper, he'd

seen his mother carefully observing them, and once, narrowing her eyes when Finn had placed his hands on Devon's shoulders as she sat down at the kitchen table.

Finn was amused by her obvious confusion but also relieved at her discretion. After the meal, which Finn scarcely registered as he'd focused mainly on Devon, his mother handed him two tickets for the pageant and said she'd drive Roxanne and Kaya, who had to be there early.

They saved seats for them in the school auditorium, which functioned as a gym by day. The pageant was charming, with the typical mishaps that school performances sometimes featured and, as far as Finn was concerned, were often the best part of such events. He was restless, shifting on the hard folding chair until his mother, sitting next to him, set a calming hand on his arm. Kaya's appearance had been heralded by her proud mother, who'd given a loud whoop that made Finn, Devon and Marion laugh. Finn thought back to that brief moment when he went to bed hours later. How their small group had fit in perfectly with all the other variations of families around them.

After the curtain went up—or in this case, the house lights came on—the audience slowly made its way to the school cafeteria, where refreshments were being served. Finn would have liked to head for home so he might catch some alone time with Devon, but he also knew Kaya would be disappointed if they weren't all at the reception. Roxanne went to the classroom to help Kaya get out of her costume and Marion headed off to chat with friends.

"Well?" Finn grinned.

"Cute," Devon said, matching his grin. "Were you ever in something like this? A pageant?"

He shook his head. "Not that my mother and teachers didn't try, but I always hated to be in the limelight. I was more of a backstage kind of kid."

"Even now, I think," she murmured, gazing up at him with her cobalt blue eyes. Appraising him.

Finn smiled but felt his face heat up and turned aside to peer down at the selection of cookies and squares on the long cafeteria table. For want of anything to say, he blurted, "How about you?" and mentally kicked himself.

"Yes, I was in a school play once, but only Dan came to see me. Ellen and Ted had seven other kids, so they had to kind of share attendance at school events. And to be honest, like you, I wasn't and still am not a person who likes attention."

"Yeah," he murmured, moving closer to her as someone attempted to reach the table behind him. "We have that in common at least."

"I'm beginning to think we have more in common than I'd have thought a week ago."

She was close enough to kiss, and Finn wished he could magically transport them to a dark, private place. Maybe on the way home, they could find a moonlit spot to park the truck and, well, kiss. He smiled at the snippet of his teenaged past surfacing unexpectedly.

"Shall we go find a quiet place to wait for the others?" he asked.

"Please."

He clasped her by the elbow as they wound their way through the crowd and had just reached the main cafeteria door when a rumble of a voice called, "Finn McAllister!"

Finn swung around to see the last person he expected to encounter at a school pageant: Walter Ingram. The older man seemed to be moving in slow motion as he headed toward them, Finn was thinking. He looked from Walter to Devon at his side. He hadn't arranged the meeting he'd suggested earlier and was tongue-tied when Walter drew near.

"I wouldn't have expected to see you at an event like this" was all Finn could think to say.

Walter grinned. "I was persuaded to buy a ticket—good cause, you know—and after an early supper made an impulsive decision to come. I liked Kaya's angel pose. Or should I say *angelic* pose?" He chuckled. Then he turned his attention to Devon.

"And you must be the young woman this fella rescued on the trail."

Devon smiled but cast a quick wink at Finn. *She's thinking about the Glen grapevine*, he thought. The timing was definitely not so great. The din around them seemed to fade as Finn instinctively ushered Devon out into the hallway away from the crowd, and Walter followed. Then Finn clasped her hand in his and said, "This is Devon Fairchild. Devon, meet Walter Ingram."

He watched Devon's face as she processed the name. Then she blurted, "I used to be called Chloe. Chloe Morrison."

Her hand slipped from his, and she rushed forward to hug the man who'd rescued her twenty-five years before. Finn kept going back to Walter's face all night long, searching for the right words to describe what looked like incredible disbelief to wonder to delight. He couldn't imagine what the two must be feeling but figured neither one would ever forget this moment.

When Devon pulled back and drew a tissue from her jacket pocket, Walter simply stood staring at her, his lopsided grin at odds with his damp eyes. Before anyone had a chance to speak, Finn noticed his mother, Roxanne and Kaya heading along the hall toward them.

"It seems our group might be ready to head home," he said. Devon and Walter turned where he was looking. Finn was torn. He figured neither one could handle small talk, and disclosing anything more right then wasn't his decision to make.

Walter came to the rescue. "How about you two come for lunch tomorrow at my place?"

"We'd love to," Devon said, then glanced at Finn as if to confirm that would be okay.

Finn patted the older man on the shoulder. "See you tomorrow."

Then Walter turned and disappeared into the crowd as Kaya ran up to Finn and Devon.

"Did you like my angel?" she asked breathlessly.

Devon reached down to hug her. "You were the best of all the angels tonight," she said. Then catching Finn's eye, she said in a lower voice, "Except for one much older angel."

Her smile was in Finn's mind the rest of the night.

CHAPTER SEVENTEEN

DEVON WAS HELPING to carry cookies from the car into the community center when Marion commented, "I noticed you met Walter Ingram last night," and Devon almost dropped the boxes in her hands.

Then Marion said, "Are you all right, dear? You look like you've seen a ghost."

"No, no. I mean, I'm fine. And, yes, I did. In fact, he's invited me to go and see his…uh…his honey production."

"Oh? Well, that's nice of him. Or should I say sweet of him?" Marion's light laugh carried off on the wind as she led the way to the center's front door. Then she suddenly stopped. "Oh, look, they're setting up for the Christmas tree lighting ceremony tonight."

She pointed across the road to the church, where Devon spotted a gigantic fir tree with garlands of red and gold intertwined among large sparkling ornaments. A group of men wearing orange safety vests were stringing red ropes around the base of the tree while others were carrying crates from a van toward what looked like a makeshift stage.

"I think Finn mentioned he was involved in something this morning," Devon said, squinting to see if he was one of the helpers. There was a lot of information sharing last night, but after his goodnight kiss, Devon scarcely remembered any of it.

"He's probably involved somewhere on his day off. That's Finn. He takes an active role here in the Glen whenever he can." She gazed thoughtfully at Devon. "I'm glad he talks to you about what he's doing."

Devon wasn't sure what to make of the cryptic comment. Was Marion probing for more information or simply being…well…Marion? Devon was beginning to see and understand many more sides to Finn's mother.

She followed Marion inside and along a hall into the large open area of the center where groups of women were setting out their contributions to the cookie exchange on long tables. The room echoed with greetings, laughter and the squeals of young children, but Devon's mind was focused on last night's surprise meeting.

She hadn't felt like talking on the short ride from Kaya's school in Wallingford back to Maple Glen, and Finn had clearly been attuned to her need for silence. When he'd dropped her off at the B and B, he'd hugged her for a few seconds before kissing her. It had been a reassuring kiss rather than a romantic one, which she appreciated. The rush of emotion when Finn had revealed Walter Ingram's identity had begun to merge with a swirl of memories, both good and bad. As she watched him head back to the Manor, she thought of Dan and how he'd have liked Finn. Even more, how he'd have loved to have met Walter Ingram. At some point during the long, sleepless night, she realized she now had two compelling ties to Maple Glen—Walter Ingram and Finn McAllister. Going back to Chicago had shifted from an expectation to a dilemma.

Paying attention to Marion's instructions about how the exchange worked was a challenge, especially after reading Finn's message he sent as she and Marion were arranging the boxes of ginger shortbread and fruitcake squares on their assigned section of table.

Text when you're ready to be picked up. Walter suggested 1:00 p.m.

The shock of meeting her rescuer had faded, and Devon was beginning to think of questions she wanted to ask Walter. Her own memories were hazy, but Dan had told her details he could recall of the day they were found, and she was eager to compare his stories to Walter's account.

At the moment, though, she was grateful for the diversion of the cookie exchange.

Once the cookies were all laid out, Marion said everyone could take their containers and start walking the rows of tables to collect their share of the cookies. "We've been doing this a long time," she told Devon. "And we're on the honor system. The rule is you're entitled to take the same number of cookies that you have contributed. I've brought six dozen, so that's how many we can take. Got it?"

Devon nodded.

"So how about you collect your three dozen on that side of the room, and I'll take this side. That way we won't have any duplicates. Try to get something we don't have at home."

Along with the two types they'd brought that morning, there were almond crescents, raspberry thumbprints and chocolate drops at the Manor. The names were all new to Devon, whose knowledge of Christmas cookies had been restricted to shortbread and gingerbread men.

"How will I know if Roxanne, Kaya and Finn will like the kind I choose?"

Marion arched a brow. "Seriously? They will eat anything, trust me. But Kaya is especially attracted to cookies with icing or sprinkles, so that could be a guide. I'll focus on ones that are unusual. Okay?"

"Okay."

"All right. Good luck and let's meet back at our own section when we're finished." She handed Devon an empty container. "Oh, there's Sue with the order from the Watson family. I want to find out how Betty's doing."

Devon watched her rush toward Sue Giordano. Looking around, Devon wondered what it would be like to know practically everyone in the room. And not only in the room, she suddenly thought, but in the village itself. As she headed to gather her cookies, she was aware that a few of the women were glancing her way, some obviously curious and others simply smiling. She stopped in front of a box of cookies cut out in Christmas shapes—trees, Santas, stars, even reindeer—covered in red, green and sparkling white sprinkles, and began to choose a selection.

"Cute, aren't they? I promised my kids to get some with lots of sprinkles and M&M's," a woman about Devon's age remarked as she waited her turn.

Devon smiled. "They are cute. Maybe I'll take two dozen of my three dozen choices."

"You can also do half a dozen at a time for more variety, though only six of these particular cookies would end in a lot of arguments and ne-gotiations in my house. I'm Leni, by the way, and aren't you the woman Finn McAllister rescued on the trail a few days ago?"

Devon had been prepared for this. Finn's parting reminder last night had been to expect at least one person to know who she was. *The Glen grapevine, remember?* Yet the comment didn't bother her as she'd expected it to. The woman was being both polite and welcoming.

"I am. My name's Devon. I came here with Finn's mother, Marion." She gestured to the other side of the room where Marion was chatting with someone.

"Yes, I saw you two come in. It's so great that you're a guest of theirs while you recuperate."

"They've been wonderful."

"Good people," Leni said. "Will you be staying on for Christmas?"

"Um, maybe, I haven't quite decided." After yesterday's emotional reveal of her story to Finn and then later, meeting Walter, Devon was positive she was going to stay but thought being vague might be a good plan for now.

"You should! There's always something happening. Tonight, they're lighting the village Christmas tree, and of course there's the bazaar tomorrow. Oh, wait, I think that was put off to Sunday because of the wedding."

"The wedding?" Devon asked.

She leaned forward and lowered her voice. "They want it to be a secret as long as possible— don't ask me why. Everyone probably knows already."

"They?" Devon found herself drawn to the gossip.

"Maddie Stuart and Shawn Harrison. I heard it's a very small, family-only affair, with not even a party after."

Devon wondered if Finn had heard and what he'd make of it. Then she smiled. *You are getting sucked into the grapevine!*

While she was choosing six of the decorated cookies, Leni said, "Anyway, nice to meet you. I'm sure we'll meet up again over the next few days."

"I hope so, and thanks for the tip...about taking six at a time." Devon watched the friendly woman move along the row to other cookie selections. *A potential friend*, was her first thought, followed at once by another, more realistic one, *if you stayed in Maple Glen.*

By the time Devon's container was full of a varied selection of three dozen cookies, she'd met too many women to keep count. Some were friends of Marion's, some Roxanne's, and there were a couple who knew Finn from high school. They were all friendly, though not as chatty as Leni had been. She skimmed the crowd, searching for Marion. Then she pulled out her cell phone to see that it was almost noon. She texted Finn to say that she was ready to leave and went to look for his mother.

WALTER INSISTED ON giving Devon a tour of his honey shed, though the honey operation itself was closed for the winter. He'd pointed to a nearby collection of beehives, stating that all the hives were also closed for the season, and when Devon asked if there were bees inside, he'd said yes. The worker bees were surrounding the queens and keeping them warm and alive.

Finn was fidgeting. He was itching to hear Walter's side of Devon's story, and he imagined Devon was, too, though there'd been interest in her face as Walter was speaking. He had to admire her for that, thinking he could never be so patient. He was beginning to see how they balanced each other out. Relief surged through him when Walter suggested they go to back to the house for some lunch and talk.

He'd never been inside the man's house before and was intrigued by the woodcarvings of birds next to shelves teeming with books of all kinds. Until the past year or so, Walter had been a solitary person. Finn had gradually come to see that the man's need for privacy stemmed not only from the unwanted publicity years ago following the Morrisons' rescue but from his nature as a quiet man who enjoyed his own company. Finn could somewhat relate. He'd always loved walking the trail by himself, in tune with all that was happening around him.

He headed along a dark hallway to a bright, cheerful kitchen, where Devon was setting spoons and a cheese plate onto the table. Walter stood at the stove ladling soup into bowls.

"Carrot ginger made with my garden carrots. Good crop this year. I'm also lucky to have what folks used to call a root cellar, which is basically a cold storage section in my basement."

Finn thought he saw a wink in Devon's smile. Was she guessing he was feeling impatient? He marveled again at her breezy chitchat as she carried the bowls to the table, and they sat down, passing bread, butter and cheese around. When she mentioned the village Christmas tree lighting, Finn remembered that he'd promised Kaya they'd get their own family tree on Saturday. Tomorrow, he realized with a sense of panic. He had yet to finish his Christmas shopping, and there were only so many days left until the actual day rolled around. He mentally counted the days to December 25 and didn't notice Walter pushing back his chair.

"I think I know something about your story, Devon," Walter began. "Are you ready for mine?"

She set her spoon down beside her partially empty soup bowl. "Yes, please."

"When you and your brother, Billy—"

"Dan," Devon broke in. "He changed his name to Dan. But please call him Billy for now."

Walter nodded thoughtfully. "Will do. I was fire chief in Wallingford at the time, and all of us—full-time crews and volunteers—helped search when the park rangers reported two missing children. The groups convened at the recreation area, where you were last seen and where your…uh… foster parents were camping." His face shifted into anger for a second. "The morning of the third day, I'd been held up by some administrative problem at the fire hall, and because I had little time to actually help search, I decided to access the trail from the Glen. I thought I'd walk for a couple of hours and then head back home."

He paused for a long moment before adding, "I was married at the time, and my wife and I lived in Wallingford." His voice dropped. "We never had children."

Finn saw concern in Devon's face, but she didn't interrupt with questions or make some token comment.

"The days were still long then in mid-September, and warm and sunny," Walter continued. "But temperatures fell at night, and the people supervising the search were worried. The two of you had already been gone two nights, and we had no idea what you had with you for protection against the weather and so on." His lip curled in disgust. "The foster parents were no help with that, either."

Finn kept his eyes on Devon. *She knows this part*, he thought, the negligence and incompetence. Yet except for a slight twitch at the corner of her mouth, she was quiet.

"I'd almost reached the junction where the off

trail to the Glen merged with the Long Trail itself and had decided to turn back. That's when I heard what sounded a heck of a lot like a sneeze." He grinned at Devon, who smiled for the first time since he'd begun to speak. "I stood absolutely still, waiting to make sure my ears weren't deceiving me. That's when it happened again, followed by a shushing sound. I guess that was Billy, trying to get you to stop."

Devon only nodded. Finn saw her eyes well up at and guessed she was replaying that scene in her head that very moment.

"My hearing was a lot better in those days, and I was able to head in the right direction. You were both quite a ways off the path under a pile of branches that Billy must have collected to shelter you overnight."

"He took good care of me," Devon suddenly said. "And he was only ten years old! Just a child himself."

"In years maybe, but not in maturity," Walter said, his voice so low Finn could barely hear. "What I remember was the expression of fear in Billy's face when I pushed aside those branches. I said everything was going to be okay now that you both were found, and right away, he cried out that he didn't want to be found. That you both hadn't been lost at all but had run away." Walter paused. "You were both sobbing by then and... and my heart just broke."

Walter stopped, took a deep breath and reached across the table to clasp Devon's hand. "That's when I made a decision that would basically change everything. Instead of contacting the search party supervisor to report that I'd found you, I lifted you into my arms, took Billy's hand and walked you here—well, to the Glen." Walter looked at Finn. "I don't know where you were that day, Finn. At school, I guess, but your folks were home, and I took Chloe and Billy into the Manor, where I called Child Protective Services in Rutland and waited until someone came to pick you up."

Finn saw Devon fighting back her tears and was desperate to get up and fold her into his arms. But Walter wasn't finished.

"Looking back, I realize that the minute my call was logged in, the search party leader was contacted. Then someone at that end probably let slip you both had been found and were safe in Maple Glen. It didn't take long for the media to get word, and by the time the social service team arrived, the first reporters and photographers had also arrived." Walter looked at Finn. "We were basically barricaded in the Manor until the state police came to escort the team from Child Protection and—" his attention shifted to Devon "—take you and your brother away." His face tightened. "But of course, I lived here, and everyone wanted my version of your story."

Finn was still processing the part about their hiding out in the Manor. His parents had never said a word about that ever, and he wondered why. And how did that part of the story escape the Glen grapevine? Unless the few people who learned it kept it a secret. His mind teemed with questions, and he suddenly realized that Devon was staring at him, as struck by this revelation as he was.

Walter's sigh broke the silence. "The rest is history, as the saying goes, and to be honest, I wouldn't have done anything different." He let go of Devon's hand to pick up his mug of tea and took a long sip.

Collecting himself, Finn thought. He knew that wasn't quite the end of Walter's story—the press hounding him once a year, the collapse of his marriage and early retirement. Not all of that was due to rescuing Chloe and Billy, but collateral damage. Finn saw Devon reach for her handbag and rummage around in it. When she pulled out a tissue, he realized that she was crying.

CHAPTER EIGHTEEN

AS THE TRUCK pulled out of Walter's drive onto the county road, Devon turned from gazing out the passenger-side window to sneak a peek at Finn. His hands gripped the steering wheel, and other than sharing a quick bear hug with Walter, he'd been seriously withdrawn. *He's still making sense of everything.* Ironically, Devon herself felt liberated. There were no tears left. Now that she had the whole story, she decided to do what Dan had told her to.

I want you to have the family we never had.

She'd never believed in fate or destiny, figuring that people's lives were guided by choices, either directly or indirectly. As a five-year-old, she hadn't chosen to run away. Dan made that choice for her, and she'd chosen to come to Maple Glen to bury the three childhood treasures because when they were older, she and Dan had read some of the online press reports of their discovery near Maple Glen. All the rest—the fall, Finn helping her and taking her to the Manor to recover—were mere coincidences. Sort of.

When Finn turned onto Church Street, Devon said, "We have to tell your mother."

He nodded but didn't speak for a long moment. "Maybe later this evening? We're taking the cookies to Dad's care home at about three, and that visit will be emotional for her. Let's give her some time to collect herself."

"What about tonight, after we get back from the tree lighting?"

Finn glanced at her, a smile breaking for the first time since Walter's talk. "You're coming to the ceremony with us?"

"If that's okay."

"Devon!"

"Yeah, yeah, I know. I have to stop saying that." She reached across to pat his arm. "I found out about it this morning, at the cookie exchange. And there's something else." She hesitated, wondering if she really was ready to make a commitment. Should she wait until everything she'd heard from Walter had registered? On the other hand, she reasoned, acting on impulse sometimes paid off.

"What?" Finn prompted. "You said there was something else?"

"This morning at breakfast, Bernie told me the B and B was booked for the whole weekend, and he was very sorry, but unless he could juggle things around a bit, I might have to stay somewhere else. And I think I know why it's all booked."

Finn grinned. "Uh-huh. And I *know* why."

"Because—"

"Maddie and Shawn are getting married, and the families are having a special dinner and spending the night at the B and B."

Devon had to laugh. "The Glen grapevine?"

"Actually, no. Shawn told me himself this morning. I went to the farm while you were at the cookie exchange. Maddie asked me to check on the donkeys tomorrow night."

"Why didn't you tell me?"

His face sobered. "I was going to, but compared to what we were hearing from Walter, it seemed a bit trivial. I'd planned to wait till later." Before she could say anything, he added, "I hope you're going to come back to the Manor."

"If that's—"

"We took a vote this morning, before Mom picked you up for the cookie thing," he quickly said. "It was unanimously agreed that one of us would ask you to come and stay through Christmas."

Devon bit down on her lip. No more tears, she told herself. "And were you the chosen one?"

"No, Kaya won that draw. And please don't let on that I already told you."

"I won't." She leaned against the seat and closed her eyes, feeling as though she'd gone through several lives since breakfast. "Would it be okay if I went with you and your mother to the care home? To meet your father?"

Finn swerved to the side of the road and shifted into Park. "Come here," he said huskily.

She slid over as far as the console permitted and he wrapped an arm around her. He lowered his head to hers and was quiet for a long minute. "I think you've become part of my family, Devon. Whatever is okay with you is definitely okay with us." He tilted her chin up and kissed her.

FINN KNEW DEVON would handle what could have been an awkward situation with sensitivity and empathy. Yet those two words failed to adequately describe her calm, gentle manner with Lewis, the way she held his hand and didn't correct him when he called her Roxie, and her grin as he bit gleefully into his cookie and then offered her a bite, too. They stayed with him while Finn's mother dropped off the rest of the cookies to the main office, and when Marion returned to the lounge, Lewis beamed with adoration. Finn knew his father wasn't exactly sure who Marion was, but his smile said he loved her. *What more do we need than love?* Finn thought as the three of them walked silently back to the parking lot for the drive home.

Except for the spontaneous hug his mother gave Devon at the news she would stay at the Manor over Christmas, Marion was deep in thought after visiting her husband—as Finn knew she would be. After he parked her car in the garage, she leaned over and patted his cheek. "Thanks, dear. I'm going up to my room for a bit," she said, as he also knew she would. And he knew she'd rally and come down to make dinner, too.

But as they walked in the front door, he changed the pattern a tiny bit by saying he was going to order pizza from Wallingford for supper to celebrate the start of Kaya's holiday and Devon's return.

"I'd love that, Finn," Marion said, and gave Devon a big smile as she headed upstairs.

"Let's go pick up your things from Bernie's," Finn suggested before Devon removed her coat. "And you can also get your rental car and park it here. I promise to make room for it," he teased.

"Sure, though I have the room until the morning."

"I won't wait till then."

THE SUN WAS already lowering in the west as Devon and Finn strolled along Church Street toward the B and B, passing the church where a few workers were still adjusting the strings of lights on the giant tree.

"We use the tree every year," Finn said, "so we don't have to cut down another one. I don't know how long it's been there on the church front lawn, but it's at least as old as I am. Hopefully it'll still be here when I…"

He didn't finish the sentence, but Devon sensed he'd been thinking about a family of his own. She didn't like the idea of Finn having a family with anyone else but her, and realized life-changing events were taking shape without any decisions on her part.

They passed the church and Devon saw that the community center on the other side of the street was lit up. "Is something happening over there?"

"The community center's social committee will be organizing something for tonight, after the tree lighting. Usually they offer hot chocolate, hot cider and coffee with leftover cookies to folks who attend."

"Your mom is on the committee, isn't she?"

"Of course." Finn chuckled. "She's been on every committee the village has had since moving here as a young bride." After a pause, he said, "But the bazaar is her focus this year. You probably heard it's been switched from Saturday at the church to Sunday at the center because of the big Ping-Pong tournament there, as well as the surprise wedding tomorrow at the church."

"I have a feeling the wedding's not much of a surprise anymore," Devon said, laughing.

Finn shrugged. "The Glen. What can I say? There are pros and cons to people knowing your business." He suddenly stopped walking. "Are you okay with my mother knowing your background?"

"She ought to know, and I want her to know how different my life turned out because of what Walter did."

"I thought you might say that," he murmured. He put his arms around her in a quick hug.

"Now we've really given the grapevine followers something to pass around. An embrace in the middle of the street in broad daylight," she teased.

Finn grinned, but she saw that he couldn't resist glancing around. "Is this…village awareness, I'm going to call it…about our personal lives going to be an issue for you?"

"How do you mean?"

"If you were to stay here."

"I think I can handle it for the next few days." She smiled to reassure him that she seriously intended to stay through Christmas.

"No, I mean if you—"

The blare of a horn cut off what he was about to say, and they both jumped. A pickup truck pulled over to their side of the street. Devon saw two women sitting up front, and when the driver's-side window rolled down, she recognized Maddie behind the wheel and her sister, Maura.

"Hey, you two love birds!" Maddie was grinning. "You're going to get the whole village all riled up with that kind of public affection. I bet my own news has already made the rounds, so the grapevine will be looking for a fresh item."

Finn smiled at Devon, shrugging as if to say, *What did I just tell you?*

She followed him to the edge of the sidewalk to talk to the women.

"How're things going for tomorrow?" he asked.

"We've just been at the church doing some more preparations. I guess you've heard...this was pretty much a last-minute impulse on our part," Maddie explained, laughing.

"Along with all of Maple Glen," Finn said.

"That's okay." She looked quickly at her sister, who shrugged and nodded at the same time. "Soon there'll be more news to go around. I know you can keep a secret, Finn, and I'm betting Devon can, too."

"Sounds about right," Finn said, winking at Devon.

"Shawn has been given a chance to lead a special project for the Green Mountain Conservancy in Battleboro for a year. We're moving there right after the holidays, and Maura is taking over Jake & Friends while we're gone."

"And living in their place while our own house is being renovated," Maura leaned over to add.

"That's fabulous! Pass on my congratulations to Shawn—and congrats to you, too, of course."

"We may or may not see you at the tree lighting tonight, depending on how much we still have to do for tomorrow. But I wanted to remind you to check on the animals. They'll be in the barn, so we just want to make sure they're all okay. Shep will be there, too, with Roger. We'll feed them before heading to the church."

"No problem, Maddie. All the best for tomorrow."

She gave a thumbs-up and continued on down the street.

Devon heard Finn sigh. "What?"

"I'm happy for her and Shawn. They went through a rough patch for a few years, and suddenly last summer, everything came together for them."

The exchange between the three friends reminded Devon that she hadn't kept up most of the friendships formed during her time with Ellen and Ted. When she'd left the foster home at fifteen to live with Dan, she'd cut off practically all ties to those foster years. Except for her annual Christmas card and a note advising Ellen and Ted of Dan's passing, there was little contact between them. She wondered what it would be like to be connected to the same group of people your whole life.

Before heading to the B and B, they made a brief stop at the post office adjoined to the bakery. "I may as well collect the mail while we're here," Finn said and ducked inside.

Devon waited on the pavement, gazing through

Tasty Delights' front window at the Christmas baked goods. She realized that Finn hadn't finished what he'd been about to say before being interrupted by the Stuart sisters. She was about to mention the lapse when he exited the post office with some mail. He was staring at an official-looking envelope that, as Devon came up beside him to see, was addressed to Roxanne. He looked up, his lips pursed, and said, "This is probably what Roxanne's been waiting for—the divorce papers for her to sign."

"Good news or…?"

"She's been expecting this, so no surprise. But the timing isn't good, you know? Christmas and all the fun events she and Kaya are looking forward to." He tapped the envelope against his hand. "This…this is going to be a hard reminder of everything both of them have lost."

"True. But she and Kaya have you and your mother to show them that the one thing that hasn't changed, and won't, is your family's love."

Finn pulled her into his arms. "To heck with grapevines and gawkers," he murmured, lowering his face to kiss the top of her head.

THEY MADE IT to the tree lighting with mere minutes to spare. Finn thought he was accustomed to the change in pace at the Manor since Roxanne and Kaya moved back, but now he was beginning to see that the pace was faster the past few days, sometimes even frenetic. Like the delivery and con-sumption of pizza for supper, followed by Kaya's recitation of the Christmas list she'd prepared to give to Santa Saturday morning. "And can you still come, Devon?" she'd asked a bit anxiously.

Kaya's concern probably stemmed from her mother's silence during the meal. His niece was no doubt picking up on the change in Roxanne's mood since Finn had handed her the manila enve-lope. Devon was right when she'd said the family would bolster them, but he still felt helpless, want-ing to do more than pass on meaningless advice.

Their moods had lifted by the time the five of them headed toward the church and the tree light-ing. Kaya ran ahead while Roxanne and Marion walked arm in arm, their heads bent together in quiet conversation.

"Is there a countdown or something?" Devon asked as they approached the knots of people min-gling and gathering on the sidewalk, the church driveway and, for those who arrived early, around the tree itself, cordoned off with red velvet ropes.

"I think so. Usually, Reverend Higgins gives a brief blessing to remind us what Christmas is supposed to mean, and then someone is given a megaphone to do the countdown. The chosen per-son varies, but this year, Ashley Watson—Betty and Ed's teenaged daughter—has the honor."

"That's a lovely touch. Will anyone else from the family be there?"

"Not Betty, but I'm guessing Ed and Scott will be." Finn paused. "That reminds me, I need to confirm Scott's hike with Luke Danby over the holidays." He suddenly took in Devon's expression. "What is it?"

"I was thinking how involved you are with so many people here and with all the events and activities in the community. Does it ever get to be too much?"

There was enough moonlight to see the worry in her eyes. "Sometimes," he admitted, "but I take breaks if I need to. And..." He hesitated to say what he was actually thinking at that moment. Was it too soon? Was this the right place?

"And?" Her smile suggested she had an inkling of what he wanted to say.

"If I had someone at my side, you know, to raise my spirits when they flag or boost my ego now and then, I'd be okay."

"Just okay?"

He smiled at her teasing grin and was about to tell her he'd be the happiest and luckiest man in Maple Glen, when a young voice rose above the chatter of the crowd. "Ten, nine, eight..."

The rest of the night rushed forward in a collage of sound, light and laughter that Finn knew he'd never forget. Not simply because the woman he'd always dreamed of was holding his hand throughout, but because he was filled with the heady knowledge that the small glen where he'd grown up was the best place in the world. Now that he'd found Devon Fairchild, he also knew he'd never want to be anywhere else or with anyone else.

Eventually, the evening came to an end. Roxanne and Kaya left the reception at the community center first, followed by Marion, who'd insisted she was quite capable of walking home by herself. Finn and Devon took their time. It seemed that most of Maple Glen had met Devon already—because some woman Finn didn't even recognize approached Devon to tell her that her cookies were delicious and asked if she could have the recipe. After a couple of glasses of mulled cider and too many pieces of shortbread, Finn suggested they go home.

They held hands on the way, and Finn was hoping everyone would be tucked inside so that he and Devon could spend some time alone, either in front of a cozy fire in the living room or stargazing from the veranda. But a premonition of bad news hit the instant they walked through the front gate and he saw a car parked behind his truck.

Two people were standing on the darkened porch, and Finn stopped to try to identify from their stances what was happening. They suddenly turned around and Finn swore under his breath.

Roxanne. And next to her, Leo.

CHAPTER NINETEEN

DEVON COULD SEE why rescue and emergency work was the perfect fit for Finn. His face was impassive and his voice quiet and calm as he told Leo perhaps he could come back in the morning for a chat. But his tightened jaw was the giveaway, she thought.

Leo took a few seconds to respond. "Fine. Kaya said she's going to the Rutland mall to see Santa and asked if I'd come, too. What time should I get here?"

"We'll meet you there," Finn said. He looked at Roxanne. "What time?"

"Her appointment with Santa is at ten."

"Ten it is." Finn turned to Leo again. "See you then."

He glanced at Devon and nodded to the door. *My cue*, she figured, as she murmured a good-night, and they moved around Roxanne and Leo to go inside.

When Finn closed the door behind him, he said, "Why don't you go up to your room? I'm going to stick around down here until he goes, then maybe have a word with Roxanne."

"Are you concerned for her? Is she afraid of him?"

"No, no. Not afraid at all. That's not the problem. She's always given in to him and doesn't realize how completely untrustworthy he is."

"Finn—" she hoped he'd take this the right way "—I'm sure Roxanne is perfectly capable of handling her ex, but you made the right call. She looked relieved when you suggested he meet her and Kaya at the mall rather than come back here."

"I don't want my mother to have to put up with him. He cost her a lot of money, bailing him out of gambling debts."

"I get that you want to save her from having to see him, but essentially, Leo is Roxanne's problem."

Finn wheeled around from peering out the front door's small window. His eyes flashed. "Not really, Devon. Collateral damage, you know? His exploits and behavior have affected all of us, not only my sister. Someone needs to give him the message that he's not wanted here."

This was a Finn she hadn't seen, though there'd been glimpses of his tendency to watch over his family since her first day at the Manor. Her work experience had taught her that adult members of families needed strategies to deal with situations much like this one with Leo tonight. But how to convince Finn that his mother and sister could manage their own lives?

"I was hoping we'd have some time alone," she said, placing her hand on his forearm as she looked up at him. "To talk about Christmas a little bit. I want to pick up some gifts for your family, and maybe you could give me some ideas."

The twitch at the corner of his mouth told her he saw through her ploy. "Sure." He shrugged. "In there?" He gestured to the living room.

"Great. Too late for a fire, I guess?" She headed for the sofa and turned on the table lamp next to it.

He hovered by the front door a minute longer, which made her smile. Finally, he joined her, taking a chair opposite the window. *So he can monitor from in here*, she guessed, though the darkness hid the couple. "First," she said, "is Kaya."

Finn's gaze shifted from the window to her. He seemed confused at first but clued in quickly. "Oh, right. She's still in her unicorn phase. Anything to do with unicorns would be fine."

Devon tried to recall what had been on the list of items Kaya had read out over supper, but her attention had been on Finn and his serene face, enjoying his family. "Okay. Guess I might have to confer with Roxanne about unicorn stuff, then." She studied him as she spoke, noticing the way he leaned forward in the chair, squinting against the reflection of the lamp to see better onto the veranda. He clearly needed more distraction from whatever was happening outside.

"Finn," she said in a low voice that got him to

look at her, "at the lighting ceremony, just before the countdown began, you were about to tell me something." At his frown, she immediately wished she hadn't used that example. Did she really want to revisit that moment? Part of her whispered, *Yes, I do*, but she'd be venturing into territory she'd spent many years avoiding. Serious romance. Love. She was about to backtrack when he smiled and seemed about to stand up. Devon held her breath.

Then the front door opened and quietly closed, followed by soft footsteps going upstairs. Devon kept her eyes on Finn. She guessed he'd want to see who was coming in—if Roxanne was alone or not—but he stayed in his chair. After a moment he said, "Thanks for...for this." He waved a hand around the room and grinned. "I needed to decompress, and you gave me the opportunity."

"Anytime," she said, smiling at him, then added, "Can I go to bed now? 'Cause I'm exhausted." She yawned as she got to her feet. An escape upstairs, and from that gleam in his eyes, was her best option.

But he moved quickly to her side, folding her into his arms. "This is what I was looking forward to as we were walking home tonight," he whispered against her cheek. "To say that you are the person I want by my side."

There was no escaping now, and that was okay. Perhaps it was time to set aside her well-preserved avoidance of love. She shifted her face, raising it so her mouth was on his, and let herself drift into the timeless wonder of his kiss.

HE WAS A charmer all right, Devon thought, as she was officially introduced to Leo in front of the mall's Santa village. Holding her hand a second too long as he flashed a toothy smile, he said, "Kaya told me about you. The mystery woman found on the Appalachian Trail."

Devon withdrew her hand from his and managed a smile. "Not so much mysterious as lucky to have been found by Finn."

"Yes. The Glen's hero."

The shift in tone said far more than those three words.

Roxanne came up to them. "I thought you were going to take a photo of Kaya with Santa? There she is." She pointed to the throne display in the center of the village where Kaya was waving shyly, standing next to the mall Santa.

He shuffled off, pulling his cell phone out of his jacket pocket.

Roxanne didn't say anything, watching him as he caught Kaya's attention and started snapping photos. Then she heaved a loud sigh. "Kaya wants him to go with us to get hot chocolate. Do you mind? It's just that she hasn't seen him since we came back to the Glen, and she won't be seeing him at Christmas—at least not if I have anything to do with it." She gave a half smile. "I guess Finn has told you all about Leo."

"Not too much," Devon said, aiming for vagueness.

"And none of it good, I bet." Then she swiftly added, "Don't get me wrong. I'm appreciative of everything Finn has helped me with since we got here. He and Mom have been… Well, I only hope I can be as wonderful a parent as my mother has been to me and my brother. And as good a parent as I know Finn will be…when that day comes." She gave Devon a sly smile.

"Don't doubt yourself, Roxanne. Kaya seems to be a very well-adjusted seven-year-old," Devon said, ignoring the hint about her and Finn.

Roxanne looked across at Kaya, who was still chatting with Santa. "I think she is, though she had some problems when we first moved here. Missing her friends, her room at our old apartment, and yes, she missed her daddy." Roxanne's face clouded. "I don't, not anymore. But in spite of Leo's many flaws, he loves Kaya and—as far as he's capable— has been a good father. I won't poison her against him. When she's a teenager or even an adult, she'll figure him out."

Devon placed a hand on Roxanne's shoulder. "She will. Don't worry about her."

"He came here because he also received the papers to sign, and this is a last-ditch attempt to resurrect something that died a few years ago. Unfortunately, I didn't admit that to myself until last spring." Then she suddenly hugged Devon. "I'm so happy you came back to the Manor. Finn was Mr. Grumpy while you were at Bernie's place. You're good for him, you know. He's often so serious, always worried about us when he's the one *we* worry about. Ironic and silly, isn't it?"

Devon nodded. "I thought he planned to come to the mall with us."

"He was going to, but Mom persuaded him against it. She was worried he might intervene or spoil Kaya's last few hours with Leo. Personally, I think she's the parent he inherited the rescue gene from. Anyway, you are the perfect person to tag along with us. Not to mention the best woman Finn could have saved on the Long Trail."

"I think I was the *only* woman he saved…that day at least." Devon felt tears welling up.

"Perhaps, though it is amazing, isn't it? That you decided to hike on a day that was forecast to be stormy and that you used such an unknown access point as the Glen."

Devon forced a shrug. How much did Roxanne know? Finn planned to tell his mother that morning, but she'd seen him speaking quietly to Roxanne in the living room before they left to meet Leo. But, no, he wouldn't have told his sister without checking with her first.

Kaya came running up to them then, followed by Leo, and the topic was dropped. Devon decided to let them have the rest of the outing to themselves. "If you don't mind, Kaya, I have some shopping to do, so I'll meet up with you and your mom at the car, okay? In an hour?" She looked at Roxanne.

Roxanne gave a grateful smile and, cajoling a slightly disappointed Kaya with the promise of a special cookie and hot chocolate, headed toward the food court with her daughter and ex.

Devon didn't mind if Roxanne knew her story, but she'd thought a lot through the night about her past and her future. Burying those items had been a token gesture, but it actually symbolized her desire to put the past behind her, to seal up her old self, the one afraid of being hurt. Now she could finally continue her life simply as Devon Fairchild, a person shaped to some degree by what happened but mostly by the encouragement and love of her brother, as well as the auxiliary people in her life back then. Ellen and Ted, along with the social worker who initiated the process to change their names.

If Finn wants me to be part of his life in Maple Glen—and I hope he does—I want a life unmarked by what happened to Chloe and Billy Morrison. She wanted that former life to be buried forever, like the treasures in the hollow tree.

FINN HAD EXPECTED SURPRISE, shock or amazement when he told his mother Devon's story, but not tears. The last time he'd seen her cry was at the medical appointment regarding his father's Alzheimer's diagnosis.

"They're tears of happiness, Finn. I'm struggling to absorb all this. The coincidence, if that's what it is," she'd said.

She was still asking questions when Devon arrived home with Roxanne and Kaya. There was an awkward moment when Roxanne might have realized something was amiss with Marion, but fortunately, Kaya was in an elevated mood, fed by the morning's excitement. The focus shifted to her then while Finn had a chance to take Devon aside. He wanted to tell her about his mother's response, though she'd seen Marion's beaming smile when she walked in the door. Even more, he wanted to get the lowdown on Leo.

"Roxanne said he's going back to New Jersey today. She said he got the message about turning up here unexpectedly, but she also promised him she'd consider more visits with Kaya after he signs the papers," Devon said when they were alone in the kitchen.

He nodded, lips pursed. "Good, and thanks for going with them after all. I'm glad she wasn't alone to deal with any undue pressure on his part. He can be both charming and persuasive."

"I think Roxanne's not taken in by him anymore, and I also think she's very happy that you let her handle him by herself."

He managed a faint laugh. "Um, I have a feeling you were involved in that decision, Devon Fairchild, so thank you. I'd have hated for our Christmas to be ruined by some kind of scene, either from Leo or—I have to admit—from me." He swiped his hand across his face and sighed. "I guess I need to work on some bad habits."

"You don't need to change anything about yourself, Finn," she murmured. "I like you just the way you are."

"Like?" he quipped.

"Not only like," she said, her face solemn, "but—"

"Devon!" Marion exclaimed as she breezed into the kitchen. She crossed the room and hugged her. "I'm still trying to understand it all. The incredible coincidence of that little girl who sat in this very room all those years ago clutching on to her older brother. I've wondered through the years what happened to that child, and now…here you are." Marion shook her head in disbelief. "I only wish Lewis could understand what I plan to tell him when we visit him next."

Finn noticed her tear up and was about to put his arms around her when Devon did just that. Roxanne and Kaya burst into the room then, and although his sister cast a questioning look at her mother and Devon gazing silently into each other's eyes, she didn't comment. Finn was grateful not to have to produce an explanation. Roxanne should know at some point, he figured, when Devon was comfortable with that.

Checking the time, he realized he'd promised to help supervise the Ping-Pong tournament at the community center. "I'm due at the tournament," he said.

"Coaching?" Roxanne teased.

"I doubt our team would want that. Referee and general problem solver will be more like it. You're welcome to tag along, Devon." Her face didn't register delight, so he quickly added, "Unless you'd rather hang out here."

"Thanks...um...but I have some Chicago business to take care of, so this afternoon would be a good opportunity to do that."

He knew not to ask what that business might be in front of his family, but he hoped it was connected to taking a longer holiday or even something more permanent. "Okay, well, I'll see you when I'm finished. It may be late, Mom, but before dinner."

"That's fine. We womenfolk will tackle that. And because the bazaar is tomorrow and we will all be far too tired to cook, I've planned our Sunday roast for today."

"But it's Saturday," Kaya protested.

"Yes, dear," Marion said, laughing. "It's good to change things up a bit, don't you think?"

Finn took Devon by the hand as he went to get his coat from the hall closet. "Maybe we can have some alone time before dinner. Or—" he had a sudden thought "—when I'm supposed to check on the donkeys later tonight. You up for joining me then?"

"I wouldn't miss it." She moved close enough for him to kiss her on the cheek, then said, "Have fun at Ping-Pong."

THREE HOURS LATER, after a successful tournament and hearty dinner, Finn was driving along Church Street with Devon at his side, when he saw that the Shady Nook B and B was all lit up. A bouquet of helium balloons bobbed in the night air from the porch pillar. "I'm not hearing the sounds of revelry," Finn remarked, slowing down.

"I imagine it's lively inside, though," Devon said.

Spotting a large sign posted on the B and B front lawn, he pulled over to the curb and rolled down his window. Devon leaned across to read along with him. Someone had sketched two cartoon donkeys standing side by side in a field with a speech bubble extending from one of their mouths:

They finally got the message, but it took a team of us to do it.

"Very good," she said, laughing. "Do you know who made the sign?"

"Not sure, but I've got a hunch. I noticed Ashley Watson and Luke Danby sneaking off to work in one of the offices during the tournament today. Their excuse was that they'd promised to tabulate scores, but there'd been a lot of giggling between them."

"I haven't met them yet. Maybe tomorrow, at the bazaar."

"They're great kids. You'll like them." He drove the truck back to the right side of the road.

"Is there anyone in the Glen who's…well… *unlikeable*?"

He had to laugh at that. "I'm sure there's someone, but no one I can name at the moment. People here generally get along most of the time. When everyone lives so close together, you learn to make concessions." Then he remembered something. "At least, that's how things usually work, but not always."

"What do you mean?"

"There are a couple of families here who live side by side at that bend in the county road, before we get to the Stuart and Danby farms, and for several years, they've been involved in—" he searched for the right word "—a feud over their property lines."

"Why haven't I heard of this before tonight?"

Finn glanced at her. "Not sure. Maybe the rest of the village is in denial about it," he quipped.

"Reluctant to admit Maple Glen isn't the utopia everyone claims it to be?"

"Maybe." As they approached the last street in the village proper, Finn slowed down again. "So this is where Church Street turns into the county road, and if you look out your side, you can see two houses there." He pointed to the right. One house was lit up with strings of Christmas lights, but the other was in darkness. "See that wide space between the two properties? It was once a shared lane. I'm not sure if you can see it in the dark, but there's a tall fence running down the center."

"Okay. So what's the big deal?"

"Before the fence was erected, the lane provided easy access to the rear of both properties."

"Then…"

"Jerry Bower, and his father before him, had a maple syrup production facility that was a family business for a couple of generations. Unfortunately, the business went bust several years ago. I don't know all the details, but there was a falling out between the Bowers and their neighbors, Tom and Inez Costa, who used to live in the house that's all lit up. I think the feud centered around an acreage of maple trees the Bowers owned right behind their place, and that was sold to Tom Costa. They recently handed the property over to their daughter, and I heard she wants to set up a business—a farm shop of some kind—at the rear of the house."

"And the problem is…?"

"The fence makes the lane inaccessible for both properties. The Bowers have access to their back acreage from the other side, so the fence isn't a problem for them, but the other side of the Costa property is flanked by Otter Creek. There's just enough space between the creek and the house for cars or farm machinery. Using the lane would definitely facilitate any construction project, but it seems that fence isn't going to come down anytime soon. Not as long as Jerry and his wife, Gert, own the place."

"That's a tough situation," Devon said. "And must be especially hard at this time of year when most people make an effort to maintain that... you know... Christmas spirit." After a pause, she murmured, "Dan and I used to joke that Christmas was for the kind of family portrayed in those holiday TV movies. Not the foster one we had."

"But you don't feel that way any longer, do you?"

The last streetlight in the village illuminated her smile. "No, Finn, I don't."

"Good," he finally said, and stepped on the accelerator, heading for Jake & Friends.

CHAPTER TWENTY

DEVON WAS THINKING about neighbors feuding at Christmas, a time when families and communities usually connect. That thought led to Maddie and Shawn and what a beautiful time of year it was to have a wedding. "Who all was invited to Maddie and Shawn's wedding, do you know?"

"Mom said Shawn's parents drove up from Florida. They'll be staying at the B and B."

"This weather must be a shock to their system." The temperature had dropped since dusk, and more snow was in the forecast.

"I'm sure, though they lived here up until Shawn went off to college. Besides their immediate families, Mom said they invited Walter, too."

"I'm not surprised," she said. "He seems to be involved in a lot of people's lives in Maple Glen."

"He is, but not in any obvious way. He's just… how to put it? Just *there* for people. Available to listen and to help if help is wanted."

That was a good summation of the man, Devon thought. Knowing exactly *when* to help was a gift.

She'd been thinking about gifts since Christmas shopping in the mall while the others went to grab something to eat. The purchases she'd made were basic ones—she'd pretty much had to guess what might appeal to Roxanne and Marion. Kaya had been the easiest to shop for. So far, she hadn't bought anything for Finn, but she wanted him to know that she loved him. She'd been on the verge of telling him in the kitchen earlier in the day before Marion came in to hug her. An official welcome to the McAllister family, she'd murmured to Devon while they were close together. *No matter what happens between you and my son.*

Obviously, the change between Devon and Finn the past several days had been observed by all in the household. Even Kaya had been giving them curious looks, trying to work out what was going on. Devon smiled. *This may be the family you were referring to, Dan.*

Her brother had been on her mind all afternoon. While Finn was at the tournament, she took the opportunity to email Dan's partner, Mike, with her decision. Yes, she'd go with his plan and sell her half of the company as well. It was what Dan would have recommended, she told herself, if he'd been able to meet and get to know the McAllisters— and Finn. If the selling price met or surpassed the offer, she'd be a fairly wealthy woman. One who could give gifts.

Finn turned off the county road onto the driveway at Jake & Friends. Except for lights at the barn and one at the side of the house, the place was in darkness.

"Want to stay here in a warm truck while I check on the animals?" he asked.

"No, I want to come and see them, too."

He smiled at her and turned off the engine.

Devon's breath plumed into the frosty air. Clouds hid the stars she'd seen last night on the way back to the Manor after the tree lighting. Now, inhaling the earthy warmth of hay and animals from where she stood inside the barn was like a dose of summer. After a few seconds, she heard the shuffling of hooves and donkeys snickering as they realized humans had infiltrated their cozy haven. The sudden yipping from the rear of the barn raised the tolerance level of the donkeys, and they began to stamp their hooves on the barn floor.

A black-and-white dog streaked toward Devon and Finn, who murmured, "Shep, here, boy." He bent to scratch the dog behind the ears and utter soothing sounds that calmed the donkeys at the same time. Devon's heart swelled. How she loved this man.

They walked between the two rows of stalls, only four of which were occupied by the donkeys. Devon paused at each stall, patting noses and telling each animal that their keepers would be back tomorrow bright and early. Finn checked water levels and made sure each trough had enough hay.

"Shep seems to be sleeping in here, next to Roger," he commented, peering into the last stall. "This is where he hangs out most of the time, right next to his best buddy. Walter brought the two of them to the farm about the end of June. If Maddie and Maura hadn't taken them in, the animals would have been separated, which would have been a tragedy."

Devon shivered, thinking how close she and Dan came to being split up when potential adoptive parents wanted a little girl but not a preteen boy. That time, they'd been rescued by their social worker. When Devon went back to Chicago to finish settling Dan's estate and deal with the company's sale, she'd search through her brother's papers to find the documents they'd received from child welfare after Dan turned eighteen. She decided to write the woman a letter, thanking her for all she'd done back then.

"Everything okay?" Finn asked, coming up to her after settling Shep down for the night.

"Yes," she said, "but I'm ready to get into that warm truck again." When he sighed, she wrapped her arms around him. "What is it?"

"Just thinking how perfectly this day is ending," he whispered. "I love you, Devon. There's no one else in the whole world I'd want to spend the rest of my life with."

"That sounds like a pledge." Her tease choked on the lump in her throat.

"It *is* a pledge. To be yours forever." He tightened his hold on her.

"I think you already are, Finn McAllister."

FOR THE FIRST time since Devon had stayed at the Manor, Finn's mother wasn't in the kitchen making coffee when she went downstairs in the morning. In fact, the kitchen was deserted and she paused in the doorway, wondering if something had happened.

Last night before going to bed, Marion had told Devon that she was heading to the community center at eight sharp to help set up for the bazaar. "Come whenever you feel like it, dear," she'd added, glancing from Devon to Finn, who had been kneeling in front of the fireplace in the living room. "If you want to sleep in."

Devon had strained to keep a neutral smile on her face. Finn had his back to her, but she thought she heard him clear his throat. *Stifling a laugh?* she'd wondered.

It was only seven thirty, and Devon didn't think Marion would have left already, but the door to her bedroom was ajar, so she must have decided to go in early. Roxanne's and Kaya's doors were closed, and as Devon walked past Finn's room, the last before the staircase landing, she noted it was empty, too. She smiled, replaying last night's hug and cuddle session while they made plans for after the holidays. She hadn't yet told him her news about the sale of Dan's company or her ideas for the windfall she'd eventually receive. Plenty of time for all that, she'd reasoned. Why distract him from holding her in his arms?

She began making coffee, thinking at some point Finn might show up. Footsteps overhead signaled that Roxanne and Kaya were up, so Devon found the boxes of cereal everyone liked and set them on the table with bowls and cutlery. She was struck for a moment at how automatically she did all this, as if she'd been living in the house for months rather than a mere ten days. So much had happened that she felt as though she'd been here a lifetime. *And maybe I will be, too.* The idea was both exhilarating and frightening at the same time. She'd only lived in cities her whole life, and recent events—especially the Glen grapevine—emphasized how small places like Maple Glen could seem.

Kaya ran into the kitchen, followed more sedately by Roxanne, who was looking at her cell phone. She glanced up, saw Devon getting coffee mugs out of the cupboard and said, "Oh, I thought you might still be sleeping. Your door wasn't open all the way, so…"

"Guess what, Devon?" Kaya burst out. "Uncle Finn is taking me to get our Christmas tree this afternoon after the bazaar."

"That's great," Devon said, smiling, but her attention shifted to Roxanne's frown. "Is there a problem? I noticed Finn has gone somewhere."

"Yeah. Mom says he and Theo Danby were called out on an emergency in the middle of the night. Someone in the Glen had a massive heart attack, and I guess it was quicker to get my brother and Theo on the scene than wait for emergency people from Wallingford and Rutland."

"Do you know who it was?"

"Mom didn't say. But she did say she wouldn't be at the community center until later and asked if we could go in her place and help organize tables. I assume she's with the family of whoever had the heart attack." Roxanne went to the counter to pour herself a coffee. "Thanks for making this, Devon." Then she noticed the table set for a quick breakfast. "Thanks for that, too. Kaya, go sit down and start on your cereal. We all have to help out this morning." Turning back to Devon, she gave a rueful smile. "So much for plans, right? I was going to make waffles for Kaya before heading over, but now that Mom can't be there until later..."

"I can go. My ankle is much better now, thanks to the brace."

Roxanne smiled. "I should be used to emergencies after living here for the last six months. Be prepared to see any of your plans go down the drain, so to speak, cause Finn gets called out a fair bit." She laughed. "Oops, I think I'm presuming too much here." She patted Devon's arm as she passed her to get to her chair. "None of us wants you to ever leave, so be warned! Mornings like this will probably happen many times in your future. If you decide to stick around, that is."

"I'll keep that in mind," Devon said, smiling. She sat down and was pouring some granola into a bowl when Kaya said, "My daddy said you were pretty."

Devon looked immediately at Roxanne, standing and drinking her coffee behind Kaya's chair.

Roxanne's eyes widened and she grimaced at Devon. "Oh, you know Daddy, Kaya. He thinks all women are pretty."

"Maybe, but he was asking me about you, Devon. He said your last name—Fairchild—means a child who is pretty 'cause that's what 'fair' means, and I agreed with him that was a good name for you. But then I remembered your other name, you know the one on the back of the photograph of the house you lived in when you were little." She chewed on a mouthful of cereal.

Devon sat perfectly still, though she suspected what was coming next.

Kaya swallowed and said, "Morris or something." Her face screwed up in thought. "Morrison!"

"Kaya, you need to mind your own business," Roxanne reprimanded. "Lots of people have more than one last name. I do!"

"I know that, Mommy. Daddy was just interested, that's all. Why are you making such a big deal out of it?"

Devon felt her heart rate slow down. Kaya was right about making a big deal out of nothing. She wondered then if Roxanne knew the truth but decided from her expression that she did not.

"Kids," Roxanne muttered, shrugging her shoulders. Then in a lower voice, added, "And ex-husbands. Both can be a little indiscreet."

The moment passed and Devon felt herself relaxing. Today was going to be hectic, but in a good way. She finished her granola and her coffee, then got up to help Roxanne clear dishes before they headed to the community center.

FINN WAS BEAT. When he turned into the driveway, he saw that all the cars were gone. Setting up for the bazaar, he remembered. Everyone would be there, except perhaps his mother, because she'd driven to the Bower place as soon as she heard the news. That was the Maple Glen way and, especially, Marion McAllister's. He wondered how Devon would respond in a similar situation. She definitely had empathy for others, but helping others in the community when there was a need demanded a kind of openness. After living in a big city for so long, how difficult would it be for her to drop all her walls?

He reached for the portable defibrillator in the

back seat as he got out of the truck. He figured Devon was at the bazaar, too, yet felt a tinge of disappointment that she wasn't there to give him a hug. That thought brought a small chuckle. If she were here, she'd reassure him big men needed hugs occasionally. Or something to that effect, he decided, as he went into the silent, empty house.

The Wallingford dispatcher had sent the alarm at about 4:00 a.m., figuring Finn would be on the scene quicker than the other emergency teams. After he hung up, he impulsively decided to call Theo. When he heard Theo's groggy voice, he felt bad for asking him to go out. The guy had been partying at a wedding the night before, but he was a professional and rallied before the call ended. On the way there, Finn had been thinking how ironic, in a bad way, that Gert Bower should have a heart attack the very night he'd told Devon the story of the feud. That sad situation was on Finn's mind all the way back to the Manor, hours later.

He stood beneath the hot shower, felt the tension easing and wondered why some people became obsessed or angry over things that were either beyond their control or, worse, trivial. No explanations or answers came to mind by the time he was dressed and heading for the kitchen, where he found, to his relief, the coffee maker still on.

He was on his second cup and making a third piece of toast and peanut butter when the front door opened. Footsteps moved along the hall, and there she was, standing in the doorway, her coat and hat still on.

"I heard what happened. At the community center. I was so shocked, especially after what you told me last night and—oh, Finn, I'm so sorry."

She moved into his arms and he held her tight, feeling the despair of his failure to save Gert Bower easing.

CHAPTER TWENTY-ONE

DEVON KNEW FINN needed to talk. When she finally let go of him, she poured more coffee for them both and said, "Let's go talk in the living room, where it's sunnier."

He took his coffee and followed her along the hall to the front room. Sun streamed through the big bay window, though Devon noticed large puffy clouds gathering on the horizon. She sat on the sofa, but Finn paced, coffee mug in one hand while he ran his other hand through his damp hair. Devon figured the adrenaline surge from hours ago was still coursing through him.

He outlined the entire night, and she knew not to interrupt with a single question. He ended his recounting of the events in a voice heavy with emotion. "Theo and I knew as soon as we walked into the room that there wasn't much hope. We tried our best, followed all the protocols…it just wasn't enough." Then he turned his back to her, drinking coffee.

Giving himself some time, she thought. She saw

his shoulders rise and fall before he faced her again.

"I'm fine," he said, turning around. "There have been other losses of life in my career, so I've been through this before. But there's always those first minutes, or longer, when I need to process what happened. Figure out if there was anything I could have done differently."

"But Theo was with you, too," Devon pointed out. "And from what you've told me, it sounds like there was very little either of you could have done." She hoped he'd accept that Gert Bower's life hadn't depended on him alone.

He set his coffee mug on a table and sat next to her, clasping her hand in his. "I know that. It's simply a matter of allowing myself to decompress without blaming myself. Know what I mean?"

"I do. When Dan died, I blamed myself for not giving more time to him those months after his diagnosis was confirmed. I kept thinking he'd be fine, that eventually the super physically fit Dan I'd always known would return." His hand squeeze helped stop her tears. After a moment, she went on, "The news was already spreading when Roxanne, Kaya and I got to the community center. Does Mr. Bower have family to call?"

"There's a son, but he's in the military and stationed somewhere overseas. Jerry's going to call him when he feels more composed. Mom showed up with one of her friends to see what they could do to help. Theo and I would have gone to ask the neighbors to come over, but...well..."

"I guess not, considering what's happening between them. I wonder if this will change anything."

"How do you mean?"

"If it might thaw the situation a bit. You know, help resolve the problem."

Finn's sigh told her he doubted that. "Been going on a long time." Finally, he added, "I'm sure you're needed at the community center, but thanks for coming back, Devon."

His smile was all the appreciation she needed. When he left for Wallingford to finish his report about the night's events, Devon drove back to the community center. Her mind was flooded with fragments of Finn's account along with images of his face as he spoke. She remembered what Roxanne had told her that morning. That emergencies and night callouts would always be part of a life with Finn. Although she felt she'd handled his reaction well and had given him the support he needed, would she always be able to do that? Would it ever become too much for her?

She remembered the time when she was about nine or ten that she'd asked Dan to tell her again how they were found because she couldn't recall all the details. He'd been engrossed in a book and had looked up with an impatient expression and said, *That's all in the past. I don't want to keep talking about it.* She'd gradually learned to stifle any further questions or concerns about their old lives. Did she want that to happen between her and Finn?

The community center was buzzing, people bustling to set up tables, signs and displays. Devon stood at the entrance to the large room, scanning the crowd for Roxanne, Kaya or even Marion, if she'd returned from the Bower home. A voice at her side got her attention, and she swung around to see the owner of the bakery, Sue Giordano, standing next to her.

"Shame about Gert Bower," she said. "Some of us are taking turns going over to the house 'cause no one knows when Jerry's son will be able to get home. And you must be proud of Finn, going out in the dead of night and doing what he does."

"Um, well, he's a professional, so I guess you could say he was doing his job" was all that Devon could think to say. The comment about being proud of him was something she decided to ignore, at least to someone who wasn't a family member.

Sue pursed her lips. "Finn is a good guy. Everyone in the Glen loves him."

Was there a message in that, Devon wondered? Or was she overreacting?

"Anyhow," Sue went on, "we're also happy he's met someone like you. I mean…assuming you and he… Oh, I guess I'm blathering here."

She took a deep breath. "Okay, I better get to my table. Oh, and if you see Marion, tell her the order for Christmas will be ready the morning of the twenty-fourth. Kringle." She smiled and walked toward the far side of the room.

Relax, Devon told herself. *She means well and is just being friendly, despite the fact that she seems to know stuff about you and the McAllisters.* Then she chuckled. *Well, that they like kringle anyway.* She spotted Kaya among the crowd and headed toward her.

"Hi, Devon! Come and see our table." She grabbed Devon's hand and led her to a table near the front windows.

Roxanne was setting out articles of used baby and toddler clothing, along with toys and books. She smiled at their approach and said, "Mom has been storing this stuff in the attic for ages, so I figured this would be a good place to dispense with it."

Kaya was browsing through the books. "Not this one, Mommy!" She held up a picture book.

Roxanne grinned at Devon. "I'm worried most of this will go back to the attic if Kaya has anything to do with it." Turning to Kaya, she said, "You can take one thing from this table. Only one!" Then to Devon, "Has Finn got home yet? I saw you leaving a while ago, right after we arrived."

"He was home, but now he's gone to write up his report."

"Right. I'm glad you went back, Devon. He probably needed to talk to someone, and unfortunately, Mom and I don't always get to hear what's on his mind."

"Maybe because he hates to burden you with... you know...more problems?"

Roxanne shrugged. "Maybe, but he ought to give us more credit. We are entirely capable of handling serious emotional things."

She continued unpacking, dropping the subject. Devon realized this was an issue in the family that had yet to be settled and hoped they weren't counting on her to do that. She hung around for a bit before deciding to wander the aisles and check out the items for sale. Maybe there'd be something for Finn's Christmas present. At least, some quirky, perhaps amusing, item. As she walked between the rows of tables, she gathered enough snippets of conversation to realize that the Bowers were on everyone's mind.

She rounded one row and started on the next aisle when she sighted a familiar face. The woman she'd been speaking to the other day at the cookie exchange, but she'd forgotten her name. As Devon drew near, the woman caught her eye, but the smile she gave was hesitant. *Maybe she can't remember my name, either*, Devon thought. She saw two children, a boy and a girl, sitting cross-legged under the table reading books. Devon smiled. That was one way to keep track of your kids.

"Hi," Devon said. "I like your makeshift play-room." She gestured to the table. Then she bent down and said to the children, "This is a cool fort, you've got. Is there room under there for a grown-up?"

The girl, who looked younger, giggled while the boy mumbled, "No, kids only."

As Devon stood up, the woman shrugged. "Sorry about that. He's a bit out of sorts this morning."

"He's a kid and entitled to moods."

"What I think, too." She held out a hand. "I'm Leni. We met at the cookie exchange."

"Devon Fairchild."

"Right! The woman staying with the McAllis-ters and found—"

"With a sprained ankle on the Long Trail. Yes."

Leni's smile was apologetic. "Sorry about that, too. You do get used to it if you stay here long enough. My problem is that I was gone for sev-eral years and am still readjusting, especially to the Glen grapevine." She glanced around at the groups of chatting people buying and sell-ing goods. "I guess you heard about Mrs. Bower since your...well...partner was one of the people who tried to save her."

"I did hear, early this morning. Do you know how her husband is doing?"

"Only through the grapevine. But I imagine

he's reeling from the shock." She stared down at the table and then, raising her head to Devon, said, "I'd have gone over if they'd asked, but no one did. I guess they were afraid to."

Devon frowned. "I'm not sure I understand."

"You don't have to keep talking to me if you'd rather not. Everyone else is giving me the cold shoulder today, so…"

"Uh, I'm really sorry, Leni, but I'm not sure what you're talking about." Devon said, confused.

"I live next door to the Bowers. I'm Tom and Inez's daughter… Leni Costa was my single name."

Devon glanced quickly around her, realizing only then that some people were staring at them and talking. "Aw, Leni," she murmured, and hugged her.

By NOON, Devon's ankle was throbbing and she knew she was ready for a break. Marion had arrived midmorning, and after a hushed update on how things were going at the Bower home, said, "There's a distant cousin coming from Burlington to stay until the son arrives." She and Marion stood next to Roxanne's table, chatting and persuading people to buy Marion's assortment of jams, chutneys and pickles.

"I spent all fall making these, just for today," she informed Devon.

They looked delicious and probably were, but

the idea of spending autumn, one of the most beautiful times of the year as far as Devon was concerned, making them was unappealing. Not that she couldn't cook. Dan always raved about her omelets. "Chef-worthy!" he used to exclaim. And she could probably produce some decent cookies for the annual exchange or ransack her condo for secondhand items to sell at a bazaar. But gazing around at the crowd, clearly enjoying every part of the event, Devon thought for the first time, *What would I do here in Maple Glen every day of the year? Devote myself to the community the way Marion has?* She couldn't see herself becoming such a public person, and yet, if it meant having a life here with Finn...

She was saved from having to finish that thought by the arrival of a tall handsome man who paused long enough at the door to chat to a couple of people while searching the room for someone. She raised an arm and waved, feeling a whoosh of relief flow through her. He headed toward her, stopping here and there to speak to people—probably giving them all the official response to the night's outcome—but keeping his eyes fixed on her all the way. Devon felt that all the other eyes in the room were on her as well, and she hoped he wouldn't kiss her.

He drew up close enough for that but must have caught Devon's body language as she folded her arms around her waist and stepped out of his reach. She thought she saw a slight grin at that but kept her distance.

"Finn, darling, you must be exhausted," Marion said when she finished wrapping two jars for a customer. "Why don't you go home for a nap?"

"I'm good, Mom. I see your jars are selling fast."

Marion shrugged. "Thank goodness, otherwise we'd be eating a lot of jams and pickles over the rest of the winter."

"I could handle that," he quipped. Then gazing down at Devon, he murmured, "Want to go for a bite to eat?"

Before she could reply, Kaya ran over from playing with some friends. "Uncle Finn, have you come to take me to get the tree?"

"Uh-oh." Finn looked at Devon and mouthed an "I'm sorry."

"That's okay." She turned to Kaya. "Can I come, too?"

"Yay! Please, Uncle Finn, can she?"

He was struggling not to laugh but gave Devon a wink and said, "I guess so."

SOMETHING WAS UP. Finn sneaked glances at Devon next to him in the pickup, while Kaya prattled away in the rear seat. She was too quiet for someone who'd wanted to go to the bazaar and barely replied to Kaya's many questions about what kind of tree they ought to get. He hoped she'd rally, because tonight he planned to ask her to marry him. He thought they'd take a late walk after dinner, check out the moon and stars…he'd bring a flask of hot chocolate, maybe spiked with a dash of brandy, and they could talk about their future together here in Maple Glen.

Now he wasn't so sure. If Kaya weren't with them, he'd ask her if something had happened at the bazaar, because she'd been her usual self before going back there. It couldn't have been the sad news about Gert Bower, because Devon had never met either Gert or Jerry.

The way she'd responded to his dark mood, rushing back just to comfort him, had confirmed she was the woman he wanted to spend the rest of his life with. She'd be there for him when he needed some comfort and he for her. Of that, he was certain. He couldn't think of a single thing he wouldn't do for her. Hopefully, there'd be a chance to talk after they picked out a tree and took Kaya back to the center.

There was a pop-up tree market on the outskirts of Wallingford that Finn thought was the best place to shop. He muttered to himself that he could have chosen one while on his way back from the fire hall an hour ago, but glancing in the rearview mirror at Kaya, her face beaming with excitement, he knew that would be breaking a promise, and he wouldn't ever do that to anyone in his family.

As he passed the Bower home, he noticed Devon

lean forward, staring out her window. "Jerry's okay," he assured her. "Some cousin is due this afternoon, and his son is apparently on the way from Germany. Should be here by late tomorrow maybe."

She turned his way, frowning. "Someone could have gone over and told the neighbors. They might have been surprised by their willingness to help."

"Well, I suppose, but like I said before when I first told you what happened, Theo and I figured we didn't want to…you know…get involved in anything. I mean…um—" he was stammering and not sure why "—sometimes things are simply best left as is."

Her frown deepened. "What does that even mean, Finn? 'Left as is'? Don't you think people should be given the chance to decide for themselves? I met Leni Costa at the bazaar—she's the woman I mentioned who was so friendly at the cookie exchange—and she was very upset. Not only about Mrs. Bower but also because people were talking about her! Making assumptions that her family wouldn't be upset about what happened. She told me she would have gone over right away if someone had come to tell them ."

Finn stifled a groan. Was this the cause of her mood? "People are upset now, Devon, but believe me, those feelings will pass. In a day or so, maybe less, folks will be speaking to her and her family again. That's the way it is here. Grudges aren't held for a long time." He kicked himself as soon as the words popped out.

"That's not what you were telling me the other night. You said they'd been feuding for years."

"In most cases, then."

She looked away again, but not before he saw that she didn't believe him. "The grapevine thing," she said, her voice low, "I don't like that one bit."

Finn checked the rearview mirror again. Kaya was still staring out the window, but he knew from experience that her hearing was excellent. He lowered his voice. "Maybe all of us make too much of it. It's become a village joke, really. A lot of people—my family included—laugh about it, but we avoid getting drawn in. We don't participate is what I'm saying."

She turned to him and said, "I know that, Finn. Your family isn't the problem."

"Then what *is* the problem?"

"I don't know. I just feel bad for Leni and her family. People probably blame them for indirectly causing the heart attack."

She was right about that, Finn thought. Someone at the bazaar had voiced that very opinion—that Gert's heart issues had been exacerbated by the feud. It was nonsense and he'd strongly dismissed the suggestion but guessed a similar sentiment was going around. He figured Devon, unconsciously or otherwise, linked the Glen grapevine with the negative media attention she endured as a kid and teenager. Yet why couldn't she understand that they were very different things? Not everyone in Maple Glen was drawn into the grapevine. People in the village represented the same cross-section as those in big cities, but the proximity to one another in a place of incredible natural beauty accounted for the differences between city and country.

He spotted the tree market ahead and began to slow down. "Here we are, Kaya."

She squealed, and for the first time since they'd left the center, Finn saw a very slight smile on Devon's face. If he was lucky, the outing might change the dark abyss Devon had apparently fallen into. Maybe his plans for the evening could still materialize. He hoped so. But a splinter of doubt punctured his expectations.

CHAPTER TWENTY-TWO

DEVON WISHED SHE hadn't asked to go tree shopping. On the way back to Maple Glen with a tall fir tree bobbing in the back of the truck and Kaya's satisfied smile, she figured she ought to have stayed at the Manor. Perhaps some time by herself away from the center might have tempered the disagreeable mood she'd sunk into and put the whole grapevine thing into perspective, which is what Finn had been attempting to do.

They hadn't spoken directly to one another since their disagreement about the Glen grapevine and its effect on situations like the Bower and Costa feud. Or so-called feud. Maybe the property dispute wasn't anything more than bad feelings, she reasoned, and the term *feud* had arisen thanks to the grapevine. When Finn pulled into the community center parking lot, she was tempted to say she'd go back to the Manor with him and the tree, but his face was closed up, letting nothing in, and she decided some time apart might be best.

Kaya hopped out of the back seat as soon as

he turned off the engine. "Thanks, Uncle Finn, for helping me pick out a super tree. I can hardly wait to decorate it tonight."

Devon watched her run inside, eager to tell her mother and grandmother about the tree. She envied that freedom from worry, thinking she hadn't been worry-free even at Kaya's age. Looking at Finn, she thought he was the most worry-free person she'd ever met. Sure, he had anxieties about his family and how they were doing, and he had a strong sense of duty and commitment. But she had a feeling he tried to diminish worries by analyzing them without emotion and then dealing with them.

"Um, thanks for the lift," she murmured as she opened the truck door and started to get out.

"Devon—"

She turned around and saw the turmoil in his eyes. She could have uttered some positive words then but decided to wait until later when they both had a chance to talk without interruption. Instead, she simply said goodbye and shut the truck door before he could stop her. Forcing herself not to look back, she marched toward the center's main door and, as she opened it, heard the truck roar off.

The place was teeming with people, and Devon jostled past new arrivals and those leaving. It was well past noon, and she wondered if she ought to see if either Marion or Roxanne wanted to be relieved for lunch. Personally, her appetite had disappeared with Finn's truck.

She stood for a moment, tracking the flow of people in the large room to see if Leni and her children had left. Perhaps she could take over their table so Leni and her kids could grab some lunch or have a break. About to enter the room, she was stopped by Sue Giordano, carrying two large baskets of baked goods.

"Devon!"

"Hi, Sue." The woman looked flustered, so Devon asked, "Want help with one of those?"

"No, thanks. They're big but not heavy." She paused to let a couple pass through the door. "But I need to tell you that someone is looking for you." Setting down one of the baskets on the floor, she took Devon by the elbow and moved off to the side, close to the hall leading to the offices. "I didn't know you had a brother. Dan is his name?"

Devon blinked, trying to make sense of Sue's last few words. Then she immediately thought, *The Glen grapevine.* How her brother's name got tangled up in it, she had no idea but told herself to stay calm. She cleared her throat and said, "Yes, I *did* have a brother."

Sue's smile vanished. "Oh, I'm so sorry, Devon. I didn't think to ask when she told me."

Devon was confused. "When who told you,

Sue? I don't understand. I just got back here after a little break and—"

"There's a woman here asking about you." Sue looked toward the doorway, raising her head as if to see above the crowd. "She's probably still inside, but I don't see her."

"Someone from Maple Glen?"

"No, no. I've never seen her before. Very professional-looking. Maybe in her midsixties? Does that ring a bell?"

"No." For one strange minute, Devon wondered if her boss had come to drag her back to work. She almost giggled at the idea but realized at once that she hadn't told her boss where she was, so...

"Want me to go look for her?"

"No, but do you know why she was looking for me?"

"Not exactly. But she told my friend Marianne that she knew you might be in Maple Glen, and she wanted to talk to you. She had a photograph, too."

Devon felt every cell in her body slow down. "A photograph?"

"Yep, of your brother from a newspaper article she had on her phone. Something about his company getting sold—to be honest, the print was too small for me to read. But there was a picture of him—your brother—Daniel Fairchild."

She hadn't seen any article about the company's sale, nor had she received a text from Mike about one. It had to be a reporter or journalist, but how did she track her down in Maple Glen? Would she ever escape her past and the media frenzy that had dogged it?

A wave of dizziness swept over her, and she reached for the doorjamb beside her.

"Are you okay?" Sue asked.

The concern in her voice helped calm Devon. She was leaping to conclusions here, assuming this unknown woman was a journalist.

"We thought she was an old friend of yours," Sue went on to say.

"We?"

"I was with a couple of other women when she came up to us and asked about you and then showed us that article on her phone, with the photo. She seemed to know a lot about you. Said she was an old friend, which is why we kind of went along with her. But then..."

"Then what?"

"She said you might be going by another name here and that's when we got suspicious. We couldn't say we didn't know you, 'cause we'd already admitted that, so we just said you weren't at the center and we didn't know where you'd gone." She took a breath. "Which was true."

A reporter accessing old news articles could have connected their former names with Maple Glen because that was the location where they'd been rescued by Walter Ingram. Yet how would someone know their new names? The dizziness gave way to nausea. "Um, I have to go, Sue. Thanks for telling me this and...um...if you see that woman again—"

"Mum's the word," she said, drawing an invisible line across her mouth. "But do you want me to tell Marion? Or maybe she's already heard what's going on from some other people."

"Please don't tell Marion. I...um... I'll talk to her later. Right now, I have to go." She swung around, pushing past newcomers on her way out.

Thoughts, ideas and suspicions vied for attention in her mind as she jogged toward the car park. Thank goodness she'd decided to drive herself that morning rather than go with Kaya and Roxanne. At the time, she'd done it so that she'd have a means to escape for some alone time with Finn. *So much for that*, she thought as she rounded the corner of the center and saw Walter Ingram standing by the end of his pickup, unloading boxes.

He looked up, startled at what he must have seen in her face. "Whoa!" He held out a palm to slow her down. "Everything okay, Devon? You seem upset."

Walter was the perfect person to encounter. When she could breathe enough to speak, she said, "There's a woman inside asking all these questions about me and Dan. But that's not all, Walter. She said I might be going by another name. I think she must be a reporter."

"Slow down, Devon. Are you sure this isn't just

some friend of yours from Chicago who knew you might be here?"

"No one knows I'm here in Maple Glen, Walter. Not a single person I know or work with. Not even Dan's former partner. We've been texting, but I never told him where I was."

"What makes you think this woman is a reporter?"

"Because she has a photo of my brother from this article about the sale of his company." At his puzzled frown, she explained, "I inherited Dan's half of a company he started in Chicago. His business partner, who owned the other half, and I just sold the business. I guess it made the news because of the buyer, but I didn't know there was an article about it."

Walter was shaking his head. "You're making a lot of leaps here, Devon. Sure, someone could connect Dan to you through the internet, but how would anyone learn your former name? Those documents are sealed."

A wild idea occurred. "Roxanne's husband, Leo, was in town on Friday. He was curious about me, and Kaya said he asked lots of questions." Devon took a breath. "The thing is, Kaya had seen a photo of mine, of the house Dan and I lived in when our parents were alive. She saw a name on the back of the photo and asked about it. I told her it was an old family name."

"Morrison."

She nodded.

"Okay. That's still a lot of conjecture. But here's what I suggest. I'm going inside to find this woman and get some information from her—directly. While I'm doing that, I think you ought to go somewhere nice and quiet and have a think. Or try to fit all this into some logical explanation, 'cause I'm darn certain there is one. Okay?"

She nodded. That was exactly what she needed. Time to put some perspective on the matter, as Walter implied.

"Then I'll text what to do when I get this information. Either come back 'cause it's all nothing or stay away until we get rid of her."

Devon almost giggled at his last phrase, picturing the crowd ganging up on some hapless woman.

He picked up a box from the end of the truck and began walking, turning back once to say, "Go!"

She ran for her car and was reversing it when she thought she saw someone come out the front door of the community center. Without checking who the person was, she shifted gears and shot out of the parking lot, turned right onto Church Street and headed out of Maple Glen.

FINN DIDN'T READ his mother's text. He stowed the tree on the veranda, untying its ropes to let the branches fall enough to be decorated later that evening. That is if anyone was in the mood for decorating. Even Kaya might not be if Devon wasn't around. He definitely wasn't in the mood.

He couldn't understand how a little disagreement could have spun out of control. Was that down to him? Of course it was, he decided. Devon was the newcomer to the Glen, still figuring it out and getting used to small-town thinking. *She's only been here less than two weeks, and you're expecting her to adjust from big-city life on top of coming to terms with the recent death of her brother—her only relative in the whole world.*

He muttered a curse word. No wonder she was confused and unsure of her place here, even her place in his family. He hoped she wasn't uncertain about him or his love for her, but could he blame her if she had doubts? He'd had a chance in the truck to explain himself with more sensitivity. His mother often said to him when he was a teen, *Come down off your high horse, Finn McAllister.* He'd scoffed at the trite phrase, but she'd had him pegged. He could be like that— all-knowing, all-enthusiastic about his passions, one of which was Maple Glen. It was time for him to start looking at the world, especially the Glen, through Devon's eyes. If he wanted a life with her here, he had to clearly understand and accept her concerns—*her fears*—about losing the privacy and independence she'd struggled so long to achieve. He needed to stand aside and let her handle the inevitable complications, however big or small, that would arise. She was perfectly capable of rescuing herself.

The right thing to do was to go find Devon and apologize for being such a jerk. Except she might not be ready to see him, and he also needed to figure out exactly what he'd say. It seemed that he wasn't very articulate recently, not since finding Devon Fairchild on the Long Trail. What he really needed right then was some physical activity, and the trail had always been the place where he could collect his thoughts and reflect on his life, from the time he first entered its dark mysterious woods with his father when he was a child. He had just opened the front door to get his hiking boots when his phone rang.

"Didn't you get my text?" his mother asked, her voice high and clipped the way it was when she was anxious.

"Um, sorry, no. What is it?"

"There's some woman here at the center who's causing a bit of a stir. She's asking everyone about Devon and showing them some article about Devon's brother. I haven't spoken with her, but I met Walter coming in, and he said Devon was upset, thinking this woman might be a reporter. Walter's gone to check her out, but I thought you ought to know."

"Where's Devon now?"

"She drove out of the parking lot as I came out

to look for her. I don't know where she was going, and she's not answering her phone. I think you'd better—"

He was already running to his truck.

SHE COULD HAVE kept on driving. A small part of her wanted to do that. Leave Maple Glen and never go back. She didn't even have to return for her backpack and clothes. New ones were always available. But Walter was right. She ought to go somewhere and wait for his call. She ought to calm down and stop jumping to conclusions. She ought to turn around and look for Finn, tell him how foolish she'd been and that if he still wanted her, she'd try her best to tolerate the parts of Maple Glen that she had difficulty accepting. But first she needed to figure out how to face Finn and his family if all the fuss at the community center was about nothing at all. That's what she was hoping. Better to look foolish than cowardly, because running away was cowardly. She knew that deep inside.

Driving by places that were now familiar to her felt years away from her first day in Maple Glen almost two weeks ago. There was the Shady Nook B and B, where Bernie had tried to warn her about hiking on the trail when a storm was on the horizon. The sign with the two donkeys had fallen to one side, and the balloons on the porch pillar sagged. The lot behind the B and B was empty of cars now, all the wedding guests departed, she presumed. Maybe Maddie and Shawn were on their way someplace warm or just back at their farm. The bakery was closed, as expected, because the owner was selling goods at the bazaar and the post office was also closed because it was Sunday.

As Church Street became the county road, Devon looked to her right at the two houses and their families that had been the topic of so much talk—sympathetic and otherwise. There were cars in both driveways but no sign of people. Sheltering inside from public view and gossip, she supposed. What she intended to do for now. *Find shelter from my thoughts.* But where in Maple Glen could she do that?

She rounded the curve in the road and saw the answer straight ahead: Jake & Friends. Tapping the brake, she slowed down to make her turn. There were two vehicles parked near the barn, and she drove up behind one and switched off the engine. She sat for a minute trying to think of an excuse for being there when everyone else in the village was at the bazaar. Deciding maybe she didn't need a reason at all, she got out and headed for the barn door, which was wide open. When her eyes adjusted from the sunny day to instant darkness, Devon realized the stalls were empty. She hadn't noticed any donkeys in the pastures abutting the farm, but then she hadn't been looking for any, either.

The murmur of voices at the end of the barn was reassuring. She didn't have to worry about being taken for a trespasser. The notion was ridiculous, given that everyone in the Glen apparently knew everyone else.

"Hello?" she called out from just inside the door.

The voices went, quiet and seconds later two teenagers—a boy and a girl—were walking along the central aisle toward her. "Hi, I'm Devon Fairchild...um...a friend of the McAllisters. We haven't met, but I...um...I came to see if Maura was here."

"We've heard about you," said the girl. "I'm Ashley Watson, Scott's sister. He told me about the day he and Finn found you on the trail."

Devon stifled a sigh. As long as she was in Maple Glen, she'd never lose that descriptor.

"And I'm Luke Danby. My dad—"

"Treated my sprained ankle that day," Devon interjected. They all laughed.

"You can't escape it," Luke said. "Maple Glen, I mean. People just know things."

"I grew up with it," Ashley commented, "and I'm kinda used to it, but there are times when I need an escape. That's why I volunteer here with the donkeys."

"Where *are* the donkeys?" Devon peered around her at the empty stalls.

"They're out in the north pasture. It's a beautiful day, but it's supposed to storm late tonight or early tomorrow. Maura thought they could use some fresh air and exercise before getting shut up in the barn again," Luke answered. "But Roger's here in the end stall. Something's wrong with a hoof, and we've been feeding him treats while Maura's gone to get the vet."

"Want to come see him?" Ashley asked.

"Sure." Following behind them, Devon thought that neither teen had asked why she was there. Perhaps they were accustomed to people—even strangers—impulsively dropping in to see the donkeys. Or perhaps they were simply demonstrating the Maple Glen welcome, accepting without too many questions. It occurred to her that although many people knew her name and how she arrived in the village, no one had specifically asked her any personal questions.

Roger's large head turned toward their footfall, his ears twitching back and forth. He gave a loud snort and Luke laughed. "He's so greedy today! Thinks we've got more treats even though he's eaten everything already."

Devon reached up to stroke Roger's snout. "Comfort food," she murmured. "We all need a little comfort at times, don't we? Food, treats or hugs? The need for comfort isn't only a human thing, is it?"

"Nope," said Luke. He seemed about to say something more when the sound of vehicles arriving got their attention.

"That's Maura with the vet," Ashley said. She headed for the barn door followed by Luke.

Devon spent another few seconds patting Roger, letting the tranquility of the barn settle over her. Then she whispered a goodbye and went to greet Maura before getting back into her car and leaving. *Leaving for where, though?* she asked herself as she met the group at the barn door.

She registered Maura's surprise at seeing her there, but the woman merely smiled and introduced the vet—"This is Kyle, from Wallingford"—and as Ashley and Luke accompanied Kyle to Roger's stall, Maura took Devon aside. "You're welcome here anytime, Devon, but... um...is everything okay? I mean, everyone in the Glen—well, *almost* everyone," she tittered, "is at the bazaar."

"I know. I've just come from there." She felt an urge to confide in Maura but held back. "I...um... I just felt an urge to escape for a bit." She tried to tone down the admission with a light laugh, but Maura's eyes narrowed.

"Uh-huh. I know exactly what you mean. That's why I'm here and not there. Some time with the animals is what I needed today."

"Therapy?"

"You got it." Then she sighed. "I'm happy for my sister, who's got an adventure ahead of her, but frankly, I'm a bit anxious about running the operation by myself." Patting her midriff, she smiled. "Junior here—or Little Miss—will be arriving this spring just when the riding therapy business ramps up. We've hired a full-time instructor who will be starting before the baby's due, but I'm still fretting about it, despite Theo's assurances that everything will work out." She took a deep breath. "Anyhow, that's me complaining, and I'm sure you've already heard some of our potential woes through the grapevine."

Devon shook her head. "Not at all."

Maura laughed. "You will eventually, but as annoying as that will be, you can be sure of one thing. The support of people here in the Glen is awesome." She patted Devon's arm. "So don't let anxiety about all that talk drive you away."

Was she reading her mind, Devon wondered, or had she already heard about the events at the community center? No, she thought right away. *Maura's been dealing with a distressed donkey and has more important things on her mind.* Like caring for those wonderful animals and operating a business that helped people deal with life's challenges. Almost single-handedly, too.

Then an idea began to germinate. There could be a solution, she thought, to her dilemma about staying in Maple Glen, a place where almost everybody knew almost everything about everyone, as Finn said his father had been fond of saying. *I can't run away from my past for the rest of my life. Perhaps I can be part of that incredible support network and, at the same time, hang on to some private alone time that's so important to me.*

"Maura," she said, "can I come and see you tomorrow? I have an idea I'd like to discuss with you."

CHAPTER TWENTY-THREE

THERE WAS SO much confusion and babble in the entrance to the community center that Finn caught Walter's eye and nodded to the door. The woman standing next to Walter picked up the cue as well, and the three of them wound their way around the people entering and headed for the parking lot.

"My truck or your truck?" Walter quipped, grinning at Finn.

"How about my car?" the woman put in, smiling.

The men followed her to a compact sedan and got inside, Finn in front with the car's owner and Walter in the back. The car was warm enough for a brief chat, but Finn was anxious to get out on the road to search for Devon, who still wasn't answering her phone. He was torn between hearing out this stranger whom he hadn't officially met and finding the woman he loved and begging her to come back.

Fortunately, the woman introduced herself before Finn had a chance to pepper her with questions. "My name is Amelia Owens. I was the social worker who took over the Morrison case when the children were returned to Boston."

Finn was speechless. His quick glance at Walter told him the man had already heard this. "Everyone thought you were a reporter nosing around to expose Devon," Finn managed to say.

"I wasn't very discreet," Amelia admitted. "I was getting desperate. I'm only here for tonight, and my flight home is tomorrow. This was an impulsive but important mission for me. A resolution, so to speak, for Chloe and her brother." She smiled. "Devon, I mean. It's been years since I had any contact with them. When Billy turned eighteen, he took over as legal guardian and at the same time, I was promoted and moved to another city."

Finn wanted to hear her story but knew Devon should hear it first. He looked at Walter. "Any idea where Devon might have gone?"

"I told her to find a quiet place to calm down and put things in perspective. I was afraid she'd simply drive away and never come back."

My fear exactly, Finn thought. Then he had an idea. "If she was heading toward Wallingford, she'd pass Jake & Friends. You think—"

"Could be," Walter said, nodding thoughtfully. "Definitely a quiet place. Well, most of the time," he laughed.

"Jake & Friends?" asked Amelia.

"Come with us and you'll see," promised Finn. He turned to Walter. "My truck or yours?"

DEVON SWERVED, pulling into the rear car park at the community center. A truck was reversing and she drummed her fingers on the steering wheel, mentally urging the driver to hurry. When it drove up next to her, about to turn onto Church Street, she glanced over to see Walter at the wheel with Finn next to him and a woman in the back seat. She honked the horn to get their attention, shifted into Park and got out of her car.

The driver's-side window rolled down, and Devon said, "Um, are you looking for me?" She made an effort not to look at the woman in the back, resolved not to lose her nerve now. Besides, why would a reporter be with them? Unless they were getting rid of her. She almost smiled at the irrational thought.

"We were going to look for you," Walter began, "but…"

He turned to Finn who leaned forward to say, "Follow us, Devon. We're going to the Manor to talk."

His tone was urgent, and Devon knew her questions could wait. She risked a quick peek at the woman behind Walter and Finn and saw her broad warm smile. Then she nodded and got back in her car, made a U-turn and followed Walter.

They were going inside the house as she parked

behind Walter's truck. Finn held back, waiting for her as she climbed up onto the veranda. "It's all good, Devon. Don't worry."

His quick hug was the reassurance she needed. He took her hand, and they went inside where Walter and the woman were taking off their coats. The woman turned to Devon and said, "You may not remember me, Devon, but I'm Amelia Owens, and I was the social worker who took you and your brother back to Boston twenty-five years ago this past September."

Devon couldn't speak. Of all the explanations for who the mystery woman was, this one would never have occurred to her. But the name suddenly took shape in her memory. "Amy?"

Amelia smiled. "You called me that from the moment I introduced myself all those years ago. And I have to remind myself to call you Devon now. It's been a long time."

"Shall we go sit in there?" Finn asked, pointing to the living room.

Devon sat next to Amelia on the sofa. She couldn't stop staring at the woman. Nor could she think of a single question, though fragments were beginning to form in her mind.

"Why don't I go first?" Amelia suggested. "I was transferred to another city shortly before Billy got legal guardianship over you, and I'm sorry to say that I was immersed in my new job and lost touch. I didn't even know that you and

Billy had legally changed your names until a former colleague in my old department sent me a copy of Billy's—*Dan's*—obituary with a note explaining the name change." She paused to compose herself. "I felt so bad, remembering what a wonderful brother he'd been to you. A hero, really, at ten years of age."

Devon tightened her lips, fighting back tears. She didn't dare speak but nodded.

"I wanted to write to you to convey my sympathy but had no idea how to get in touch. You were nowhere on social media and my colleague said your file hadn't been updated since the name change years ago. In fact, she'd been about to archive it permanently when she learned about Dan's passing. The two of us decided to track you down but weren't having much luck because the obituary provided little information, other than he was survived by you and a nameless friend and business partner. We were about to give up when the article about Dan's business was published."

Amelia held up her phone. "I downloaded it. So now I had the business partner's name, Michael Thomas, and knew where I could contact him. He didn't know where you were and from his manner, I doubt he would have told me anyway. But he did say you were out of town on important business—he actually used the word *mission*—and, remembering this year was an anniversary of sorts for you and Dan, some critical thinking along with a wild guess on my part, brought me here, to Maple Glen. The place where you were carried out of the woods, twenty-five years ago." Amelia stopped and looked across the room at Walter. "You can imagine my surprise to find out that Walter Ingram still lives here. We never met back then, though I'd heard how he'd found you."

Words failed Devon. There was a lot to process but fragments of memory soon began to shift together, forming pictures and emotions from the past. When Amelia smiled, the dimples in both cheeks reminded Devon of warmth, and her voice, with its Boston accent, brought back the soothing words Amelia—*Amy!*—had whispered when they met.

Devon looked at Finn, whose eyes were shining. *From tears, or for love of me?* She smiled at him, hoping he'd pick up the love in her silent message. She wanted to know as much about their rescue as possible and also hoped Amelia might have information about her mother and her mother's family, if any existed at all. But Amelia's next words turned everything upside down.

"There's one more thing," she said. "That colleague of mine went through your files again and found a letter." Keeping her eyes on Devon, she said, "From your father. It was written long before the day you and Dan ran away, shortly after your mother passed. I have it with me. Perhaps there's a place where you and I—"

"Yes," Finn broke in. "Sorry to interrupt, and forgive me if I seem pushy, but I have an idea. My family will be coming home from the bazaar soon, and my mother will want to start preparing something for dinner. How about if you and Devon went to the B and B—you said you have a room there?"

Amelia nodded.

"Go there for the rest of your talk and…um… if you both feel up to it, come back to the Manor for dinner. I can text you a time."

It was the perfect solution, Devon thought, and a glance at Amelia told her she thought the same.

On their way out, Finn took her aside. "I didn't mean to force my idea on you, Devon. It just seemed like…well…a good one."

His laugh was sheepish, and she reached up to touch his cheek. "It was an excellent idea, Finn, thank you. Will you fill your mother and Roxanne in on all this?"

"I will. And listen, I want to say something before you leave." He looked around as Walter and Amelia were opening the front door. "I love you. Please think about staying through Christmas. Please give us and Maple Glen another chance."

His eyes pleaded and Devon whispered, "I love you, too."

DEVON'S HANDS SHOOK as she held the photocopied letter that Amelia took from her suitcase.

"It won't make you unhappy," Amelia said, "but maybe a bit sad." Then she got up from the arm-chair in her room at the B and B. "I'm going to see if Mr. Watson can rustle up some tea."

As the door closed, Devon began reading.

To whom it may concern,
My name is Blake Morrison, and I'm the fa-ther of Billy and Chloe Morrison, who are currently in your care in Boston. I would like to petition for their guardianship. I am currently serving in the United States Army in Germany but will be on leave next week and intend to come to Boston to fill out any papers required for this. I have documen-tation and can get any references you will need. Please advise as soon as possible.
Yours truly,
Lt. Blake Morrison

Amelia returned with a tray of tea and cookies as Devon finished wiping her tears.

"I'm sure you have questions," she said quietly, setting the tray down on the small table next to Devon's chair.

"Where do I begin?" Devon heard the wobble in her voice and paused a moment. Then taking a breath, she said, "His tone here. He doesn't sound like the man I have a vague memory of. At least, the memory I have of his voice. He was loud, and it seemed like he was always shouting."

Amelia nodded. "Apparently neighbors reported a lot of arguments and shouting before he left your mother. She applied for social welfare, and that original report was added to the file we had for you and Dan. But one of the neighbors, who claimed to be a friend of your mother's, later said the arguing was a new thing, and she felt it stemmed from your father's admission of an infidelity." She paused, meeting Devon's eyes. "Plus, your father had reenlisted, and I guess your mother…"

"Couldn't handle it anymore," Devon murmured. "Dan remembered more than I did and told me he figured our mother was depressed. At least, he realized that as an adult, looking back at the memories. So what happened after your department got my father's letter?"

Amelia pursed her lips. "That's what I feel obliged to apologize for. The letter was basically overlooked as it meandered through the system. Apparently, your father showed up unannounced at a local office in Boston, and the case worker he met with took an instant dislike to him. I have no idea why, and of course, this was a few years before I was involved in your case. The letter was filed in a separate folder under your father's name and was never collated with yours and Dan's. When the files were updated after Dan turned eighteen, yours was renamed Fairchild. My friend Andrea eventually managed to figure it all out."

Devon could relate to the woman's obvious exasperation over the bureaucratic mishaps. Her own department sometimes had similar issues. "And my father? After he left that office?"

"I assume he went back to his squadron in Germany. But after learning about Dan's death, Andrea did some more digging. She loves detective fiction, so she was very keen to get the answers." Amelia softened her voice and said, "She eventually found that Lieutenant Blake Morrison passed away ten years ago. I don't know the cause of death, but he was living in New Hampshire somewhere." Amelia paused a beat. "He left behind a wife and young daughter. You have a half sister, Devon."

The words scrolled over and over in her mind. A half sister. She could be a Morrison again, with a sibling. The past was gone, and now, there was only the future.

"WHAT IS YOUR most vivid Christmas Eve memory from childhood?" Roxanne suddenly asked.

Fortunately, she directed the question to Finn and not to her. Devon's Christmas Eve memories were all the same—takeout from any place that happened to be open and watching television with Dan. Devon looked at Finn, whose face was pink, as he was clearly searching for a way to get out of answering. She poked his arm. "Well? Confess," she teased.

His long sigh echoed around the room. "You know this one, Roxanne. You tell it. You were a willing accomplice as I recall."

"I was about ten," his sister began, "and we had this rich second cousin——"

"Your father's first cousin," Marion interjected.

Roxanne shrugged. "Whoever. She was wealthy and always sent somewhat eccentric gifts. Hers had arrived by mail a week before Christmas, and Mom had hidden it, unwrapped, in a bedroom closet, thinking we'd never find it. But of course, we knew all the hiding places, didn't we, Finn? Anyway, we found it and managed to open it up without leaving too much evidence that it had been tampered with."

"What was it?" Kaya asked.

"The cousin had been out west and sent us cowgirl and cowboy outfits, with toy pistols and all the rest. Lassos. The worst part was now that we knew, we had to pretend to be excited about them on Christmas Day. That was hard. Also, Mom took away the toy pistols, and as for the outfits…"

"They didn't exactly fit into the local and current fashions of Maple Glen," Finn added.

"You shouldn't have peeked," Kaya scolded. She looked at Devon. "What's your favorite Christmas Eve memory, Devon?"

Devon smiled at all the faces turned her way.

Marion, who looked tired after preparing a big meal; Roxanne and her peaceful smile since breaking the news that she and Kaya were moving to Wallingford in January. *Close to my work and her school*, she'd said. Then there was Walter, her childhood hero, and beside him, Amelia, her other hero—*heroine*, she amended—who'd agreed to stay for Christmas after much persuasion.

The absent person, still unmet and unknown, was the half sister Devon hoped to meet in the months to come. Annika was her name, and she was five years younger than Devon. That's all she knew for now.

But it was Finn that her gaze lingered on the longest. The man who'd handed her a wrapped gift hours ago when they were out behind the house collecting more firewood from the shed. The ring was gold with a small canary-yellow diamond in its center. "My great-grandmother's," he said, "handed down from my mother to you. Will you marry me, Devon Fairchild, and grow old with me and our children here in Maple Glen? I promise you'll learn to love it, too."

She'd flung her arms around him and said, "As long as you can put up with a wife who's going into business here." She'd wanted to wait until it was official, determined that no one—not even Finn—would talk her out of it. "I'm investing money and going to be a partner in Jake & Friends." His huge grin had expressed what words couldn't, and he'd held her so tight she could feel his heart pounding against hers.

"Devon?" Kaya repeated.

"Hmm?" She suddenly realized everyone was waiting for her answer.

"My favorite Christmas Eve memory is this one—right here and right now—with all of you. My family."

Finn took her hand, the ring sparkling in the candlelight, and kissed it. "I second that," he said, his warm dark brown eyes gleaming with love.

Their blended family—old, new and adopted—cheered as he kissed Devon.

* * * * *

HARLEQUIN
Reader Service

Enjoyed your book?

Try the perfect subscription for Romance readers and get more great books like this delivered right to your door.

See why over 10+ million readers have tried Harlequin Reader Service.

Start with a Free Welcome Collection with free books and a gift—valued over $20.

Choose any series in print or ebook. See website for details and order today:

TryReaderService.com/subscriptions

RSBPA24R